MW01193445

ELIZABETH FAIR
A WINTER AWAY

ELIZABETH MARY FAIR was born in 1908 and brought up in Haigh, a small village in Lancashire, England. There her father was the land agent for Haigh Hall, then occupied by the Earl of Crawford and Balcorres, and there she and her sister were educated by a governess. After her father's death, in 1934, Miss Fair and her mother and sister removed to a small house with a large garden in the New Forest in Hampshire. From 1939 to 1944, she was an ambulance driver in the Civil Defence Corps, serving at Southampton, England; in 1944 she joined the British Red Cross and went overseas as a Welfare Officer, during which time she served in Belgium, India, and Ceylon.

Miss Fair's first novel, *Bramton Wick*, was published in 1952 and received with enthusiastic acclaim as 'perfect light reading with a dash of lemon in it ...' by *Time and Tide*. Between the years 1953 and 1960, five further novels followed: *Landscape in Sunlight*, *The Native Heath*, *Seaview House*, *A Winter Away*, and *The Mingham Air*. All are characterized by their English countryside settings and their shrewd and witty study of human nature.

Elizabeth Fair died in 1997.

By Elizabeth Fair

Bramton Wick (1952)

Landscape in Sunlight
(1953, published in the U.S. as *All One Summer*)

The Native Heath
(1954, published in the U.S. as *Julia Comes Home*)

Seaview House
(1955, published in the U.S. as *A View of the Sea*)

A Winter Away (1957)

The Mingham Air (1960)

ELIZABETH FAIR

A WINTER AWAY

With an introduction
by Elizabeth Crawford

DEAN STREET PRESS

A Furrowed Middlebrow Book
FM18

Published by Dean Street Press 2017

First published in 1957 by Macmillan & Co.

Cover by DSP
Cover illustration shows detail from *Halstead Road in
Snow* (1935) by Eric Ravilious

ISBN 978 1 911579 41 0

www.deanstreetpress.co.uk

INTRODUCTION

'DELICIOUS' WAS John Betjeman's verdict in the *Daily Telegraph* on *Bramton Wick* (1952), the first of Elizabeth Fair's six novels of 'polite provincial society', all of which are now republished as Furrowed Middlebrow books. In her witty *Daily Express* book column (17 April 1952), Nancy Spain characterised *Bramton Wick* as 'by Trollope out of Thirkell' and in *John O'London's Weekly* Stevie Smith was another who invoked the creator of the Chronicles of Barsetshire, praising the author's 'truly Trollopian air of benign maturity', while Compton Mackenzie pleased Elizabeth Fair greatly by describing it as 'humorous in the best tradition of English Humour, and by that I mean Jane Austen's humour'. The author herself was more prosaic, writing in her diary that *Bramton Wick* 'was pretty certain of a sale to lending libraries and devotees of light novels'. She was right; but who was this novelist who, over a brief publishing life, 1952-1960, enjoyed comparison with such eminent predecessors?

Elizabeth Mary Fair (1908-1997) was born at Haigh, a village on the outskirts of Wigan, Lancashire. Although the village as she described it was 'totally unpicturesque', Elizabeth was brought up in distinctly more pleasing surroundings. For the substantial stone-built house in which she was born and in which she lived for her first twenty-six years was 'Haighlands', set within the estate of Haigh Hall, one of the several seats of Scotland's premier earl, the Earl of Crawford and Balcarres. Haigh Hall dates from the 1830s/40s and it is likely that 'Haighlands' was built during that time specifically to house the Earl's estate manager, who, from the first years of the twentieth century until his rather premature death in 1934, was Elizabeth's father, Arthur Fair. The Fair family was generally prosperous; Arthur Fair's father had been a successful stockbroker and his mother was the daughter of Edward Rigby, a silk merchant who for a time in the 1850s had lived with his family in Swinton Park, an ancient house much augmented in the 19th century with towers and battlements, set in extensive parkland in the Yorkshire Dales. Portraits of Edward Rigby, his wife, and sister-in law were inherited by Elizabeth Fair, and, having graced her

Hampshire bungalow in the 1990s, were singled out for specific mention in her will, evidence of their importance to her. While hanging on the walls of 'Haighlands' they surely stimulated an interest in the stories of past generations that helped shape the future novelist's mental landscape.

On her mother's side, Elizabeth Fair was the grand-daughter of Thomas Ratcliffe Ellis, one of Wigan's leading citizens, a solicitor, and secretary from 1892 until 1921 to the Coalowners' Association. Wigan was a coal town, the Earl of Crawford owning numerous collieries in the area, and Ratcliffe Ellis, knighted in the 1911 Coronation Honours, played an important part nationally in dealing with the disputes between coal owners and miners that were such a feature of the early 20th century. Although the Ellises were politically Conservative, they were sufficiently liberal-minded as to encourage one daughter, Beth, in her desire to study at Lady Margaret Hall, Oxford. There she took first-class honours in English Literature and went on to write *First Impressions of Burmah* (1899), dedicated to her father and described by a modern authority as 'as one of the funniest travel books ever written'. She followed this with seven rollicking tales of 17th/18th-century derring-do. One, *Madam, Will You Walk?*, was staged by Gerald du Maurier at Wyndham's Theatre in 1911 and in 1923 a silent film was based on another. Although she died in childbirth when her niece and namesake was only five years old, her presence must surely have lingered not only on the 'Haighlands' bookshelves but in family stories told by her sister, Madge Fair. Another much-discussed Ellis connection was Madge's cousin, (Elizabeth) Lily Brayton, who was one of the early- 20th century's star actresses, playing the lead role in over 2000 performances of *Chu Chin Chow*, the musical comedy written by her husband that was such a hit of the London stage during the First World War. Young Elizabeth could hardly help but be interested in the achievements of such intriguing female relations.

Beth Ellis had, in the late-nineteenth century, been a boarding pupil at a school at New Southgate on the outskirts of London, but both Elizabeth Fair and her sister Helen (1910-1989) were educated by a governess at a time when, after the end of the First World War, it was far less usual than it had been previously to educate daughters at home. Although, in a later short biographical piece, Elizabeth mentioned that she 'had abandoned her ambition to become an architect', this may only have been a daydream as there is no evidence that she embarked on any post-schoolroom training. In her novels, however, she certainly demonstrates her interest in architecture, lovingly portraying the cottages, houses, villas, rectories, manors, and mansions that not only shelter her characters from the elements but do so much to delineate their status *vis à vis* each other. This was an interest of which Nancy Spain had perceptively remarked in her review of *Bramton Wick*, writing 'Miss Fair is refreshingly more interested in English landscape and architecture and its subsequent richening effect on English character than she is in social difference of rank, politics, and intellect'. In *The Mingham Air* (1960) we feel the author shudder with Mrs Hutton at the sight of Mingham Priory, enlarged and restored, 'All purple and yellow brick, and Victorian plate-glass windows, and a conservatory stuck at one side. A truly vulgar conservatory with a pinnacle.' Hester, her heroine, had recently been engaged to an architect and, before the engagement was broken, 'had lovingly submitted to his frequent corrections of her own remarks when they looked at buildings together'. One suspects that Elizabeth Fair was perhaps as a young woman not unfamiliar with being similarly patronised.

While in *The Mingham Air* Hester's ex-fiancé plays an off-stage role, in *Seaview House* (1955) another architect, Edward Wray, is very much to the fore. It is while he is planning 'a "select" little seaside place for the well-to-do' at Caweston on the bracing East Anglian coast that he encounters the inhabitants of 'Seaview House'. We soon feel quite at home in this draughty 'private hotel', its ambience so redolent of the 1950s, where the owners, two middle-aged sisters, Miss Edith Newby and widowed Mrs Rose Barlow, might be found on an off-season evening darning guest towels underneath the gaze of the late Canon Newby, whose portrait 'looked down at his daughters with a slight sneer'. By way of contrast, life in nearby 'Crow's Orchard', the home of Edward's godfather, Walter Heritage, whose butler and cook attend to his every needs and where even the hall was 'thickly curtained, softly lighted and deliciously warm', could not have been more comfortable.

Mr Heritage is one of Elizabeth Fair's specialities, the cosseted bachelor or widower, enjoying a life not dissimilar to that of her two unmarried Ellis uncles who, after the death of their parents, continued to live, tended by numerous servants, at 'The Hollies', the imposing Wigan family home. However, not all bachelors are as confirmed as Walter Heritage, for in *The Native Heath* (1954) another, Francis Heswald, proves himself, despite an inauspicious start, to be of definitely marriageable material. He has let Heswald Hall to the County Education Authority (in 1947 Haigh Hall had been bought by Wigan Corporation) and has moved from the ancestral home into what had been his bailiff's house. This was territory very familiar to the author and the geography of this novel, the only one set in the north of England, is clearly modelled on that in which the author grew up, with Goatstock, 'the native heath' to which the heroine has returned, being a village close to a manufacturing town that is 'a by- word for ugliness, dirt and progress'. In fact *Seaview House* and *The Native Heath* are the only Elizabeth Fair novels not set in southern England, the region in which she spent the greater part of her life. For after the death of Arthur Fair his widow and daughters moved to Hampshire, closer to Madge's sister, Dolly, living first in the village of Boldre and then in Brockenhurst. *Bramton Wick*, *Landscape in Sunlight* (1953), *A Winter Away* (1957), and *The Mingham Air* (1960) are all set in villages in indeterminate southern counties, the topographies of which hint variously at amalgams of Hampshire, Dorset, and Devon.

Elizabeth Fair's major break from village life came in 1939 when she joined what was to become the Civil Defence Service, drove ambulances in Southampton through the Blitz, and then in March 1945 went overseas with the Red Cross, working in Belgium, Ceylon, and India. An intermittently-kept diary reveals that by now she was a keen observer of character, describing in detail the background, as she perceived it, of a fellow Red Cross worker who had lived in 'such a narrow circle, the village, the fringes of the county, nice people but all of a pattern, all thinking on the same lines, reacting in the same way to given stimuli (the evacuees, the petty discomforts of war). So there she was, inexperienced but obstinate, self-confident but stupid, unadaptable, and yet nice. A nice girl, as perhaps I was six years ago, ignorant, arrogant and capable of condescension to inferiors. Such a lot to learn, and I hope she will learn it.' Clearly Elizabeth Fair felt that her war work had opened her own mind and broadened her horizons and it is hardly surprising that when this came to an end and she returned to village life in Hampshire she felt the need of greater stimulation. It was now that she embarked on novel writing and was successful in being added to the list of Innes Rose, one of London's leading literary agents, who placed *Bramton Wick* with Hutchinson & Co. However, as Elizabeth wrote in her diary around the time of publication, 'it still rankles a little that [the Hutchinson editor] bought *Bramton Wick* outright though I think it was worth it – to me – since I needed so badly to get started.'

However, although Hutchinson may have been careful with the money they paid the author, Elizabeth Fair's diary reveals that they were generous in the amount that was spent on *Bramton Wick*'s publicity, advertising liberally and commissioning the author's portrait from Angus McBean, one of the period's most successful photographers. Witty, elegant, and slightly quizzical, the resulting photograph appeared above a short biographical piece on the dust wrappers of her Hutchinson novels. The designs for these are all charming, that of *The Native Heath* being the work of a young Shirley Hughes, now the doyenne of children's book illustrators, with Hutchinson even going to the extra expense of decorating the front cloth boards of that novel and of *Landscape in Sunlight* with an evocative vignette. Elizabeth Fair did receive royalties on her second and third Hutchinson novels and then on the three she published with Macmillan, and was thrilled when an American publisher acquired the rights to *Landscape in Sunlight* after she had 'sent Innes Rose the masterful letter urging to try [the book] in America'. She considered the result 'the sort of fact one apprehends in a dream' and relished the new opportunities that now arose for visits to London, confiding in her diary that 'All these social interludes [are] extremely entertaining, since their talk mirrors a completely new life, new characters, new outlook. How terribly in a rut one gets.' There is something of an irony in the fact that by writing her novels of 'country life, lightly done, but delicately observed' (*The Times Literary Supplement*, 1 November 1957) Elizabeth Fair was for a time able to enjoy a glimpse of London literary life. But in 1960, after the publication of *The Mingham Air*, this interlude as an author came to an end. In her diary, which included sketches for scenes never used in the novel-in-hand, Elizabeth Fair had also, most intriguingly, noted ideas for future tales but, if it was ever written, no trace survives of a seventh novel. As it was, she continued to live a quiet Hampshire life for close on another forty years, doubtless still observing and being amused by the foibles of her neighbours.

Elizabeth Crawford

CHAPTER ONE

"I AM SMALL and insignificant," said Maud, "but this room is going to make me feel much more so."

She gazed at herself in the speckled looking glass which hung on the wall. A giant's wardrobe near the window cut off the daylight and the single electric light was behind her at the other end of the room. As well as the wardrobe the room contained a white-painted iron bed, a chest of drawers, a chair and a carpet. The carpet had once been crimson with green and yellow flowers. The wallpaper, as faded as the carpet, had been striped brown and beige, with blue flowers dotting the beige part. The bedspread had never been anything but cochineal pink.

"I expected something better than this," she said gloomily. She spoke aloud, addressing her speckled image in the looking glass; but she spoke softly, in case there was anyone outside on the landing. "Not even a dressing table," she added, thinking of her new brushes and the powder bowl and the box that held manicure things and little jars for face cream.

Still, she must unpack. She had come to stay; she would be here for a long time; she must put up with it. Perhaps when she had settled in she could make some improvements.

"Wilbraham!" called Cousin Alice, from the head of the stairs.

Downstairs, another voice called for Puppy. Cries of "Wilbraham" and "Puppy" resounded through the house, as Maud struggled with the awkward lock of her trunk. But there was no response to the cries, and presently the voices grew squeaky and hoarse, died away into mutters, and were then heard, more faintly, outside in the garden.

Maud had been in the house less than an hour, but she had already made out that Puppy and Wilbraham were alternative names for the same animal. He was Wilbraham to Cousin Alice and Puppy to Miss Conway. She had not yet seen him but she gathered from their talk that he was their joint property and that they had had him for seven years. Puppyhood must be far behind him, but perhaps he was exceptionally skittish for his age; or perhaps Miss Conway disliked being reminded of the passage of time. Hearing the cry of "Puppy" grow louder, Maud straightened up from her unpacking and walked to the window to take another look at Miss Conway if she was in sight; she had already guessed that Miss Conway was a person to be reckoned with. Cousin Alice had written of her as "my companion," but they were so different that one could hardly imagine it as a companionship based on common interests, and yet Miss Conway quite lacked the docile air of those who are paid to be agreeable. Moreover, her hearty welcome to Maud had not wholly concealed a defensive—or possibly offensive—vigilance.

Miss Conway was standing in the middle of the small lawn and loudly beseeching Puppy to emerge from a clump of rhododendrons. She wore a very brightly patterned cotton frock, no stockings, and scarlet sandals. Her brown hair was streaked with grey, but like the rest of her it looked full of life. She was plump, but not flabby; her plumpness, Maud thought, was probably kept in check by vigorous daily exercises. She was middle-aged; or, at any rate, she was a good deal older than Maud, who had recently celebrated her twentieth birthday.

But she's much younger than Cousin Alice, she thought, dismissing the idea that they had been friends from childhood. At this moment Miss Conway swung round and saw her. She smiled and waved, and Maud was forced to open the window wider and enter into conversation.

"Ahoy there," Miss Conway began it, like a mariner hailing a castaway. "Finished your unpacking?"

"Almost," Maud said, untruthfully.

"Splendid. Do you want a bath?"

"No, thank you. I had a bath this morning."

"I thought you might like one after the journey."

"I don't seem dirty. But perhaps I could wash my face."

"Yes, do. The bathroom at the end of the passage—remember? And then come down and join us. We might go for a walk—I expect you're longing to stretch your legs."

"Perhaps you could show me Glaine."

"Oh, not this evening. Time enough for that tomorrow—you'll be seeing quite enough of it once you start the job, you know! And then, old—your boss doesn't encourage people to drop in casually."

"I meant, just show me how to get to it from here."

"Wilbraham!" called Cousin Alice, appearing from the other side of the rhododendrons.

"He's in there," said Miss Conway. "Right in the middle. I saw him for a second but I can't get him to come out."

"I think we shall have to try a bribe. Have you got a biscuit?"

"Here," said Miss Conway, fishing in the pocket of her dress.

"A sugar one? We mustn't disappoint Wilbraham, or he won't trust us in the future. Besides, it's morally wrong to use bribery . . . so the least one can do is to make the bribe worth taking."

Maud, at the window, pondered this remark with interest. She also seized the chance to take a good look at Cousin Alice, who was now directing Miss Conway to lie on the grass and hold the biscuit at the edge of the rhododendron clump where Wilbraham could see it. But her scrutiny was brief; she had an uneasy feeling that Cousin Alice, though apparently intent on retrieving Wilbraham, was perfectly aware that she was being watched and might at any moment, without raising her voice or turning her head, come out with another remark about spying being morally wrong even if the person being spied on was well worth her young relative's attention.

Maud did not have to guess Cousin Alice's age, for she knew her to be sixty-three. But her hair was still dark and her tall figure was youthfully supple; she did not look as if she needed to do exercises to keep plumpness at bay. Unlike Miss Conway she dressed with considerable formality; she wore stockings, and laced shoes with pointed toes, and a dark red dress which was neither fashionable nor frumpish. The disparity between the two women was most evident in their faces; the face of Miss Conway was square, fresh-complexioned, and easy to read, while Cousin Alice's was a pale, finely lined mask which gave nothing away.

"Wilbraham!" Cousin Alice commanded, having got Miss Conway, and the bribe, into the right position.

Maud withdrew. She found her sponge-bag among the strewn possessions on the floor, and went off, still brooding on the totally different faces of Cousin Alice and Miss Conway, to wash her own.

There were two bathrooms in the house and Miss Conway had told her to use the one at the end of the passage. It had been a conservatory, built on top of the flat roof of the scullery, she explained, but Alice had turned it into a bathroom because it was so awkward having only one. (Maud wondered why.) She had pointed out the door, without opening it; and so the glassy peculiarity of the second bathroom was not revealed to Maud until she went to wash her face.

It had been a conservatory, and to her first startled glance it still seemed one; a conservatory with a bath along one side and a hand-basin at the far end. On the side not occupied by the bath there remained the staging which had once held plants in pots, but to spare the occupant's blushes the walls had been lined with plywood for a height of about five feet and the glass above was white-washed to its junction with the roof. The roof was like any other greenhouse roof, transparent though rather dirty. The floor was covered with coconut matting.

"Well!" said Maud.

She looked at it again; and saw it, this time, as a product of Cousin Alice's inventive mind. It was truly ingenious of her to have contrived a second bathroom so simply and economically; and one could only hope that she had arranged some way of heating it in winter—an oil stove perhaps, or a charcoal brazier. On this warm autumn evening there was a bizarre charm in the glass roof and the streakily whitewashed walls, but in winter the bathroom would be icy. Still, it was cheering rather than depressing, and it made up for the ugly little bedroom and for the absence of enthusiasm in Cousin Alice's greeting. Looking at it, she recaptured the feeling of excitement she had experienced when the taxi turned off the main road and descended the lane into the combe: the feeling of entering an enclosed world where everything would be odd and yet delightful.

She washed her face and hurried back to her bedroom, where she made the shortest work possible of putting away her crumpled clothes—Maud's attitude to her clothes was at all times brutal rather than loving—before going down to join the others in the garden. They were not in sight when she stepped out of the french window, and she stood for a moment on the verandah, looking about her.

The front door of Combe Cottage opened on to the lane, but the window was at the end of the house and she was facing the sea. Higher hills on either side defined the valley where she stood, and yet she was high above the sea; the valley was like a wide saucer, gently tilted towards the south, and the sea was a pale, gleaming line beyond a rim of hedge and wood. Maud was enchanted; she wondered whether there was a way down to the sea and whether she would have time to bathe before breakfast. She remembered, with a slight tug of anxiety, that after breakfast she would have to face an employer and start to earn her living, but the prospect in front of her diminished her fears. The people—the person—who lived at Glaine must surely be amiable.

She walked to the corner of the house and looked at the lawn behind it. It was quite a small lawn, half enclosed by rhododendrons, and she could see beyond it the tops of apple trees; she remembered that an orchard had bordered the lane as she approached the house. A path led off between the rhododendrons; she followed it and came to a wicket gate leading into the orchard. Cousin Alice and Miss Conway were now in view, actively engaged in driving a number of hens towards a wooden hen-house. Puppy-Wilbraham was attached to an apple tree by a long lead, and he barked very fiercely at her as she came through the gate.

"Down, Puppy!" Miss Conway shouted, and added reassuringly, "He won't bite."

He won't have the chance to, Maud thought, keeping out of Puppy's range. She found him repulsive—a fat smooth-haired fox terrier with sly little piglike eyes—and she at once sided with Cousin Alice and thought of him as Wilbraham.

"Come and help us. The hens don't like going to bed so early, but that's only because they're new. Our old hens always went to bed at half-past five."

"In the summer," said Miss Conway. "In the winter they go to bed before tea."

"We have to take great care of them, there are so many foxes. Old M. did say he would have them shot, but I suppose he thought better of it. Or worse," Cousin Alice added thoughtfully.

Maud pursued the hens. They were accustomed to evading only two pursuers and could not cope with three; quite soon they had all been driven into the hen-house, and Miss Conway shut the door on their protesting cackles.

"Who is old M.?" Maud asked.

"Marius Feniston. Our landlord, you know. The owner of Glaine."

"Your employer," Miss Conway said pointedly. She somehow made it clear that she was not going to encourage Maud to speak of him as old M.

"Oh. And what is he like? Is he really very old?"

"Not really," Cousin Alice said. "Or perhaps, yes," she corrected herself, eyeing Maud as if she were the standard by which age was to be measured. "At any rate he has a grown-up son."

"Who doesn't live here," said Miss Conway.

Maud guessed this remark to be another discouragement; she was being discouraged from hopes of matrimony, just as she had been discouraged from speaking of Mr. Feniston as old M. She thought Miss Conway was being silly and officious. But when Cousin Alice said that young Mr. Feniston's name was Oliver, and then paused reflectively, Maud waited with interest for what she already thought of as "the postscript"—the afterthought which Cousin Alice added to most of her statements.

"He specialises in economy," Cousin Alice said.

"Oh," said Maud. She just had time to feel disdain—because a young miser sounded even more repellent than an old one—when Miss Conway rapped out:

"Economics!"

"It's the same thing," Cousin Alice said firmly.

Miss Conway did not argue the point. Young Mr. Feniston's name dropped out of the conversation as abruptly as if Cousin Alice had forgotten having mentioned it; with no obvious intention of changing the subject she asked Maud if her father still liked sardines.

Maud did not know. She couldn't remember sardines ever appearing on the table, or her father commenting on the lack of them. She explained this, but added (catching the trick from her questioner) that perhaps he ate them when he was alone.

"I daresay he does. Dear Alec—it is the thing I remember best about him. When he stayed with us at Wolfering he used to buy tins and tins at the village shop. We ate them for tea."

It threw an odd light on a parent Maud thought of as permanently middle-aged and interested in nothing but living conditions in backward native areas. "I suppose that was before he became a doctor," she said, tentatively.

"Oh, but I don't think they're indigestible," said Cousin Alice. "Yes, it was a long time ago . . . and I suppose it's different in the colonies. And of course, he's a government official, too."

"Yes," Maud agreed; though she did not grasp what was different, or why being a government official mattered. "I haven't seen him for two years," she continued, to forestall further awkward questions. "And then I only saw him for a short time, when he was home on leave."

"Con hopes you like eggs," Cousin Alice said. "There are two hundred and eighty-three ways of cooking them."

Maud answered politely that she liked eggs very much.

"Splendid," said Miss Conway, who had been walking Wilbraham round the orchard while they talked and who hurried towards them like another (but more obedient) dog, when her name was mentioned. Maud supposed it was tact that had taken her up to the far fence while Cousin Alice was touching on family matters.

"I'm the cook, you know," Miss Conway continued. "And I thought we'd have eggs for supper tonight—if you like them. It seemed a good idea—something nourishing and yet light—after your journey."

The fatigue and confinement which—in Miss Conway's eyes—she had endured on her journey from London seemed to give it the epic character of a transcontinental migration. Maud wondered if this was because Miss Conway never left the secluded neighbourhood of Combe Cottage. But she thanked her for her thoughtfulness, and she was surprised to see a fleeting, ironical smile cross Cousin Alice's face. It was gone in an instant; she thought afterwards that she must have imagined it.

After supper, and after further reference to her long, tiring journey, Maud was encouraged to go early to bed. They would follow her in half-an-hour, Cousin Alice said; but it was no good their coming up too soon because Wilbraham would not settle if they did. Wilbraham got more considerate treatment than the hens, Maud thought; and she asked where he slept.

"He sleeps for a month in my room, and then for a month in Con's."

Cousin Alice made her habitual pause. Maud hoped the postscript would not be an offer of a month of Wilbraham's company, and to avoid it she said quickly, "I don't think I should like a dog in my bedroom. He would keep me awake."

"Are you a light sleeper?"

Committed to being one, Maud nodded. "I have very vivid dreams," she said, which was moderately true.

"How interesting. Con and I are making a culture-study of dreams and keeping a record of our own. Unfortunately ours are generally fragmentary and prove very little. You may be a great help to us."

Maud wondered what her dreams would be required to prove; she wished she had not boasted of them, and she determined to edit them very carefully before offering them as a contribution to culture.

"I'm frightfully sleepy tonight," she said. "I don't suppose I shall dream at all."

"Off you go, then," said Cousin Alice, taking up the book had momentarily closed.

She seemed to have lost interest. As Maud walked to the door she remembered her arrival, Cousin Alice's almost casual greeting, her own sense of disappointment. She felt that Miss Conway would be easier to get on with, but she found herself wondering if Miss Conway's apparently friendly overtures, her beaming smile and her concern for the effects of the railway journey, were not a little forced, a shade unnatural. It was as if Cousin Alice had quite lost touch with the exterior world outside

Glaine combe, while Miss Conway was still dimly aware of it and trying to remember its rules.

She looked back. Each of them was deep in her book, and Wilbraham was snoring. But nothing had been explained to her, no plans for the morning discussed, no directions given; perhaps they had even forgotten that she was to start her new job tomorrow. To recall them she spoke loudly, using words which should at least catch the ear of Miss Conway.

"By the way, does old M. expect me with the milk?"

Miss Conway looked up reproachfully. "Mr. Feniston expects you to be there at nine o'clock," she replied.

"But you haven't shown me where it is. And you said *breakfast* at nine. I don't see how—"

"You won't be going at nine tomorrow," Cousin Alice interposed. "Old M. said I could bring you about half-past ten—then I can show you the way and introduce you. The next day you will have to have breakfast earlier, by yourself. Or perhaps Con will get up early too, the first day. Will you, Con?—the first day she has to have breakfast by herself."

"But it won't *be* breakfast by herself, if I'm having it with her," Miss Conway protested.

"Well, we'll see. I do hope you will suit old M.," Cousin Alice said gently.

Maud hoped so too. She had an obscure feeling, from the way they spoke, that old M. might turn out to be deaf, or incomprehensible, or afflicted with some physical deformity about which he was hypersensitive.

"Isn't it rather silly to talk about 'introducing' Maud to old M.?" Miss Conway said. (The suggestion of early rising seemed to have upset her.) "After all, it's the same as going to an office, for her. People don't take relatives along to introduce them to their employers. They just go."

"Yes, Con. But old M. doesn't know the rules either. He's never had a secretary before, except that local girl who thought she could type and couldn't."

Cousin Alice paused.

"The one who got so hysterical and broke all the Spode," she added. "I know you won't do that, Maud. Good night."

CHAPTER TWO

"I'M CERTAIN she will do beautifully for old M.—once she learns to stand up to him," Alice had told Con.

Con hadn't been so sure. Edging away from direct criticism—for it wasn't her policy to disparage Alice's relatives—she had muttered something about Maud's being rather too young and inexperienced.

They had said no more; for Alice was well aware that Maud's coming was a dangerous innovation which might upset the balance of their lives, and that a deliberate avoidance of discussion would be safest at this stage. But now, as she and Maud set off to walk to Glaine, she wondered anxiously if Con was right. For Maud did look ridiculously young in her schoolgirl's blue raincoat, and of course it was true that she had had no experience. Fresh from a secretarial training, from a delicate childhood and a silly but solicitous stepmother, how on earth would she stand up to old M.? One could only hope, Alice thought—seeking refuge in optimism—that he might take a liking to her.

It was raining, which was a pity because Glaine would not look its best on a wet morning. But the combe, in wet weather or fine, had an unfailing charm for Alice Grayson and she was pleased to think that Maud liked it too. They walked down the lane in silence, because conversation was rather difficult for Alice in her wet-weather coat, which was made of stiff black oilskin and had a hood like a cowl. Unless she turned her head she could not see Maud, and unless she threw back the Cowl she could not hear her, nevertheless she was aware of having an appreciative companion, whose silence had nothing to do with sulks.

Immediately beyond the cottage the lane turned a sharp corner and ran across the combe towards the woods on the farther side. Glaine must be in those woods, Maud decided; for neither of the two houses in view could possibly be the residence of old M. They were too ordinary, and too exposed; they hadn't the air of mysterious dignity which Glaine, in her imagination, already possessed. And the nearer one certainly was not large enough to contain a library which had got out of hand. This library, where she was to sort and catalogue books when her other duties permitted it, had pleased her the more since Cousin Alice had mentioned its out-of-handness; she pictured it as full of treasures only waiting to be discovered, dusty and neglected books only waiting to be loved. Her secretarial training had not included instruction on the cataloguing of books, but Cousin Alice had told her it did not matter. Mr. Feniston had been warned not to expect a librarian, and what he really needed was a secretary. He would teach her how to catalogue the books, when there was time.

"Does Mr. Feniston write books himself? Is that why he needs a secretary?" she asked.

Only the last words got through the cowl, and Alice nodded her agreement. "Yes, he needs a secretary." She added, "But you knew that already."

Maud abandoned the attempt to extract more information and began to recapitulate the facts she already knew. Old M. needed a secretary but he did not want one living in the house. It might have been possible to get a secretary to come out daily from Yeomouth, the small seaside town over the hill, but after one trial of the local talent (about which she longed to hear more) he had professed a dislike to having anyone who belonged to the district; he did not want his affairs discussed in the town, as they would be if he employed someone local. In this impasse Cousin Alice had been consulted, and she had found a way out.

Maud could only guess at the network of family communications through which Cousin Alice learned that Alec's daughter had always been delicate but was growing out of it, that she wished to earn her living and had recently completed a secretarial training, and that her father and stepmother did not want her to work in London; but somehow or other the existence of this candidate had become known to Cousin Alice, and her intervention had solved the difficulties of more persons than one. Old M. was to be provided with a secretary who would come daily, but who was a stranger to the district; Alec and his wife were to be satisfied that Maud's rebellion, against living at home and being delicate, would transport her to a healthy country neighbourhood; and Maud herself was to have the pleasure of earning her living instead of being her stepmother's dependent.

"It couldn't be better," said Maud. She spoke aloud, in an effort to shake off her nervousness.

"It *is* wet—yes. But it could be wetter, Maud. It often is."

"Oh—the rain! But I don't mind that at all."

I hope she means it, Alice thought. But she'll have to get a proper mackintosh, a really heavy one, like mine. And good, heavy shoes too. Her thoughts trailed off to Wolfering, and then came back with a leap to Maud's financial position. Could she afford a new mackintosh? Were they charging her too much for her room and board at Combe Cottage? The idea of making ends meet by taking one or two paying guests had seemed excellent as first, and had dovetailed in perfectly with old M.'s wish for a non-residential secretary. But there were difficulties she had not foreseen.

Seeing them now she unconsciously slackened her pace, as if they were physical obstacles, and Maud gave a cry of dismay.

"Not here!"

"Oh no," said Alice, coming back to reality.

They had reached the first of the two houses that lay between Combe Cottage and Glaine. It stood on the right of the lane, at the top of a steep bank, with the fields rising behind it to the wooded head of the combe. It was a small stone cottage and Maud guessed that it had been "done up" fairly recently. The thatch came down like thick eyebrows over its two dormer windows and all the exterior woodwork had been painted bright blue, except the water-butt which was a deep purple. A rock garden covered the steep bank, gay with dwarf dahlias and late summer annuals.

"Pixie Cot," said Cousin Alice, turning her cowled head so that Maud could see and hear her.

"Is that its name?"

"Yes. It used to be Ivy Bank, but they changed the name. They only rent it, just as we rent ours . . . and of course they cleared away the ivy when they made the garden. Though I was rather surprised. . . . It isn't the sort of name one would expect a clergyman to choose."

"Perhaps he wanted a complete change from 'The Vicarage,'" Maud suggested. "Is the tenant an old, retired clergyman? Does he live there alone?"

"He has retired—yes. A difference of opinion with his bishop; but nothing scandalous, you know. Something about a fine point of heresy, old M. told me . . . and luckily he has private means. And a daughter to look after him."

"How nice," said Maud, looking at Pixie Cot with more interest. The gay paint somehow suggested a quite youthful household, and if the clergyman was not old but merely contentious his daughter might be a girl of her own age. "What is her name?" she asked, quickening her pace to catch up with Cousin Alice.

"Ensie Martin."

"I meant the daughter's name."

"Ensie," Cousin Alice repeated. "Not N. C." She spelt it aloud, and added that she had never been able to find out what it was short for.

"A minor saint?"

"Well, it's possible. But *Pixie* isn't short for a saint. Of course a man who can call his house Pixie Cot is *capable de tout*."

"Yes, indeed."

The second house was on the other side of the lane and was screened by a wall and a tamarisk hedge. It looked a good deal bigger than Pixie Cot, but as it faced south Maud could see nothing but its garage and back premises.

"The Woodfidleys," said Cousin Alice, walking swiftly on. It was not possible to question her; she had retreated into her cowl and her mood of silence. Maud looked at her watch and hoped Glaine was not far away. She did not want to be late, even though Cousin Alice was there to introduce her. She must make the best possible impression on old M., right from the start.

The lane curved to the right. They passed a clump of wind-bent thorn and hazel, and a new aspect of the combe lay before her. On the right the rising ground had been terraced into two long gardens, one above the other, lying parallel with the lane and separated from it by a stone balustrade topped by a few strands of wire. A low retaining wall divided the two terraces, and the whole area was enclosed, except for the side abutting on the lane, by old walls of rosy brick. The terraces sloped gently towards the south, and were sheltered from cold winds by the high wall and the hanging woods behind. Though it was raining when Maud first saw the Glaine gardens she thought of them, then and thereafter, as warm and sunlit; for even on a dull day the old brick walls and red earth gave them colour, and even in winter they seemed to hold the summer's stored heat.

She had exclaimed aloud as they rounded the corner, but now it was Cousin Alice who looked at her watch and hurried on; there was no time to stop and admire, or to ask her, as Maud longed to, whether old M. had a very big family. So many rows of vegetables, so large a display of Michaelmas daisies, dahlias, budding chrysanthemums; could an old man and one grown-up son possibly need them all? But the problem was solved when they reached the far end of the long terraces. Beyond the end wall was a gate, from which a rutted drive went up the hill towards some sheds and a big greenhouse. By the gate was a signboard saying: Glaine Gardens. Vegetables—Bedding Plants—Shrubs—Cut Flowers. Open daily 9 to 12, 2 to 5.

Cousin Alice turned into the drive. But almost at once she left it and disappeared between two clumps of azaleas. Maud quickened her steps; she saw a mossy, almost overgrown path and followed Cousin Alice along it, between azaleas and rhododendrons whose wet leaves brushed her coat, past the wreck of a wooden summer-house and the ghost of a paved garden. They seemed to be walking uphill into the high woods, but suddenly the path flattened out and she glimpsed open ground ahead. They emerged on the edge of an extensive green clearing which had once been a lawn. She looked across it, and there was Glaine.

At first sight the house appeared neither as beautiful nor as old as she had expected. It stood on a higher level than the lawn; a long, flat-fronted house with flanking stucco walls and small-paned sash windows. A narrow verandah of wrought-iron ran the whole length of the façade, hiding the lower windows and half hidden in its turn by a huge wistaria which covered most of its roof. Behind and on either side of the house were tall old trees, oak and ash and Spanish chestnut, which towered above it and enclosed it in a dark frame. Remote, secret, mysteriously charming in spite of its shabby exterior, Glaine neither welcomed her nor frowned on her. It simply waited, while she and Cousin Alice squelched across the soft grass, green as a bog, towards it.

Steep and slippery brick steps took them up to the terrace, where they turned to the left and walked round the corner of the house to the front door. A wrought-iron porch offered little protection to visitors awaiting admittance, for the rain dripped through its roof in a dozen places, but the door stood open and Cousin Alice walked straight into the stone-paved hall.

"We'll leave our raincoats here," she said. "But I shall ask him to let you have one of these little rooms as a cloakroom."

There were doors leading off the hall; Maud wondered what the little rooms were like, and wished Cousin Alice would give her time to make herself tidy and efficient-looking. But Cousin Alice, thinking about punctuality, hurried her through an arch-way into the inner hall. She found herself facing a fine oak stair-case which was being dusted by a middle-aged woman wearing a striped print frock and a white cap and apron. Maud had never seen a domestic helper in this traditional uniform, and she was impressed. But she could not help noticing that the hall and staircase were little the better for the helper's ministrations; cobwebs lay thick on the picture frames, and the black-and-white marble floor was coated with dirt. It was only the treads of the staircase which were getting dusted.

"Good morning, Mrs. Hatball. Will you tell Mr. Feniston we are here, please." Cousin Alice spoke loudly, and then dropped her voice to add, "She's rather deaf. And very stupid."

Mrs. Hatball did not reply, but she descended the stairs and ambled away down a passage that led off from the back of the hall. A door opened creakingly, some distance away.

"I wonder if she heard me," Cousin Alice murmured to herself.

Seizing her chance, Maud went over to a big looking glass and peered anxiously, through a veil of dust, at her face. As she had feared, she looked quite at her worst, with her straight fair hair dishevelled by wind and rain and a splash of mud on her chin. She hurriedly wiped away the mud and hunted in her bag for a comb, listening intently for the creaking distant door.

But the door that suddenly opened, close to where she was standing, did not creak and gave her no warning at all. Comb in hand, her hair still dishevelled, she stood paralysed before her employer; her alarmed eyes saw him as seven feet high with a fierce, beaky face which reminded her of an affronted eagle. "Hey!" he exclaimed, towering over her. Silence and self-effacement seemed the only possible reactions to so terrifying an apparition, and she felt deeply grateful to Cousin Alice for accompanying her to Glaine. Stepping aside, she waited for Cousin Alice to advance and introduce her; but after a prolonged pause it became evident that Cousin Alice wasn't going to play her part. Perhaps she too had been struck dumb, or perhaps—

As the thought occurred to her Maud cast a wild glance round the hall. Cousin Alice was nowhere to be seen.

"You're Maud Ansdell. Must be."

"Yes, I am," she replied, somewhat reassured by the comparative mildness of his voice. He held out his hand; she extended her own, and perceived too late that she was still grasping the comb, which, lacking several teeth, looked a peculiarly drab object to be brandished as a propitiatory offering.

"Put that away," old M. said sharply. He waited while Maud, blushing in embarrassment, returned the comb to her bag, then he held out his hand again and wished her good morning.

"You must have a room upstairs for prinking," he added. "I'll tell Mrs. Hat. How's your aunt?"

"Which aunt?"

Even as she spoke she realized that he must be referring to Cousin Alice.

"I mean she isn't," she blurted out. But that sounded quite idiotic and she feared he would dismiss her on the spot. The fear of it drove her to face him and to pour out a rapid explanation.

"I feel it would be belittling her to call her Aunt when she's really my father's cousin and far superior to my flesh and blood aunts."

"There's something in that—don't gabble," old M. said. "But where is she? Did she come with you—hey?"

"I don't know. Yes, she did, but I don't know where she is now."

"Must be somewhere."

"Well, yes, she must be."

He advanced to the foot of the staircase and called very loudly, "Alice!" The staircase led to a gallery which ran round three sides of the hall, and Maud half expected to see Cousin Alice come popping out of one of the many doors which opened on to it. But she appeared at the other side of the hall, emerging from the long passage down which Mrs. Hatball had gone in search of her master. Serene, indifferent to Maud's sufferings, she wished old M. good morning and explained that she had been to the estate room to look for him.

"I was sure you would be there, or in the library. Mrs. Hatball went off to the gun room, but I knew you wouldn't be in the gun room. Were you in the drawing room? Of course neither I nor Mrs. Hatball thought of looking there. Not at this time of day."

"Why shouldn't I sit in my own drawing room at any time of day I like?"

"But you never *do*. And it doesn't get any sun."

"There isn't any sun to get," old M. retorted irritably. "It's been raining since six o'clock, the sky is completely overcast, you can hardly see across the combe. I shall sit where I please."

"Well, I suppose there is no need to introduce you," Cousin Alice said, after a pause during which Maud had been willing her not to irritate old M. still further. "This is Maud, and I must admit she doesn't look as old as I said, but I know she is. I remember quite well the day Alec showed me a photograph of her, because it was just after my father's death and that was twenty years ago this month. Alec came to Wolfering for the funeral and he had Maud's photograph in a wallet and showed it to all of us. She looked sweet—quite naked and much fatter than she is now, sitting on a white rug and her hair standing up in a wonderful quiff."

Maud felt bitter shame. She had come to Glaine to escape from her family, and here was Cousin Alice behaving just like those aunts to whom she had been judged superior. Worse than the aunts, for they had kept their reminiscences for family reunions and had not inflicted them on strangers; moreover no employer, least of all old M., could possibly want to know what his secretary had looked like in early infancy. Miss Conway had been right; it was a great mistake to bring relatives with one. She prayed for Cousin Alice to depart as fervently as she had prayed, ten minutes ago, for her return.

"So she is twenty and a bit," Cousin Alice said.

"My last secretary was thirty-five," old M. said gloomily, "and no more sense than a child of ten. Or else she wasn't all there. *You* all there?" he asked suddenly, giving Maud a searching look. "No banging your head on the table? No throwing the china at me? Hey?"

"No, no, I promise," she replied, more unnerved than ever by this glimpse of the state to which he had reduced her predecessor.

"Good. Then we'd better begin."

Cousin Alice took the hint. "I'll see you at lunch," she told Maud. "Straight back along the lane, you know. It'll take you about twenty minutes so you must start at twenty to one."

"I shall walk must faster when I'm alone," Maud said hastily.

"Well, don't be late. Con doesn't like being kept waiting."

Maud foresaw daily difficulties; Miss Conway's demands and old M.'s were bound to clash. But this problem must wait, she was only concerned now to get Cousin Alice away before she said anything else—anything about her being delicate and needing regular meals. She could almost see this remark shaping itself on Cousin Alice's lips.

But old M. spoke first.

"The stables are full of bicycles," he said. "Saw them last time I looked round. Take one of those. Bound to be a lady's among 'em."

"Thank you very much."

As she followed him along the passage Maud wondered how the stables came to be full of bicycles.

CHAPTER THREE

"He is most considerate," Maud had said at lunch.

But by four o'clock old M. no longer seemed a considerate employer. Or perhaps it was that having talked to her in the morning and found her more intelligent than the head-banger he had overrated her secretarial ability. The speed with which he had dictated his letters had left her breathless, and as he had not dealt with the letters till after lunch she had little time to type them out—even if her shorthand outlines had been perfectly clear to her. The post went at six, and he was coming back at five to read the letters and sign them.

It was like a nightmare. Every time she looked at the clock the hands had jumped forward, and on each page of her shorthand pad there were indecipherable squiggles where she had been left behind in her race to keep up with old M. The empty hours of the morning, when she had been shown his filing system, his account books, and the various peculiarities of the three typewriters, seemed heaven in retrospect, though at the time she had been too nervous to enjoy them. The charming room, looking out across the lawn, had the oppressive atmosphere of a dungeon. But I shan't be in it long, she thought sadly, seeing herself disgraced, instantly dismissed, when old M. came back and found his letters untyped, his rapid eloquence all wasted.

"Maud, you are far too easily discouraged. You could do much better if you tried."

The words seemed to sound in her ear; they had in fact been spoken some years ago, by a schoolmistress to whom delicate, fanciful children were antipathetic. She had not believed Maud's ingenious excuses; she had said headaches were just imagination and idleness. That she was partly right had not endeared her to Maud; but now, remembering Miss Lambert-Smith's angry face, recalling her hectoring voice, she was suddenly inspired. It was as if the ghost of Miss Lambert-Smith had risen from the grave encourage her in her hour of need. (But surely so robust a personage could not be dead.)

There were five letters, three short ones and two fairly long. She tackled the easiest; it was an order for a pair of boots, like the last pair but with studs in the soles. It appeared that old M. had his boots made for him, and there was an interesting digression about why boots were so much healthier than shoes. Omitting this, because she supposed it to have been addressed to herself, she typed out the letter and laid it aside. Perhaps if she could produce three letters, or even two, he would give her another chance.

"Finished them? That's right."

It was ten minutes past five, and old M. stood in the doorway. The ghost of Miss Lambert-Smith faded away and left Maud trembling; if she could have torn the letters up and thrown them in the wastepaper basket she would have done so. But it was too late, he had seen them lying neatly beside her and he was already hunting for his pen.

"Good, good," he said. "Bring them here, please."

He sat down at his big desk. Quaking, she advanced and laid the letters before him. All would now be discovered, and her childish deception—as it now seemed—would certainly infuriate him far more than an honest confession of failure. He would find out that the letters she had typed were not—except in spir-it—the letters he had dictated.

"The stamps are in the right-hand compartment of that tin box on the third shelf by the fireplace," said old M. He looked up. "Hey!" he said, sharply but not unkindly.

Maud recovered the use of her legs, and of her wits, and be-fore going in search of the stamps she snatched up the letters and carried them back to her own table, where she anchored them safely under a glass paperweight. They must not be left lying about, they must be folded up and fitted into envelopes and entrusted to the security of the G.P.O. as soon as possible, before her luck changed.

Old M. had signed them all without so much as glancing at what he was putting his name to.

The letter-box was set in the wall close to Cousin Alice's cot-tage. It was therefore Maud's duty to post the letters, when she went home. She carried them in one of her raincoat pockets, and in the other pocket were the carbon copies, which she meant to hide tomorrow in some part of the filing system where old M. was unlikely to find them. That should not be difficult; for the intricacy of the home-made filing system, which filled three long shelves and five large boxes, had defeated him even when he was trying to explain it to her. Miss Goose had botched it all up, he had said, and they would have to sort everything out one of these days and start again. Maud blessed Miss Goose, whose hands (when they weren't throwing china) had thrust letters into the files at random, or who had banged her head on her desk so often as to dull her remembrance of the alphabet.

She wondered if the recipients of the letters—two of which were personal ones, apparently to relatives—would notice any difference. Old M. had dictated long, rambling sentences, full of digressions and of words whose shorthand outlines bore no resemblance to any word in her vocabulary. Her own style was terser, but in the longer letters—the ones to relatives—she had drawn on her imagination and had included some noncommittal remarks about the weather, so that the letters should not look suspiciously short. It had been a desperate expedient, and it had worked.

She did not mean to go on deceiving old M.; deception had been anathema to Miss Lambert-Smith and her ghost would certainly not lend its support to a career based on guile. Today had been an exception; tomorrow, when she was less nervous and more accustomed to her surroundings, it would be easier to follow his dictation. Tomorrow she would be able to concentrate, or she would bravely interrupt him if she got left behind.

Thinking these thoughts, Maud reached the end of the back drive, and then she remembered that she had not yet located the stableful of bicycles. She turned and walked back up the drive towards the outhouses and greenhouse, where the drive curved out of sight. There, beyond the towering clumps of laurels, she supposed she would find the stables.

Before she reached the laurels she passed an open door in the high wall, the wall of the terraced gardens, and paused to look through it. There was no one in sight, and she assumed that the gardeners had gone home. But why had they left the door open? An open door was almost an invitation to enter, to walk round and explore ... at least it was to Maud. She walked a short distance into the garden and stood still to admire it.

Here on the upper terrace the enclosing walls seemed higher, the garden more sheltered and cut off, than she had expected; although she could see the lane below her it had shrunk between its steep banks, and beyond the lane the fields sloped gently away, towards the silvery horizon of the sea. The garden was like a world of its own, or the very heart of the world that was Glaine combe.

Solitude was bliss, after the nerve-wracking day with old M. She walked the length of the garden and back, slowly, deep in a happy dream where failure and stupidity had no place. She looked at the distant sea, and up to the wooded hills at the head of the combe; but she did not look at the door in the wall until she was close to it again. The shock of discovery came instantaneously: the door was now shut.

Though she could see that it was locked she rushed to it and rattled it furiously, hoping that the person who had locked it might be still within earshot. "Hey!" she called, imitating old M. No one replied, no footsteps sounded. She ran back to the middle of the long garden and down the steps to the lower terrace. There was another door in the wall, opening on to this terrace, but it too was locked. She was locked in.

"Oh, misery me!" she exclaimed. It was an exclamation which went with wrung hands, tears, despair; but Maud had not yet begun to despair. She was distraught because she knew she had been stupid and because this was the kind of misadventure that caused other people to despise one, but she did not despair of getting out of the garden. On the fourth side, along the lane, there was only a balustrade and some wire. She would be rather conspicuous, climbing over it, but surely escape would be possible.

The lowest bed on the terrace was filled with rows of Michaelmas daisies. They were tall and solidly massed, but she pushed her way through them and came out only a few feet from the balustrade. There it was, not very high, with five strands of wire supported on iron stanchions above it.

But between her and this surmountable obstacle there was a deep ditch, filled from end to end with great coils of barbed wire, like something left over from the war.

She stood and gaped at it. She turned and looked back at the high walls. Frantically staving off the moment of despair, she hardly heard at first the faint, familiar sound coming from beyond the wall. It had grown much louder before she recognised it and sprang into action.

A car was coming along the lane; there wasn't a second to be lost. She ran along the edge of the flower bed, away from the end wall, so that she could more easily be seen. She waved and shouted, her handkerchief in one hand and her handbag in the other; she brushed the Michaelmas daisies aside as she ran, and then grabbed several of them and waved them with the handkerchief.

"Help!" she called. "Hey, help! Please stop!"

It was undignified, but some cars went very fast. This one, however, was going quite slowly and went even slower as it got nearer. It drew to a halt just below her, and there was a moment's complete inactivity while the driver presumably sat wondering if she was mad. It was a big car of a famous make, but so old that it did not suggest riches. Presently the door opened and the driver got out and came round the car to the near side and stood staring up at her.

"How did you get there?" he asked.

"I'm locked in. Please help me to get out."

As she spoke Maud dropped her hands to her sides, hiding the Michaelmas daisies behind her back. Of course it was too late, because he was almost certain to have seen them, and among the many regrettable aspects of the situation this irrationally struck her as the worst. It was bad enough to be locked up in someone else's garden, to be reduced to hailing total strangers and imploring their help. But it was quite appalling that the total stranger should turn out to be a Feniston—old M.'s son, and one who specialised, according to Cousin Alice, in economy.

She didn't doubt that this was Oliver Feniston. He was a tall, lean man, and his likeness to old M. was striking. He had the same beaky nose, the same stubborn chin and jaw. His hair was black and short, whereas old M.'s was white and shaggy, and this of course made him look more civilised and slightly less terrifying. He was shabbily dressed in clothes a scarecrow might have blushed to own—a ragged tweed jacket and muddy corduroys—and his face was so tanned as to suggest that he led an out-of-door life. That did not fit in with her idea of him as a city-dweller, but since the idea had only come from hearing Miss Conway say he did not live at Glaine she at once abandoned it. He lived in the country, perhaps not far away, and he had been over to see his father; and except for old M. himself he was the last person on earth whom she would have wanted to rescue her.

"I'm very sorry," she said, "but I got locked in accidentally. Someone locked the door while I was inside. The door was open, when I went past it, and I just went in to look round. And I'm in a great hurry because I have some important letters to post and it goes at six so please let me out quickly."

He glanced at his watch. "A pity you didn't think of that before you started looking round. And where were you going, when you walked past the open door?"

"To the stables, to borrow a bicycle."

"So that you could ride swiftly to the post with these important letters? But you weren't going in the right direction, for the stables."

"I didn't know. How could I know, when I'm a stranger? I just thought I'd walk up the drive and *look* for the stables."

"And pick a few flowers while you were about it? I must say you seem an unusually enterprising stranger. But I'll go back and let you out."

He got into the car without another word; and Maud was too mortified to speak. She had overlooked the fact that it was only a one-way recognition, that although she had identified him as Oliver Feniston he could not have known she was his father's new secretary; and now his first impression of her was even less favourable than it would have been if she had explained things properly. And first impressions were important, and second impressions did not wholly obliterate them, and it would be dreadful if Oliver Feniston disliked her and prejudiced his father against her. She wanted to stay at Glaine, though it seemed a place where her usual run of misfortunes occurred with even greater rapidity than at home.

He had backed the car along the lane to the end of the wall. Retracing her steps to the door Maud composed a short, explanatory, propitiatory speech—the best she could manage in the time available—and as soon as he unlocked the door she fired it off at him.

"I am extremely sorry to have given you so much trouble. And I ought to have explained that I wasn't stealing the bicycle—and I only picked the flowers to wave. I had to have something to wave. But you see I've come to live here, to live with my cousin, Mrs. Grayson, at Combe Cottage and to be a secretary—to work at Glaine. And it was really all right about the bicycle because your father told me I could borrow one. He said the stables were full of them."

"My father!"

"Yes. And thank you very much for letting me out. Now I must run, because of the letters."

"Did you say my father told you you could borrow a bicycle?"

He stood in the doorway, staring down at her with an expression which wasn't so much sceptical as absolutely incredulous. Maud lifted her head and stared back, fortified by the knowledge that she was speaking the truth.

"Yes, your father," she replied with dignity. "Old M."

The awful ease with which "old M." slipped out alarmed her hardly less than the thought of what would be its effect. "I don't mean—I mean—" she added wildly; and the tall man said:

"Yes, you do. Everyone calls him old M. But my father died when I was ten. Who do you think I am?"

"But you're Oliver—you must be!—I mean Mr. Oliver Feniston. You look so like him!"

"Like Oliver!"

"No, no!"

"Oh—like old M.?" For an instant he looked even more like old M., as the expression of an affronted eagle came and went, but then he smiled. "We-ll . . . I suppose there's a family likeness. But you're quite wrong. I am Charles."

"Charles?" she echoed falteringly.

"*Charles* Feniston. Not Oliver," he said, as if explaining things to a backward child. "Oliver is my cousin."

"Oh," said Maud.

How could she have been so stupid as to mistake him for Oliver? She saw at once that he was a Charles.

"And who are you?" he asked, still speaking to a child.

"I told you—"

"No, you didn't. You told me you were Mrs. Grayson's cousin and old M.'s secretary. That doesn't give me much to go on—and anyway, I don't jump to conclusions."

Being laughed at by Charles was almost more humiliating than being scolded by Oliver. "I am Maud Ansdell," she said. Her hateful name, which she associated with great-aunts in the opulence of their Edwardian youth, sounded more ridiculous than usual after the rightness of Charles. "And now I really must go, or I shall miss the post."

He was walking beside her back to the lane. As they reached it he said, "You have missed the post already, but I'll post those letters for you in Yeomouth. There's a late collection at the post office."

"Oh misery me!"

He was startled, not unnaturally, by this cry of anguish, but he said reassuringly, "The letters will go tonight. I'm going past Combe Cottage, so I'll give you a lift home."

"Thank you, but it is most important that I post these letters myself."

Not for anything would she trust the letters to another hand; she knew too well the tricks Fate could play on her.

"But if you post them here, they won't go tonight," he argued.

"I know—but you see, I shall have *posted* them."

"I won't forget, I promise you. Come along. You can give them me when we get to Combe Cottage and think of them arriving tomorrow."

There was nothing for it but to detach herself from this masterful man, who was now as determined to post the letters as she was herself. He held the car door open; she saw herself trapped, out-argued, made to give in.

"Thank you—but I don't want a lift," she said. "I have to walk, I have to take lots of exercise. My doctor—I mean my father—says it is essential. My father *is* a doctor, so of course he knows."

"I hope he also approves of bicycling," Charles Feniston replied.

He shut the door and went round to the driver's side. Maud stood still, waiting for him to get in, waiting for the moment when it would be safe, and also polite, to say a friendly last word.

But Charles wasn't one to delay his departure. The car seemed to start the instant he had taken his seat, and the last words, called through the open window, came from him.

"Don't think I should have told old M. about those letters—or whatever you're up to. We haven't spoken to each other for years."

CHAPTER FOUR

MAUD WAITED till after supper to ask who Charles Feniston was. The edited version of her afternoon's work, the details of the walk which her companions and Wilbraham had taken, the discussion of the new supper dish (largely made of eggs), filled up the time till then. Besides, she was wary of Miss Conway, whose silly mind might leap to the conclusion that she was "interested" in Charles Feniston if she spoke about him at once.

Her stepmother—whose unvarying kindness had sometimes caused the ungrateful Maud to long for a wicked one—had given this word, "interested," its quotation marks and its specialised meaning. Her stepmother was always rounding up young men and hoping Maud would be interested in one or the other of them (she should not, of course, be interested in more than one at a time); but her kindness, like the lavish icing on a cake, covered everything with a layer of sickly make-believe. She could never see—or she could never be brought to admit—that none of the young men was remotely interested in Maud.

Maud knew she was small and insignificant, delicate and unlucky. But she had her pride. After an early disillusionment she did not permit herself to be interested in any of the candidates, and she resented other people thinking she was. Miss Conway, so unlike her stepmother in every other way, resembled her in this; she showed a tendency to suspect "interest" when masculine names were mentioned. It had come out when she spoke of Oliver Feniston, and again at lunch when they had talked about the Woodfidleys. Maud's stepmother hoped she *would* be interested, and Miss Conway seemed anxious to discourage her; but Miss Conway's manner was as maddening as her stepmother's because it assumed that she was foolishly susceptible.

So she waited for the right moment to seek information casually, which came after supper when they had settled down in the sitting room with their books. Cousin Alice and Miss Conway were obviously glad to find that Maud could read; so many people, Cousin Alice said, needed the wireless all the time. It occurred to Maud that even if she had needed the wireless she couldn't have had it, since it was placed on a high shelf and had the forlorn appearance of a thing that was out of order, but she supposed they had feared she might be restless without it.

"You must join the library in Yeomouth," Cousin Alice said.

"How do I get to Yeomouth?"

"You can walk up to the main road and get a bus. Or you can walk all the way by a path along the cliffs."

"A man offered me a lift, this evening, and he was going to Yeomouth," Maud said casually.

"Oh. I wonder who that would be. What was he like?"

"Like Mr. Feniston, but younger. Very tall, and black-haired."

"That would be Charles," said Cousin Alice. Miss Conway, who had already opened her book, looked up and said, "Charles Feniston."

"And who is he?"

"He's a nephew of old M.'s. He has rented that big walled garden we passed this morning and turned it into a market garden—I daresay you saw the notice as we went through the gate."

"Does he live at Glaine with old—with Mr. Feniston?"

There was a short pause; she felt that Cousin Alice and Miss Conway were silently consulting each other and that Miss Conway was counselling caution.

"No," said Cousin Alice. "He lives in rooms in Yeomouth. Such a pity, when Glaine is so large and full of moth."

"That Mrs. Hatball is a slut," Miss Conway said vigorously. "Last time I was in the drawing room at Glaine I could have written my name in dust everywhere. And her husband is no better—what does he *do* all day, when he's supposed to be a chauffeur-gardener! The weeds on the terrace—"

"No, Con, he's not a chauffeur-gardener. He's a gardener-chef."

"He's not a gardener, anyway."

"I expect he doesn't care for it. Old M. says he's quite an artist at sauces."

Miss Conway snorted. "It wouldn't take *me* all day to cook for one old man and my wife and myself."

"I daresay not." Cousin Alice found her place in her book and settled back in her chair. "But you're a remarkably quick cook."

Miss Conway seemed to take this as a compliment.

"Oh, I don't believe in fiddle-faddling," she said.

Maud did not like to bring the conversation back to Charles. She had already noticed that neither of her companions was a gossip; they did not pour out a flood of information, as her stepmother would have done, about everyone in the neighbourhood, they did not even try to help her by telling her about Glaine and old M. It was as if they expected her to know, as if they had forgotten what it was like to be a stranger in a new place. But their reactions to Charles's name had been subtly different from this; instead of expecting her to know about Charles, they had deliberately decided to withhold information. It was intriguing; it added the little touch of mystery that was needed to make Glaine a perfect world in miniature.

I shall find out, she told herself. She would unveil the mysteries, she would explore the valley, she would become an efficient secretary. She would be herself, not the kind of person her stepmother had wished her to be. The first day was over, and she had survived it, and she was quite looking forward to tomorrow.

At ten o'clock Miss Conway left the room to give Puppy his evening run. At twenty past ten Cousin Alice, accompanied by Maud, joined her in the garden to look for him. Maud had yet to discover that this was a nightly routine, though she had already guessed that Wilbraham did not love his owners as much as they loved him. It was she who caught him; he showed himself for one moment in the dim light of Miss Conway's electric torch and she grabbed him before he could slink into the rhododendrons. "Well done!" said Miss Conway, advancing with the lead. Wilbraham, surprised and indignant, uttered a growl, and Maud promptly slapped him.

"Oh dear, he won't like that," Miss Conway said.

Maud did not mind about hurting Wilbraham's feelings, but she remembered it was wrong to chastise other people's dogs when their owners were standing by. She apologized to Miss Conway, who forgave her at once. They returned to the house, where Miss Conway told Cousin Alice about Maud's swift grab and nobly refrained from telling her about the slap.

"How quick of you, Maud. But you *are* quick. I noticed it at once."

Cousin Alice sounded as if she were referring to more than physical agility. But she had been up to the orchard, looking for Wilbraham, and of course she might have been thinking of Maud's first-night success with the hens.

"I am fairly quick," said Maud, hoping Cousin Alice wasn't thinking of the hens.

"It's because you are interested," said Cousin Alice.

"Cocoa?" said Miss Conway, waving the tin towards Maud.

"No, thank you. Yes, I am."

With Cousin Alice there wasn't any suggestion of quotation marks; Maud felt she could safely admit to being interested in life in general. At that moment she was finding even the kitchen interesting; it was the first time she had entered it, and she was struck by the large number of bits of paper—newspaper cuttings, typewritten lists, handwritten memoranda on envelopes—pinned to the doors of cupboards or propped on shelves. Some of them were recipes, others were more scientific and gave information about calories and proteins. A printed card above the stove listed the times for cooking different sorts of food in the pressure-cooker, and at the foot of the card someone had written in ink: "Reduce all times by 2 minutes to preserve vitamins."

This must be why everything she had eaten at Combe Cottage seemed slightly underdone.

"We have a milk drink every night," said Miss Conway. "But one mustn't *boil* the milk. That destroys all its value."

She took the pan off the stove; it had been there less than a minute, Maud judged, and the milk could barely be warm. Feeling rather sorry for Cousin Alice—for tepid milk must be even nastier than hot milk—she bade her goodnight.

She was halfway through the door before Cousin Alice added the postscript to her goodnight wishes.

"I'm glad you're going to have a bicycle. It will avoid any awkwardnesses about lifts. Though it was kind of Charles to offer one—but of course he couldn't know who you were."

Maud spun round, to catch Miss Conway making a warning face at Cousin Alice, who, however, was gazing in the other direction.

"Alice means he didn't know you were old M.'s secretary," Miss Conway said briskly, forgetting, in the heat of the moment, to give old M. his proper name. "That's what would be awkward, if it came out. He wouldn't like it."

"Because they have quarrelled, you see."

"But who wouldn't like what?"

"Con means old M. wouldn't like it. Don't you, Con?"

"Of course I do. And he is difficult, Alice."

"Sometimes he is *un peu difficile*," Cousin Alice said reluctantly, as if she hoped to conceal old M.'s faults by veiling them in French. "And as he is our landlord—"

"—and your employer—"

"Well, you *see*, Maud. It's better not to be involved."

The explanation was inadequate, but Maud did see, up to a point. She saw that old M. would strongly disapprove of anyone who fraternised with his enemies. She would have liked to know why Charles and his uncle had quarrelled, but she was not going to be told. Cousin Alice and Miss Conway had sat down at the kitchen table and were bending their heads over the biscuit tin, which lay between their tepid cups of cocoa. The subject was closed.

The next morning she had to be at Glaine at nine. Her alarm clock went off and Miss Conway cooked her breakfast (though she made it clear that in future Maud must cook it herself) and

Cousin Alice came down in her dressing gown to see that she wasn't going to be late. Before half-past eight Maud had been pushed out of the house. She had time to loiter, but she walked briskly, anxious to find the stables and choose a bicycle before she started work.

At least, she walked briskly until she reached Pixie Cot. But there her pace slackened; for the front door stood open and a shouted conversation was taking place between the girl outside on the terrace and the man leaning out of the dormer window, who must of course be Ensie Martin and her Papa. The girl was wearing a dressing gown, like Cousin Alice, and her dark hair hung down in two long plaits, but as she had her back to the lane Maud could not see her face.

"She was here two minutes ago," she called defensively.

"You shouldn't have let her out," said the man at the window.

"She—she wanted to go."

A dog, thought Maud; another joker like Wilbraham. She looked round to see if the dog was hiding under the hedge.

"She won't have gone far. It's been raining, and she simply hates damp grass," the girl continued.

"My poor little Pixie, braving the dews of morning!"

"But that's just what she won't do. She's probably in the lane."

"Then seek her out, Ensie. Seek her out."

He had a rich, well-modulated voice full of clerical intonations and a plump, rosy face which needed a round collar and a black coat to set it off; the striped pyjama jacket destroyed his dignity. Ensie, when she turned to obey him, looked older than Maud had expected—the long plaits were an early-morning deception—and had not inherited her Papa's pink rotundity. She was sallow, with big, protuberant eyes and a worried, even a slightly alarmed, expression. But the next instant Maud realised that she herself was the cause of the alarm; for with a startled hiss (a warning to her Papa?) Ensie gathered her dressing gown round her and retreated into the house. Almost simultaneously the window slammed shut, and a hand and striped pyjama sleeve were briefly visible jerking the curtains together.

They will have to get used to me, she thought, walking on. She turned the hypothetical dog into a cat and the contentious clergyman into a whimsical cat-lover. She felt quite sorry for Ensie Martin and quite prepared to make a friend of her.

The house where the Woodfidleys lived was called Chestnut Lodge. It had been a farm, then a dower house, then a farm again; but now the Home Farm had all the land in the combe and the Woodfidleys had taken a long lease of Chestnut Lodge and modernized it. At present they were away, travelling on the continent with their married daughter and their youngest son (the one who was said to be musical), but they would be coming home quite soon and then they would give a party. Oh yes, they always gave a party when they returned from their travels, Cousin Alice had said, and they asked everyone. But she did not know what kind of a party, because she and Con had always refused.

Maud had not been able to learn much more about the Woodfidleys. Cousin Alice and Miss Conway were quite talkative at meals, but they did not always answer her questions; she had to pick up what information she could before they started another subject. She did not know how many Woodfidleys there were, or what they did for a living, but she had formed the opinion that they were rich, restless, and slightly uncongenial. She hoped, however, that if they asked everyone to their party she might be included.

She walked quickly past the terraced gardens, giving them one quick glance to see if Charles was there. He was not. She did not approach Glaine by the back drive but walked on till she reached the main entrance, a little further along the lane. The front drive was as reedy and rutted as the back one, and it led her through a tunnel of overgrown shrubs and trees, curving uphill to the hidden house. If there had been a garden on this side, no trace of it remained; she saw the house close in front of her as she rounded the last bend, and she was struck anew by its melancholy charm. She walked on, following the drive to its end in a derelict stable yard where grass and thistles hid the cobblestones. In the middle of this yard, gazing up at the blue sky in a happy trance, stood a man in a chef's white cap and apron.

"A good morning, yes?" he said as she approached him.

"Yes, it is."

He must be Hatball, the gardener-chef; she had thought Hatball was a curious name but she had not realized till now that he was a foreigner. It must be a corruption of his real name. He was a fat, cheerful-looking man, and he appeared to be a good deal younger than his wife.

"I'm looking for a bicycle," she said. "Mr. Feniston said I could borrow one. Do you know where they are?"

"There are everywhere bicycles. They are for the women in the war and for the conscientious men, who work here. So I am told. Some are left behind and I think it is because they do not go. For me I prefer auto-bicycle and this one is mine, in harness room. But most other bicycles are in stables and some all-broken ones in pigsty. No pumps are here any more but my wife has pump for her bicycle which is in washing room at back of the house, and that you shall use. None of the doors are locked."

"Thank you," said Maud, dazed but grateful. "Then I'll just go and see—"

"You shall find bicycle and put here. I shall bring pump and do tyres. So shall be ready for you at luncheon time and so—"

"Thank you very much."

"—and so you have time to eat and enjoy and digest. I think yesterday you have no time, running there and running back, to eat and enjoy and digest. No one is happy, so. You are disagreeable inside."

"I see what you mean. And thank you very much. Now I must look for the bicycle or I shall be late for work."

"You still have much time, for I see Mr. Feniston first to discuss food. This is important—more important than letters."

He turned and walked away, whistling, and Maud hurriedly began her search for a bicycle. Whether or no old M. thought food more important than letters, it would not do to be late.

She was at her desk by nine o'clock, but her employer did not appear for another twenty minutes. It gave her time to try all three typewriters and to begin cleaning the one that seemed the best. All were old, each had different faults, they were only one degree better than the bicycles. She wondered if they too had been left over from the war; but old M., coming in suddenly, enlightened her.

"Bought them all at different sales," he said proudly. "Got them for practically nothing. Astonishing what bargains you can pick up if you know where to go."

"Yes," said Maud, wondering why he had needed three.

"Did you find a bicycle?"

"Yes. I went round to the stables this morning—"

"Saw you from my bedroom window, talking to Hat. You mustn't let him talk, you know. He talks far too much, and too fast. You must tell him to stop. Was there one that would do?"

"Yes. Of course it wants oiling and cleaning, but I'll do that this evening."

"Good. I can see you're a believer in oil."

Maud looked at her hands. They were black with oil—though it must have come off the typewriter because there had been none on the bicycle. She looked at old M., who said fiercely:

"Go and wash them. Are you another Miss Goose? I even had to tell her to wash her neck."

She fled. But it was in a milder voice that he called after her, "Find Mrs. Hat. Tell her to show you your room."

Mrs. Hatball was dusting the stairs. (Perhaps she had a thing about them; perhaps they were the only part of Glaine that ever got dusted.) She had been told that Maud was to have a room upstairs, for "prinking," and she led her to a large, sheeted front bedroom, which had been prepared for her by removing the dust-sheet from the dressing table and leaving two coat hangers on the bed. She also showed the way to the bathroom, and its immense mahogany-encased bath and brass taps delighted Maud as much as the view from the bedroom windows—the lovely view of the valley in the morning sunlight. But she did not linger; quite soon she was back with old M., half expecting him to tell her to hold her hands out for inspection.

He ignored her hands, but he gave her a hard, penetrating stare. It was not wholly disparaging, but rather suggested that he had found out something about her; that she had become more interesting, more a person to be reckoned with. Maud hoped her swift unhesitating flight had shown him that she was more obedient than Miss Goose (who perhaps had resented being told that her neck was dirty), but it did not quite account for the stare. And anyway it had been really necessary for her to wash her hands. Miss Goose's neck couldn't have been black with oil.

Nevertheless, she and old M. were getting on much better. He opened his letters, read bits out to her, discussed them, and showed her how to keep the household accounts by his special system, which seemed very complicated and quite unlike the bookkeeping she had been taught. In the afternoon he dictated seven letters; and either because he spoke more slowly or because she was less nervous she found it much easier to keep up with him. But she began to wish he would leave her to type the letters, for it was already after four.

"They can wait till tomorrow," he said suddenly. "Give you something to do in the morning if I'm late."

Maud gladly agreed. It seemed a good arrangement; and henceforth it worked well. There were to be times when she and old M. took at least four days to acknowledge what he considered to be really urgent letters, and far longer to deal with the rest. But by then they had begun a task so engrossing to him that most letters ranked as a tiresome interruption.

"When shall I start cataloguing the library?" she asked now. It was as if the claims of the library had been in both their minds; old M. looked at her with unmistakable approval.

"That what you want to do?" he asked.

"Oh, yes."

"Good. I'll show it you tomorrow. Too late now—and I want to walk down to the farm. We'll stop for today."

She looked at the clock. "Isn't there anything else? I know—I'll clean the type—"

"*Stop!* I said stop and I mean it. Can't you understand plain English?"

Perhaps Miss Goose couldn't. But Maud had at any rate begun to understand old M.

CHAPTER FIVE

'WE CAN'T START today," old M. said, "because Oliver is coming. My son, very clever feller but a bee in his bonnet. Very *nice* feller," he added, with a touch of anxious pride. Maud found it endearing; but she could not really concentrate on Oliver. Her first glimpse of the library was still making her feel slightly giddy.

The library appeared to be an immensely big room, though she could not see it very clearly because old M. had opened the shutters in only the nearest of the four long windows. A shaft of sunlight, solid with motes of dust, stretched between her and the more distant recesses, but she could just make out that these recesses were deep bays, like miniature rooms within the big one, shelved from floor to ceiling. At the end where she stood there were no bays, but the shelves continued in an unbroken line from the door to the chimneybreast. Between the windows there were tall bookcases with glass doors. Down the middle of the room stood smaller bookcases, back to back for want of wall space, and all different. They looked as if they had been wonderful bargains, like the typewriters.

"Nice lot of books, aren't there?" said old M.

"Yes. Yes, indeed."

She had expected a lot of books standing higgledy-piggledy on shelves, all in the wrong order and waiting for her to come to their rescue. But she had not expected that there would also be books all over the floor; piles of books stacked in high, tottering towers; rivers of books winding about their feet . . . and everything thick with grime and cobwebs.

"We'll start on Monday. Oliver is sure to stay till Monday once he's here. Don't see much of him these days . . . pity to chivvy him too much. . . ."

Old M. went on muttering to himself, while Maud looked at the library and wondered where they would begin. It would be the work of a lifetime, of several lifetimes—how on earth could she and old M. hope to reduce this chaos to any sort of order! She stooped and picked up the nearest book, and then put it down again and wiped her hands on her skirt. Old M. would have to get used to dirty hands, after Monday.

"But where—I mean, did you inherit them?" she asked.

"Some of them. Oh yes, my grandfather collected books," he answered proudly. "He built this library when he enlarged the house. Twenty-one, he was, and he'd just come into his money. Not the sort of thing you'd expect an orphan to build, is it?"

"I don't know what I should expect an orphan to build."

"Nothing, of course. Or something frivolous—a gazzy-boo or a turret. If he'd been brought up by mad Methodists like my grandfather you'd expect him to gad about, instead of settling down in a library."

"I suppose he went on buying books all his life."

"No, he didn't. He lost interest in books, later on. Took to drink, as a matter of fact—but that's between you and me. No, the library was half empty when I came in for it. A great pity, I thought. Room doesn't look properly furnished, with a lot of empty shelves, does it?"

"No," Maud said, weakly. "But do you mean that *you* bought all these books?" She pointed to the rivers at her feet.

"Got a lot of 'em at sales. Books are amazingly cheap if you buy them in lots—get them for next to nothing. And then I was very lucky in my aunts."

His crowing laugh showed that the aunts were indeed a happy memory. "How? How?" she cried, too enthralled to remember that secretaries should not be inquisitive. But old M. had also forgotten it, in the pleasure of having acquired an attentive listener.

"Three of them," he explained triumphantly. "One old maid and two barren widows, and all as fond of reading as a nest of owls. Very like owls, they were—tawny hair and blinking eyes, you know, and no necks—and they all lived to a good old age. But it was worth waiting for."

"You mean they left you all their books?"

"The last one did. That's what I'm telling you. She knew there was room for them at Glaine, you see. As I said, I had to wait a long time. They all lived together in the end, and the youngest one—the spinster—outlasted the others by twenty years. I thought she'd see her century, but she didn't quite make it. She died three years ago."

Maud could hardly believe that some of the books had been there only three years. The room looked as if it hadn't been touched since the youngest aunt's first birthday.

"I suppose it wasn't a surprise," she said. "Getting the books, I mean. You knew your aunt was going to leave them to you?"

"Yes—but I didn't expect the money. Didn't think she'd got so much to leave. Not that it was a fortune," he added hastily. "But still—a tidy sum."

"How exciting."

She thought old M. regretted having mentioned the money, for he broke off rather abruptly and walked away to close the shutters. In her own family, too, money was not a thing one discussed with strangers—or, she supposed, with secretaries— so she was able to sympathize with him although she longed to know what the tidy sum amounted to. To change the subject she asked him, as they left the library, what time Oliver was expected.

She referred to him as "Mr. Feniston," and at first old M. seemed not to understand her.

"Who—who?" he demanded. "Oh—Oliver. He'll be here at tea time. Takes him all day to drive down. I tell him I could do it in half the time with one eye shut."

Maud thought this did not sound very safe; but somehow the thought of Oliver driving slowly and carefully was putting-off. She had been put off in the first place by Cousin Alice's saying he specialised in economy, and now she could not help wondering if he drove slowly to save petrol. But she tried hard to keep an open mind and found it easier to do so as the day wore on. For old M. was clearly looking forward to Oliver's arrival; and his excitement, disguised though it was by mock grumbles, communicated itself to Maud.

"He hasn't been near me for three months," he complained. "Not as if he was married, either. Some excuse for spending his holiday at the seaside if he'd a wife and children, you know—but as it is, he might just as well have come here."

"Where did he go instead?"

"Venice. Odd-shaped boats, lions, people in fancy dress, all that poppycock. I've been to Venice myself so I know what I'm talking about. Mediterranean seaside places aren't any good anyway, because they haven't got proper tides."

Maud had not thought of Venice as being a seaside place; but if Oliver had spent his holiday there he must be less economical than she had feared.

By half-past three old M. had become restless; after pacing up and down the room several times he abruptly announced that he would show her his aunts. Or rather, their portraits, upstairs in the long gallery. She guessed why he had wanted to visit the long gallery when they got there; it was at the end of the house, above the library, and from its windows one could see some distance along the lane. The lane was not visible from the windows on the ground floor.

"There they are. Painted in the drawing room here, when they were girls. Feller from Exeter did it. Looked like owls even then."

They did look like owls. The Exeter painter had given them fixed stares, and they were perched in a row on a spindly sofa with a trail of greenery hiding their knees. Three dear little owls. And old M. was an eagle; and Charles was an eagle too, when he was offended. She wondered whether Oliver would be an eagle or an owl.

"That's my grandfather. And that's his wife. And that's my great-grandfather, in the blue coat. He was like me—he married twice and outlived both of them."

But he wasn't really interested in his ancestors; his glance kept straying to the windows, and presently Maud walked on by herself and left him standing at the end window pretending to be lost in thought. She did not like to leave the gallery, since he had come there on the pretext of showing her the portraits, so she paced slowly on, past a row of indifferent family portraits, and amused herself by pairing the ladies with the gentlemen and deciding whether their marriages had been happy. Great-grandfather in the blue coat had been a charmer, and his wives were worthy of him; grandfather, on the other hand, had a weak, frightened face, and it was hardly surprising that he took to drink to escape from that bullying wife. . . .

"Why, there's Oliver! Saw his car in that open bit of the lane," old M. added hastily, turning away from the window with ill-concealed excitement. "Come along! Tell you about the others another day. The light's going anyway."

Maud followed him through the house; she almost had to run. "I'll go back to do those accounts," she said, as they reached the foot of the stairs. But old M., striding through the archway to the outer hall, made a brusque, beckoning gesture, as if she were a dog that was attempting to stray from his side. "Come along," he commanded. Needing no second bidding, she followed him to the open door.

The car had drawn up in the middle of the drive and Oliver was standing beside it, looking, not at the reception party but up at the exterior wall. He wore horn-rimmed spectacles, but although this instantly suggested the owl there was also a trace of the eagle in his recognisably Feniston nose, especially when, as now, he stood with his head thrown back. He was neither as tall as his father nor as dumpy as his great-aunts, but he had the lean figure of the one and the tawny colouring of the others. So much she had time to perceive, before his gaze shifted and the first greetings were exchanged.

"That gutter's rusted right through. Why on earth don't you get it mended?"

"You ought to have been here an hour ago. Mean to say you started just after breakfast?"

These reproaches, uttered simultaneously, were not what she had expected to hear; their tone could hardly be interpreted as one of affectionate badinage. Even the speakers seemed to regret their acrimony and hastily resolve to start again. Oliver walked forward, smiling, and old M. stepped out of the porch to meet him.

"Well—nice to see you at last," he said.

"You're looking very fit," said Oliver.

"Got a new car—hey?"

"No, still the old one. But I've just had her resprayed."

"Sprayed? D'you mean painted? What's the point of that! I've had my car seventeen years and the paint's practically as good as new. Except where it's got dented, of course—mudguards and places like that. Bound to happen, when you've had a car seventeen years."

"Modern paint doesn't last like the old stuff. But in any case . . ."

Oliver stopped. It was as though he was determined not to be drawn into an argument. He went back to the car and lifted a suitcase out of the boot; while he was doing this old M. looked round and called to Maud.

"Hey!—where are you? Oh, there you are. Thought you'd run away. Come here."

She came. Oliver, turning round, suitcase in hand, looked extremely surprised. Old M. said:

"This is Oliver. No need to tell you though. Oliver, this is Miss Maud Ansdell."

Puzzled but polite, and hampered by his suitcase, Oliver gave her a slightly lopsided bow.

"Shake hands!" said old M., roaring at Oliver as if he were a deaf and ill-mannered child. "Put that thing down and shake hands properly! Bowing and scraping as if you were at court—"

He checked himself with an effort; but Maud, unused as yet to family life with the Fenistons, felt that no words of hers, no social adroitness, could now reconcile Oliver to her presence. She was surprised and relieved when he calmly put the suitcase down and clasped her hand. She had expected him to get it over quickly, but he seemed quite unabashed; he looked her full in the face, said primly that this was an unexpected pleasure, and asked if she was staying in the neighbourhood for long.

"Yes, she is," said old M. "She has come to live at Combe Cottage with Alice Grayson. And she is my new secretary."

He spoke with triumph, and Maud at once suspected that Oliver had been discouraging about his chances of getting a secretary who would be both non-residential and a stranger to the district. She was his answer to Oliver, his proof that he knew best; but she wished her existence had not had to be visibly demonstrated.

"Splendid," said Oliver, in a tone of vague enthusiasm which covered everything. He picked up his suitcase again, stood aside for Maud to enter the house, and could be heard asking his father if it was too late for a cup of tea.

"Of course not. Tea's in the drawing room—told Hat to have it ready. Ring the bell—no, there he is. Come along, Maud."

Maud was swept into the drawing room. Her position had changed, her employer—though perhaps without thinking—addressed her by her Christian name, and the discovery that there were only two cups provoked him as much as if she had been a daughter of the house. It was no good ringing the bell in the drawing room because it did not work, and anyway it would be quicker to fetch a cup oneself than waste time talking to Hat—feller who talked far too much and couldn't hurry if his life depended on it. Muttering dark threats, old M. went off to fetch the cup, and Maud, seated on the spindly sofa which had served as a perch for the three little owls, waited for Oliver to reveal more of his character.

He revealed some of it at once, by looking round the drawing room and saying fretfully that it was reeking with damp. Then, remembering that she wasn't really a daughter of the house, he asked some conventional questions: had she come quite recently, did she like the neighbourhood, did she find it lonely? Maud gave conventional answers, and expanded the last into an explanation of how she had got the job. She thought he was both interested and pleased to learn that she was a relative of Mrs. Grayson.

"Of course I know her well," he said. "And Miss Conway too."

Maud thought this sounded pompous and patronizing. She remarked rather pointedly that they had lived at Combe Cottage for twenty years.

"You mean it would be strange if I *didn't* know them well? I don't agree. One can live next door to some people for a lifetime and not know them at all. I suppose it's really a failure of the imagination."

"Yes, that's true. And it works both ways. I mean, if you think people are too dull to bother about, you can be sure they're thinking the same about you."

He looked startled, as if this idea had never before occurred to him. She felt she had neatly repaid him for being condescending towards Cousin Alice and Miss Conway.

"Glaine is very beautiful," she said, to end the silence her last remark had caused.

"Do you think so? Yes, I suppose it is—to a newcomer. But from my point of view there's little to be said for a picturesque ruin. Can't you see it's falling to bits?"

It was a *cri de coeur*; it was like the lifting of a kettle lid to disclose the bubbling water inside. At this interesting moment Maud frankly regretted the return of old M., but she had time to give Oliver a swift glance by which she hoped to convey intelligent concern and limited sympathy. The limitation was imposed by her admiring Glaine as it was; sympathy was for his sufferings. It was silly of him to be driven to frenzy by the sight of a broken gutter or a damp patch on the ceiling, but silliness was more likeable than smugness, and till now she had thought him rather smug. It was nice to know that he wasn't like that through and through.

"Here we are," said old M., putting the cracked cup beside the others. "You been talking about Venice?"

They had not, but they did. Old M.'s determination to keep the talk on Venice was strange, considering how poorly he thought of it; but it was explained when she took her leave. He accompanied her to the front door, and when they reached the porch he looked back and listened.

"It's all right," he said. "He's gone upstairs."

Maud waited, almost expecting another kettle lid to lift. But old M. spoke in a soft rumble, and was more coherent than usual.

"You didn't tell him about the library? . . . Good. Just as well, you see, because he's got a bee in his bonnet. I meant to warn you it wouldn't do. We've had it all out, but he won't see reason. . . . Well, that's all. Just keep it to yourself that we're starting on the library."

"I won't mention it."

"Good, good. No point in upsetting him when he's only here till Monday."

CHAPTER SIX

By MIDDAY ON Saturday Maud felt quite thankful that Oliver was leaving on Monday. She was not supposed to work on Saturdays but she understood why old M. had asked her to come in that morning; it was to give him an excuse for not being with Oliver. Pottering about in the estate room, reading letters, hunting for his diary, he could pretend to be urgently busy. The presence of his secretary made it more convincing. She did not know whether Oliver was deceived, but at least she was helping old M. to deceive himself.

He had looked forward to Oliver's arrival, but now that he was here they did nothing but bicker. Or so it seemed; the echoes of the bickering rang down the passages and were reflected in old M.'s temper when he entered the estate room. Oliver had been late for breakfast again; he had torn the sheets to pieces ("Said he put his toe in a slit. Feller's too old to be twiddling his toes like a baby!"); he had nearly blown them up by having two baths in less than twenty-four hours and so emptying the cistern—and it wasn't as if he didn't know they had to pump all the water. Everything he did was wrong, every opinion he uttered showed he had a bee in his bonnet. And on the few occasions when she encountered Oliver it was fairly clear to Maud that he was thinking exactly the same about old M.

Oliver was polite but fretful; he controlled his tongue but he couldn't control his gaze, which wandered to the cobwebby corners of rooms, to broken chairs, to the mass of papers and letters, old account-books and half-used note-books, which covered his father's desk and quite a lot of the floor. She had not yet had time to cope with all this muddle and she feared that Oliver thought her dreadfully inefficient; but the real reason for wishing him gone was that he upset his father. Glaine had cast its spell over Maud, and although old M. still unnerved her she understood how he felt about Glaine. She did not want him to be upset.

"How do you occupy yourself when you're not working?" Oliver asked.

He had come into the estate room to tell his father that the bailiff from the home farm wanted to see him. Old M., who usually walked down to the farm every day, had said at first that it would wait, and then (perhaps to escape from Oliver) had gone off to see what the bailiff wanted. Oliver had remained in the room, and Maud guessed that he would have liked to prowl round and examine things but that he did not care to do so in her presence.

"I've hardly had time yet to see anything," she replied. "I'm going to walk into Yeomouth this afternoon—or perhaps I'll go by bus and walk back, along the cliffs."

"Do you like the country?"

"I like this country. I've only lived in imitation country, till now. Green-belt country, you know, with electric trains at a convenient distance and self-conscious village inns and everyone rushing madly about saying it must be preserved. And that's what it *is*—like tinned fruit compared with real fruit."

"Oh. I thought your father was a doctor in Nigeria or somewhere."

"So he is," she said. It wasn't Nigeria, but no matter. "But my stepmother lives mostly in England. She only goes out there in the cold weather now, because it didn't suit her. I live—I used to live—with her, and when she's away I live—lived—with my aunts. And they were all very kind to me. Kindness itself."

"Oh. And did you find that oppressive?"

Maud raised her eyes from her typing. Oliver was sitting in his father's chair, but he did not look in the least like an eagle. He looked remarkably sympathetic, as if he understood what it meant to be pestered by well-meaning aunts and—

"Of course you had a stepmother too," she said.

"No, I hadn't. What made you think so?"

She was embarrassed. There was nothing for it but to explain that old M. had told her he had been married twice and that she had jumped to the conclusion that Oliver was the child of his first marriage. The explanation was given reluctantly; she remembered that this was the second mistake she had made over Oliver and that Charles Feniston had laughed at her for jumping to conclusions.

"We were in the long gallery," she added. "He was showing me the portraits and he just happened to say that he was like the man in the blue coat because of it, and that's how I happened to know."

"What man in a blue coat? And what has a blue coat got to do with being married twice?"

Maud's embarrassment gave place to a feeling that Oliver was being rather dense. "Your great-great-grandfather, of course. *He* was married twice, like your father—and in his portrait he wears a blue coat."

"Sorry," said Oliver, accepting the rebuke quite humbly. "But I can never remember which of those portraits is which. And anyway they're all atrocious."

"But they're your ancestors!"

"I see you have already been indoctrinated. But I'm not Chinese—and neither are you, come to that. You didn't sound piously respectful when you spoke of your stepmother and your aunts."

"At least I can tell them apart."

He laughed. *"Touché,"* he said, and Maud gave him a bad mark for being affected. But affectations could be a sort of shyness; she had already seen a natural and friendly Oliver behind the stiffly polite one, and now she was to see him again.

"Yes, my father married twice," he said, "but I'm the child of the second marriage, not the first, so I never suffered from a stepmother. There weren't any children of the first marriage, nor have I any brothers or sisters. My mother died nearly ten years ago, just before my twenty-first birthday—but until recently I still had an aunt, and she was just as tiresome as yours. She was kindness itself and she never forgot that I was a motherless boy."

"My aunts never forgot that I'm delicate."

"Are you? I hope—"

"I mean, I *was*," she interrupted hastily. "I've grown out of it—just as you've grown out of being a motherless boy. But aunts never forget."

"And they make it certain that you don't either."

Maud knew she was being unfair to her excellent aunts, but she could not resist making them out as worse than Oliver's. The tiresomeness of aunts was a subject that interested him, and she succeeded in making him laugh; towards the end, however, she began to feel that her own laughter was not the response he wanted. He expected to be taken more seriously, as a misunderstood nephew.

From being a misunderstood nephew it was no distance at all to being a misunderstood son. Maud did not suppose that Oliver would actually present himself as a misunderstood son, to his father's secretary, but she felt that this dreary figure was hovering in the air, mutely appealing for attention. She looked at the clock and was glad to see it was after half-past twelve.

"Do you think Mr. Feniston is coming back?" she said. "I've finished everything I had to do."

"He's probably at the farm. What do—"

He checked himself and said instead that she had better go, and that he would tell his father. Maud, having re-established herself as a secretary, hoped the misunderstood son would fade away. A twinge of conscience, which really referred to her poor aunts, made her point out to Oliver, as she had to old M, that Alice Grayson was not an aunt but a cousin.

"I know," he said. "And a very nice one too. I was hoping to come and see her this afternoon, but I have to go to Yeomouth first. I could drive you there, if you're going."

"Thank you very much. What time are you starting?"

They arranged a time to suit both of them and Maud rushed off to appease Miss Conway, who was undoubtedly being kept waiting.

Halfway through lunch she told them that Oliver was giving her a lift into Yeomouth. Even Miss Conway could not find it inappropriate that Oliver Feniston should give his father's secretary a lift, but she voiced her surprise that he should be going to Yeomouth on a Saturday afternoon.

"Perhaps he's going out to tea," Maud said. "He didn't say he would bring me back, and anyway he knows I mean to walk back along the cliffs."

She had forgotten that Oliver had spoken of calling on Cousin Alice when he returned from Yeomouth.

"As you're going to Yeomouth you could get me some needles," said Miss Conway. "Crewel needles for my great work. I've mislaid the packet, though I know I had one."

Maud gladly agreed to do so. Miss Conway's great work—always known by this name—had not been touched since her arrival, but she supposed that was because the needles were mislaid. It was a large piece of canvas stamped with a very ugly Jacobean design, and it was stretched in a big embroidery frame which filled one corner of the sitting room. Only a flower and a half had been completed, and Maud did not care for the colours Miss Conway had chosen, each of which seemed to clash with the others. But it was certainly a great work, judged by size and complexity. She added crewel needles to her short shopping list; and then Cousin Alice remembered that she needed some soap, and Miss Conway came back from the kitchen and said they were out of tomatoes and mixed spice. Before three o'clock Maud's shopping list had grown quite long.

"I'd better take a basket," she said. She had meant to explore Yeomouth, but she feared there would not be time. And the basket, filled with tomatoes and soap and spice and hair oil and haberdashery, would be a burden on her homeward walk. But this had not occurred to them; nor did it occur to them that she would not welcome Wilbraham's company.

"He doesn't get enough exercise," Cousin Alice said. "And I know he will be perfectly good in the car if you hold him on your lap. But don't let him off the lead while you're in Yeomouth."

With a basket in one hand and Wilbraham's lead in the other Maud waited for Oliver. To wait in the lane had been her own idea; it stressed the inequality between them and thus would keep Miss Conway calm. She had not foreseen, however, that the first car to come along the lane would not be Oliver's.

"Would you care for a lift today?" Charles Feniston asked. "Or are you still under doctor's orders?"

He had stopped the car beside her, and it blocked the narrow lane. Maud's first thought was that Oliver would be coming at any moment and that nothing could be more awkward than to be found talking to his outcast cousin. A family feud aroused strong feelings, and Oliver would certainly tell his father; she saw exactly what Cousin Alice had meant about the desirability of not being involved. Her second thought was that Charles had blue eyes; like his ancestor in the blue coat, who had obviously chosen it because it became him.

"Well, you see—" she said. "I mean, no, I'm not. But I don't need a lift, thank you. I am waiting for—I am waiting."

It sounded rather odd, but she had thought it better not to mention Oliver. If Charles had old M.'s temperament it might annoy him.

"A nice afternoon for waiting," he said.

"Yes. Yes, isn't it?"

"But rather disappointing for your dog. He seems to expect to be going somewhere."

She glanced with distaste at Wilbraham, who was tugging at the end of his lead. "He is Cousin Alice's dog," she said, disowning him. "At least, half of him is, the other half belongs to Miss Conway. They're so *fair* about sharing things."

"An admirable quality, but rather confusing for the shared object."

"I expect that's what's wrong with him. It's made him nervous."

"You seem rather nervous too, if you'll forgive my saying so. Are you expecting something very terrifying to come along the lane?"

Maud had not realised that her quick glances toward the sharp bend had been so revealing. But what she resented was that Charles should tease her as if she were a child.

"Of course not," she said, coldly. "I thought I heard Oliver's car. He is taking me to Yeomouth."

"Oh," said Charles. He looked at her. She was already regretting her impulsive rebuke, and in particular the unwarranted familiarity of alluding to Oliver by his Christian name after so short an acquaintance. The aunts had held strict views about this sort of impertinence; and the influence of the aunts was still strong enough to make their niece feel ashamed. She stared back at Charles, trying to appear at her ease, but apparently not succeeding.

"Well, don't cry," he said. "Oliver is a nice, kind chap, if rather boring. To the best of my knowledge you have nothing to fear."

"I'm not crying!"

"But he's never punctual. Always late for everything, even when he was a boy. He breaks his shoelaces or loses his spectacles or just forgets to start. So next time he tells you three o'clock you needn't expect him till a quarter past."

With this advice he left her; not a moment too soon. His car had hardly disappeared over the hill before Oliver's came round the corner. Oliver had a good excuse for his lateness, but after Charles's parting words she rather doubted its sincerity. Perhaps he had just forgotten to start.

It was a relief, however, that Oliver did not object to Wilbraham. "I'm very fond of dogs," he said, stroking Wilbraham's unresponsive head. "I always wish I could have one of my own."

"Why can't you?"

The answer lasted them to Yeomouth. But Maud, who was enjoying her first view of new country, did not listen to every word. Her stepmother would have noticed that she was being inattentive and would gently have remarked on it, but Oliver did not appear to notice and needed the minimum of encouragement to continue talking. Maud said Yes and No and How interesting, and registered the facts that he taught economics at a college or university in the Midlands, that he lived in very comfortable rooms, well anyway one couldn't grumble, that his landlady was a bank manager's widow and adored cats and had bred several champions, and that with so many cats about, and many of them pregnant, it would have been antisocial of him to insist on keeping a dog.

"Not that she wouldn't allow it, but naturally ones tries to fit in. Some landladies are absolute dragons. A colleague of mine told me that *his* landlady . . ."

"How tiresome for him," said Maud.

"And I don't really mind the cats, though I'm not particularly fond of them. They seem to me . . ."

"Yes, that's true."

Pink bungalows appeared, at the top of a long hill. Beyond the bungalows the road narrowed, and they drove down the hill between walled gardens and houses by whose architecture one could measure the town's growth. The yellow Victorian brick was succeeded by Regency stucco, the detached villas gave place to a steep street where all the shops seemed to be competing to sell clotted cream, shrimping nets, and picture postcards. Behind the huddled roofs of the lower town Maud saw the curve of the bay. Yeomouth was quite a small place, and as different from Eastbourne or Folkestone as she had hoped.

She exclaimed in delight, and Oliver agreed that the town had charm. In happy unanimity they arrived at the car park, which was a tiny square at the foot of the hill. The Marine Parade, narrow and unpretentious, curved away to the right, leading to a small harbour, and on the left the oldest part of Yeomouth clung to its terraced cliff. Oliver pointed out some local landmarks and Maud listened with more attention than she had given to the account of his life in the Midlands. Wilbraham, roused from the torpor which car travel had induced, clamoured to be taken for a walk.

"I mustn't let him off the lead," she said. "And anyway I have a lot of shopping to do."

She looked sadly at the beach, and Oliver said sympathetically that that was the worst of living in the country. You couldn't go anywhere without being given a list of commissions as long as your arm, by the people who stayed at home.

"One does so resent the waste of time," he said. "With a little planning they need never run out of anything. The shopping could be done once a month, as a regular routine. If everyone in the household kept a list and co-operated . . ."

"Planning," she thought scornfully, rejecting Oliver's sympathy as a mere offshoot of economics. Her attention wandered again, but presently she discovered that he was planning their afternoon. She was to shop for an hour and to meet him for tea; afterwards they would exercise the dog, and then he would drive her home.

"And what are you going to do?" she asked.

"I'll wait for you here. I've brought a book with me. I should only be in your way if I came shopping," Oliver said humbly.

It did not occur to Maud that other people had found him an encumbrance and told him so. He could have carried the basket, she thought. But she had not realized that he had no reason to come to Yeomouth, except to drive her there, and although Charles had described him as a nice, kind chap she could not believe he would give up a whole afternoon to unprofitable kindness. Obsessed by her preconceived image of Oliver as a planner, a specialist in economy and a man with a bee in his bonnet, she was sure he had a plan and a purpose.

He wanted to find out what she was like, to decide whether she was a suitable person to be his father's secretary. The explanation occurred to her at tea, when Oliver stopped talking about his career and started asking about hers, and the more she thought of it the more probable it seemed. It fitted in with what she thought of as his fussiness. It accounted for his willingness to listen to all she said.

She exerted herself to please; not by charming him but by giving him an impression of reliability and competence. She enlarged on the thoroughness of the training she had so recently undergone. She tried to sound modest but confident; and she was thankful that old M. had warned her of Oliver's views on libraries. Sternly repressing her tendency to frivolous chatter—which seemed at times to be shared by Oliver himself—she brought the conversation back to serious, impersonal subjects; and finally, in desperation, to the Midlands, where Oliver, also looking rather desperate, kept it.

"It was nice to see Oliver again," Cousin Alice said. Oliver, refreshed by a glass of home-made cordial brimming with vitamins, had just left Combe Cottage, and perhaps it was the sight of the empty glass that caused her to add, "Though he's not at all like his father."

Maud judged that old M. would be allergic to home-made cordials. "Oliver is more co-operative," she said, using a word that went with the preconceived image. Cousin Alice gave her an appreciative glance and said that most Fenistons were famous for going their own way. Or perhaps it should be infamous.

"I do wish Charles—" she began.

Miss Conway appeared in the doorway, looking rather put out.

"Maud, this isn't the right kind of hair oil," she cried. "This one is *perfumed!*"

"I'm sorry. I couldn't get the kind you said and I thought that one would do."

"But it won't. And I didn't notice till I'd rubbed it on him."

Wilbraham, oiled and scented, came mincing into the room. Maud had not known the hair oil was for Wilbraham and she at once agreed that it wouldn't do. It was bad enough to have a scented dog at one's feet, but worse still when the dog was so obviously enjoying his new experience.

CHAPTER SEVEN

WHEN SHE FIRST saw it Maud had been depressed by the ugliness of her bedroom, but within a month she discovered its great advantage. Combe Cottage had no central heating, or gas fires, or power points for electric ones; and her room, next door to the hot-water cistern, was, if not warm, the warmest bedroom in the house.

Cousin Alice and Miss Conway did not seem to feel the cold. The last few nights had been chilly, but they had sat without a fire and Maud had been quite glad that they kept early hours. This evening threatened to be even chillier, and after washing in the greenhouse-bathroom she was anxiously surveying her party frock and wondering if Chestnut Lodge would be as draughty as Combe Cottage.

In the adjoining bedroom, which was Con's, Alice and Con were speaking in whispers for fear she should hear them. It was not really necessary to whisper, but they were still unaccustomed to the presence of a third person in Combe Cottage and they felt as exposed and overcrowded as they had done in the war, when the evacuees were there. Or at least, Con did; and when Alice pointed out that Maud was far less trouble Con retorted, in a fierce whisper, that they hadn't had to take the evacuees to parties.

"It's only this once, Con. Just so that she can get to know people."

Con sighed deeply and heavily, a sigh of self-pity.

"All this fiddle-faddle," she said. "Dressing up and going out, and feeling ridiculous when we get there."

"I shan't feel ridiculous."

"I believe you want to go."

This was Con's real grievance: Alice was no longer content with a life of seclusion, Maud's presence was corrupting her. It took so long to deal with the grievance that Maud spent twenty minutes watching the clock in the sitting room before they appeared.

"Just as well we had something to eat," Cousin Alice said. Maud took this to be an oblique reference to their lateness, but Miss Conway made the words an excuse for picking up the invitation card and reading it through for the umpteenth time, aloud and very slowly.

"Yes, it doesn't say anything about supper," she remarked. With supper—or at least, high tea—inside them it seemed to Maud pointless to reopen the argument about whether the Woodfidleys would provide food, but she listened to it quite patiently. She realised that her companions' marked reluctance to start was aggravated by their having had a tiff, but she could not help being infected by their despondency, and the unknown Woodfidleys began to loom before her as horrible rather than hospitable.

"Well—I suppose we'd better go," Miss Conway said glumly.

"We'll walk quite slowly," said Cousin Alice.

Chestnut Lodge was as hot as an orchid house, and intensively well-lit. Even in the hall where they left their coats, the lighting was brilliant, and in the drawing room it was positively dazzling; as if the Woodfidleys could not bear shadows and had invested in standard lamps by the dozen to illumine every corner where the central lighting might not prevail. As the invitation had said, it was only a small party, but everyone seemed to be making a lot of noise, and to Maud's disgust they were making it in unison. They were singing, or attempting to sing, a tune which was being thumped out on a piano and accompanied by a raucous brass instrument. The instrument was being played by a gawky youth and the piano was being played by Mrs. Woodfidley, who waved a welcoming hand and then, when the song ended, came forward to greet them.

"Just a little sing-song to get us going," she explained. "You're *late*."

Mrs. Woodfidley was a small, anxious-looking woman with an over-emphatic voice. Mr. Woodfidley was tall, thin, and completely bald. The gawky youth was the youngest son, Garson (the musical one), and the very pretty young woman was Annabel (my married daughter). Maud was introduced to all of them and was then led across the room to be introduced to Ensie Martin and her Papa.

"All you young people must get together," Mrs. Woodfidley commanded, sweeping Garson along too. "I know you've got lots to say to one another."

But it did not seem so. Garson said nothing at all, and soon drifted away. Ensie said something that was quite inaudible, and her Papa, who wasn't, in any case, a young person, was led off a few minutes later by Mrs. Woodfidley and attached to another group; for the sing-song was now over and the party had been split up into small groups for conversation. Ensie and Maud were left marooned under a glaring standard lamp in an isolated corner of the large, half-empty room.

"The day we lost Pixie," Ensie said, suddenly becoming audible.

"Oh . . . oh yes. That was the day I saw you in the garden."

"And I was in my dressing gown. You see, we didn't expect anyone to be passing."

"I suppose not."

"But I've been looking forward, ever since, to meeting you again—clothed and in my right mind," Ensie said with a laugh. "I somehow feel that we're going to be friends."

Maud tried to make cordial sounds of agreement. But her own hopes of finding a friend had rather dwindled, for Ensie, clothed and in her right mind, was less appealing than she had appeared in her dressing gown. It must have been the dressing gown that made her look downtrodden and sympathetic, she thought; and she wondered how anyone in her right mind, and as sallow as Ensie, could choose a party frock of deep, rich purple. But then she remembered the water-butt at Pixie Cot, which exactly matched the frock. It must be Ensie's favourite colour.

"And now you flash by on your bicycle," Ensie was saying. "Gone like the wind, in fact! But I expect you simply daren't keep Mr. Feniston waiting. Of course some people say he's mad, but I tell them he's just eccentric."

"Very neighbourly of you," said Maud.

Ensie wasn't listening, and Maud saw that she was looking across the room at a group which consisted of a young clergyman, a very old clergyman, and the daughter of the house, Annabel. Both clergymen were giving Annabel the attention that pretty young women can count on getting, and she was treating them with perfect fairness, turning from one to the other and bestowing charming, impartial smiles as she related what seemed to be a ruefully humorous tale of woe. Maud recognised Annabel as a practised performer who was merely keeping her hand in, but Ensie seemed to be watching the performance with some anxiety, and since neither of the clergymen was her Papa it seemed possible that she was, as Maud's stepmother would have put it, "interested" in one of them. The young one, naturally; for the other was much too old to awaken the kind of interest that betrayed itself in an anxious stare and an inability to attend to anything else.

"Have you been here long?" Maud asked, feeling awkwardly conspicuous beside the silent, staring Ensie, in their isolated corner under the glaring lamp.

Ensie looked round and said vaguely: "Yes . . . since Father retired."

"And do you like it?"

"Oh, yes. I think so."

At the other side of the room, Mrs. Woodfidley had pounced on the young clergyman and was leading him off to talk to someone else. As he went he looked up, looked round about him, looked, unmistakably, across the room at Ensie, giving her a glance which wasn't exactly meaningful or "interested" but which seemed to restore her confidence. She turned to Maud with a bright smile, as if she was ready to start making friends all over again.

"I do hope you settle," she said. "As I was telling you, I've been looking forward to having another girl here. Of course there's Annabel Woodfidley—Annabel Curtis, she is now—but she doesn't live here all the time, and anyway. . . . And Garson, well, he's at school and anyway boys don't count. It's been sort of lonely for me, being so much younger than anyone else in the combe."

"But there are a lot of people here tonight," Maud argued, looking round for a way of escape. "Even if they don't live in the combe they must live somewhere fairly near. And it's not very far to Yeomouth."

"But I'm frightfully tied. I mean, there's Father and the garden and so on. It'll be lovely having someone who can just drop in."

For an instant Maud recaptured her first impression of Ensie—a drooping figure with an overbearing Papa—and heard herself weakly agreeing to drop in as soon as she could manage it. Perhaps it would satisfy Ensie; perhaps their tête-à-tête could now be brought to an end. Other people were being moved about, given new conversational partners and fresh opportunities; it didn't seem fair that she should be stuck with Ensie for the whole evening.

It seemed even less fair the next moment, when Mrs. Woodfidley went hurrying across the room to greet the last arrival and tell him he was *late*. Charles Feniston was an acquaintance, and in a roomful of strangers he had almost the status of an old friend; she could have gone across and talked to him, if only she weren't marooned in this distant corner. But it seemed impossible to abandon Ensie, just to walk off and leave her sitting there under the lamp, downtrodden and possibly lovelorn and certainly lonely.

"Do you like walking?" Ensie asked, and began to tell her about all the nice walks in the neighbourhood. Charles was still talking to his hostess and Maud had a moment's hope that he was going to be brought across to talk to her and Ensie, for Mrs. Woodfidley was looking round with a hostess's eye as if calculating which group needed fresh blood. But before she could move the pretty Annabel had stepped forward, detaching herself from the old clergyman with an ease which Maud could only admire, though she did so reluctantly.

"I haven't seen you for *ages*, Charles. Simply ages," Annabel cried. Her voice, as emphatic as her mother's, had much more warmth, and she sounded as if she were truly delighted to see him again, after all those ages of not seeing him. Charles was lost—lost, at least, to Maud, who perceived that being a good mother counted for more, with Mrs. Woodfidley, than being a good hostess. Charles was handed over to Annabel, and Mrs. Woodfidley took charge of the old clergyman whom Annabel had discarded.

". . . That's almost my favourite walk of all. But it means being out for the whole day and starting early—because of getting the bus for the first five miles—so I can hardly ever go. Well, not in the winter, anyway. It's impossible for me to leave Father alone all day, in the winter."

Maud was glad to think that this long expedition with Ensie could not possibly take place before next summer. Moreover the conversational interlude was now at an end; Mrs. Woodfidley was inviting the guests to assemble for drinks, which were being handed out by Mr. Woodfidley and Garson from a long table in the bay window. The bottles and glasses had been visible from the first and their serried ranks must have drawn longing glances from more persons than herself—it would have been so much easier to sing and talk if even a single drink had been given one at the start of the party. But now she had guessed that the party was organized in set figures, like a formal country dance, and that the delay in serving drinks must be due to this plan. The figure in which drinks were consumed had just begun; it would be succeeded by another after a fixed interval of time, and therefore she had better make sure of a drink before the music changed.

Ensie too had heeded the beckoning finger and the breakup of the formal groups, and as they walked across the room together Maud feared that even in the throng round the table she would not be able to shake Ensie off. But that was done for her by Ensie's Papa, who called his daughter to his side as she walked past him and began to question her about Pixie. Was she sure that Pixie was indoors when they started out? Dutifully reassuring him, Ensie got left behind.

"What will you drink?" asked Mr. Woodfidley, waving his hand towards the row of bottles.

"I expect Maud would like something with gin in it," said Cousin Alice, who was standing close by. She explained afterwards that the sherry was dreadful, and even at the time Maud guessed that there must be a hidden reason for her interference. She accepted the drink with gin in it, and exchanged a few polite words with her host. When she turned away from the table Cousin Alice had withdrawn and was surrounded by total strangers; or rather, she was standing there with total strangers all round her but just out of easy conversational range. They were not strangers to one another and they all seemed to be exchanging items of local news or discussing local personalities whose names meant nothing to her, so that even if she had been near enough to any of them to join in she would have found it difficult to do so.

Pretty women, confident and admired, can impose their own rules; the insignificant, the shy and self-conscious, have to make the best of what a party offers. Maud preferred crowded parties, where her stepmother could not keep a kindly eye on her, where people talked to her because they were all jammed together in a mass, or where she could watch other people talking without feeling conspicuously neglected. But at Chestnut Lodge there were not enough guests to crowd the room, nor was there enough gin to diminish the barrier between local residents and new arrivals. Cousin Alice and Miss Conway were at the other side of the room, standing together, perhaps making it up after their tiff, and she was too proud to walk across and join them. Ensie and her Papa and Annabel and Garson, to whom she had been introduced, seemed to have disappeared. But a minute or so later she noticed that other people were also disappearing, through the open door and across the hall. Another set figure in the party dance was about to begin.

"Supper, I think," said Charles.

A moment ago he had been talking to Mr. Woodfidley. Maud hoped he hadn't been told by his host to come and talk to her; she was resigned to being an object of charity at her stepmother's parties, but she resented it here. She would rather have had nature-notes from Ensie than prompted politeness from Charles.

"The invitation didn't say there was supper," she objected.

"Didn't it? Well, we shall soon find out. They're all going into the dining room and it will be a poor joke if there aren't even sandwiches."

"But I'm not sure if Cousin Alice will want to stay," said Maud, still fighting off the last humiliation of being an object of charity. "She—they both keep very early hours."

"She can't leave as early as this. In fact, she's already in the dining room—I noticed that both of them were quick off the mark when the Woodfidleys gave the signal." Apparently thinking this might sound derogatory, he added: "Our hostess must have been grateful for their lead, because she wanted to get us moving. Chestnut Lodge parties always have to run to time."

"Like perfectionist trains. Yes, I guessed that. At least, I saw that it had all been carefully planned. First the sing-song—but you missed that. . . ."

It occurred to her that he was going to miss supper too, if she didn't move. "I'm sorry," she said, hurrying after the vanishing figure of Mr. Woodfidley, who had looked back from the door and had then seemingly given up the attempt to attract their attention. There was no need to be sorry, Charles replied, and added, half to himself, that it would not have hurt any man to wait for his guests.

The dining room glittered as brightly as the drawing room. The table was elaborately set out, but there were no chairs; for this was a fork supper, Mrs. Woodfidley proclaimed, and they must all walk round and help themselves. Everyone else was already doing this, and as they passed her Ensie gave Maud a beaming, friendly smile and said rather archly that it served them right for staying behind.

Maud supposed her to mean that the choicest dainties had already been snapped up. If this were so they must have been in short supply or the other guests must have been very greedy; certainly there seemed nothing to eat but dishes of thin little anchovies and mounds of cold baked beans. Other dishes, now bearing only a garnish of lettuce leaves, had perhaps held sausage rolls, tongue, or sardines, which she noticed on other people's plates or being conveyed to other people's mouths.

"Here you are," said Charles, reappearing at her side. He handed her a plate which contained, among other things, a sausage roll and a hard-boiled egg. "I'm sorry I couldn't consult you, but there wasn't time."

He looked round to make sure none of the Woodfidleys were within earshot, before adding, "I sometimes think the shortage of food is a device for getting the guests to move quickly when the time for food arrives. But it's bad luck on those who haven't been here before."

"It's bad luck on you. I have deprived you of your supper," she said, thinking that Charles would have moved much quicker if he hadn't been delayed by arguments.

"No, you haven't, because I shall have some sandwiches when I get home. I made sure of that."

Maud felt more and more conscience-stricken.

"Oh, dear! Do have my egg," she exclaimed. "As a matter of fact I had an egg for tea, so I really don't need another."

She looked round in her turn. Cousin Alice and Miss Conway were nowhere near.

"We have so many eggs," she confided, thrusting her plate towards Charles who had nothing but two anchovies and a bit of lettuce. "I know there are two hundred and eighty-three ways of cooking them, but they're still *eggs*. Only please don't think I'm grumbling, because I've never been so happy in my life. I mean, it's so wonderful to be free and independent."

"Free from what?—And thank you, I will have that egg if you really don't want it. Glaine seems an odd place to choose for—"

A prolonged blast on the raucous instrument drowned his words. Garson Woodfidley had blown it to obtain silence, otherwise the quiet voice of his father would not have been heard. It seemed to Maud that the time allowed for eating had been very short, but perhaps the perfectionist train was running late, and if this were so it was partly her fault. Charles had been delayed by her reluctance to accept his help; it was most unjust that a kind action should result in his missing supper.

"Take it," she whispered, tipping her plate so that the egg should slide on to his. Unfortunately she tipped it too steeply, and before Charles could restrain the egg it slithered off and went bounding across the polished floor. Mr. Woodfidley, in the middle of expressing his pleasure at being home again, was distracted by its approach; and the break in his speech, which had been flowing on at an even pace, drew everyone's attention to it.

This was the kind of comic incident which Maud's impulsive actions often produced, and which never failed to fill her with shame. Other people did not drop eggs, or fall downstairs, or spill bottles of ink all over the drawing-room carpet; yet if these things had to happen to her she was stoically prepared to be laughed at.

The respectful silence which greeted the bounding egg was partly respect for Mr. Woodfidley, who was in the middle of making a speech; and those who knew him best were well aware that the waste of good food was no laughing matter. But to Maud it appeared that they were too shocked to laugh and that she had ruined forever her chances of being accepted in this new world. She had disgraced herself. She had resumed the personality of the past, which could be briefly described as "poor Grace's stepdaughter."

"I'm so sorry," said Charles, stepping forward and addressing the room in general. "I was juggling, and my hand has lost its cunning."

He retrieved the egg and put it on a pile of dirty plates, where it could not catch anyone's eye. All eyes had been turned on him while he did it, but politeness required that they should be turned back on Mr. Woodfidley as soon as he started speaking again. The incident was closed; and no one seemed to have seen its true beginning. As they trooped back to the drawing room she overheard Ensie telling someone that Charles Feniston was almost as eccentric as his uncle.

And now the party was over, except for the grand chain in which all the Woodfidleys threaded their way through the guests exchanging a few words with each of them. In this figure the guests were required to stand still and Maud soon saw that it wouldn't be possible to get near Charles and thank him for his self-sacrifice. She had not been able to do it in the dining room because Annabel and two other people had come up to him immediately after the speech, and now he was standing at the far end of the room with Annabel and these others, and she was between Cousin Alice and Miss Conway. They had closed in on her so that they could all get away quickly; Cousin Alice whispered that Con's shoes were pinching her, and Miss Conway whispered that Alice had a headache.

Maud hoped that Charles might round off his good deed by offering to drive them home, but she had not realised how quick a quick getaway could be when carried out by two determined sufferers. Cousin Alice had stationed them close to the door, and no sooner was the grand chain completed than she was shaking Mrs. Woodfidley by the hand. In a matter of minutes they were outside the house, with Miss Conway muttering her relief at having exchanged her party shoes for her walking ones.

"We'll go by the field path, shall we?" she continued, leading the way across the Woodfidley lawn to a wicket gate at one side.

Cousin Alice agreed that with so many cars about the path would be safer than the lane.

CHAPTER EIGHT

"NICE TO SEE Oliver again so soon," old M. had said. Nevertheless his announced arrival tomorrow was not an unmixed blessing, and the drawbacks had been confided to Maud at intervals during the rest of the day.

It was *too* soon, not a month since his last visit, and all the more awkward because tomorrow old M. wanted to go to a sale at a house thirty miles away. The bees in Oliver's bonnet buzzed loudly when sales were mentioned. Then too, it would mean stopping work in the library, where Maud could have carried on alone while old M. was at the sale. Strange that the feller should come on a Thursday, and it just showed that being a professor wasn't as hard as it looked; even a clever feller like Oliver didn't realize how lucky he was being able to get away whenever he liked, upsetting everybody—well, no, not upsetting them because naturally they were glad to see him, but interfering with their work. And remind him to remind Oliver to look at the dingle-dangle before he started wallowing.

Maud knew that Oliver wasn't a professor—though this did not explain his coming on a Thursday. She also knew that the dingle-dangle was a wooden bobbin on the end of a cord which hung down from a hole in the ceiling of the upper landing and showed, by its rise and fall, the amount of water in the cistern. She wrote "dingle-dangle" in her note-book, to remind herself to remind old M. to remind Oliver. Little by little she was becoming the kind of secretary old M. had dreamed about.

Or so she hoped, because the better she knew old M. the better she liked him. At first she had wanted to please him because it was so important to make a success of this, her first job; the humiliation of being sacked was something not to be borne. But now she wished to please him because she liked him; and since her friendships were always conducted with partisan fervour she agreed that Oliver's visit was "a bit too soon."

She stayed later than usual that day, and when she reached the end of the back drive Charles was just turning out of it in his car. She had not seen Charles since the Woodfidley party and this was the chance to thank him for saving her from disgrace.

"It was *noble* of you," she began abruptly.

"What was?"

Charles might be forgiven for sounding startled; she realized that her silent approach, free-wheeling downhill, had taken him by surprise. The car was halfway into the lane and she had come racing round the bend and had swerved out to stop beside the driver's window.

"You ought to have lights on that bicycle," he said sharply. "Or ring the bell."

"Or you could look before you drove out," Maud retorted. "It isn't dark yet. *I* can see beautifully. Anyway it isn't lighting-up time."

"No doubt it isn't, at Glaine. Did old M. put the clocks back last week?"

"Of course he did."

"It's more surprising really that he ever put them *on*," Charles said, relaxing into tolerance.

Maud explained that the Hatballs had insisted on keeping Summer Time because of the cinemas and the buses. He asked what the Hatballs were like, and she told him about Mrs. Hatball's penchant for dusting the stairs. In some way this led on to telling him about the excitement over the brass image of Buddha. It sat, cross-legged, on a tall chest at the top of the stairs, and old M. had recently read that another such image had been found to have rubies concealed in its hollow centre. He was planning to get his Buddha down—only it was too heavy for Hatball to lift unaided—and examine it. How thrilling it would be if there were fabulous jewels hidden inside!

"You can tell him from me that there aren't," said Charles. "Oliver and I read that tale years ago, and we didn't waste a moment. But if there ever were rubies hidden in our Buddha someone had got there before us."

"You and Oliver!"

"I was brought up at Glaine, after my father died. Still, you'd better *not* tell him from me—as things are. Tell him from Oliver."

"Oliver is coming tomorrow."

She spoke almost at random, untroubled by aunty admonitions because her thoughts were elsewhere—fixed on the surprising fact that Charles as well as Oliver had grown up at Glaine. It was this fact, and something in Charles's voice, that suddenly revealed to her his pleasure in talking about Glaine. He wasn't like Oliver, he didn't fume at the thought of the dust and the cobwebs, or struggle to keep the irritation out of his voice when speaking of old M. He loved Glaine as it was.

But he and old M. had quarrelled. It seemed rather sad to Maud that Charles should be camping at the gates of a place he loved and not on speaking terms with its owner.

"Is he?" Charles was saying. "Good—you can ask him about the Buddha. He's sure to remember, because he got his fingers squashed. That'll save old M. the trouble of inventing a patent rope-and-pulley system to get the Buddha down."

Old M.'s patent systems for doing things in a complicated way were already familiar to Maud, but she wanted to know how Oliver had got his fingers squashed. By the time she parted from Charles she had heard all about it, and the episode of the ten-year-old Oliver and the fifteen-year-old Charles struggling with a recalcitrant brass statue in the watches of the night seemed a delightful addition to her knowledge of Glaine. In the interest of hearing about it she quite forgot her real reason for stopping to talk to Charles, and not until his car had disappeared down the lane did she remember that she had not thanked him properly. But she hoped he would understand, if he thought about it, why she had hailed him as noble.

The evening meal at Combe Cottage was known as supper in the summer and high tea in the winter. The only difference seemed to be that high tea was served earlier than supper, and the change took place as soon as the ending of Summer Time brought dark evenings. Maud had hardly grown used to the new timing, and this evening she was dismayed to find Cousin Alice and Miss Conway at the table and her own portion of the hot dish cooling rapidly under its pudding-basin cover.

"Did old M. keep you late?" Cousin Alice asked.

"Yes, a little late. And then I met Charles in the lane."

"Had he enjoyed the party?"

"I didn't ask him. He said my bicycle ought to have lights."

"Con has some lights," Cousin Alice said helpfully. "Con, where are those lamps you had when you were a warden?—In the war she had to go out at night," she explained to Maud. "And wear a blue uniform. But luckily it was very quiet here. They never seemed to notice us."

Maud wondered whether "they" meant the enemy, or the neighbours who might have observed Cousin Alice and Miss Conway at their war-work.

"I sold my bicycle," Miss Conway said triumphantly.

"But you kept the lamps. They must be somewhere. Unless I put them in a safe place."

To Miss Conway this was a challenge. Things which were somewhere had been stored by herself and could be located, but things which Alice had put in a safe place were often lost forever; the safeness of the place seemed to absolve her from the necessity of remembering where it was.

"They were my lamps, so I must have been the one to put them away," she declared. "And I'm sure I can find them."

After tea had been washed up she went off to the attic to hunt for the lamps. Maud and Cousin Alice were left alone.

Maud had come to think of Miss Conway and Cousin Alice as inseparable; from the moment of her arrival when they had stood side by side to greet her she had seldom had a chance to talk to either of them for long without the other joining in. She felt that Cousin Alice might be more communicative without Miss Conway, and she hoped the hunt for the lamps would last some time.

"Charles Feniston told me he was brought up at Glaine," she remarked.

"Yes. He was here when we first came. That was before my father died, but of course we'd left Wolfering ten years before that. He turned into a recluse, it was very sad, and lived at his club and never answered our letters."

"Did you mind very much?" Maud asked. Politeness demanded that she should show a passing interest in her great-uncle's behaviour.

"It was very difficult for my brother, because Wolfering ought to have been sold and my father wouldn't agree to it. Or disagree either, for that matter."

"I wonder if Oliver thinks that Glaine ought to be sold."

"Of course he was buried there. But even if it had been sold I suppose we should still have had the use of the vault. One can hardly sell a family vault. Or does one?"

"I don't know. Has old M. got a family vault?"

"Probably," said Cousin Alice. "Oh yes, of course he has, in the parish church at Yeomouth. I remember how—But he only told me about it, I didn't go to the funeral. When I was young, women never did."

"Whose funeral?"

"His wife's—that is, his second wife, Oliver's mother. I don't mean I was young at that time . . . but one gets set in one's ways."

"Yes," said Maud. She felt depressed. Getting set in one's ways, owning family vaults, attending or abstaining from funerals, were not the things she wanted to discuss, but it was very difficult to keep Cousin Alice to the point.

"I once dreamed I was going to my own funeral," Cousin Alice remarked. "As a spectator, I mean. And that reminds me, I've never given you a note-book to write down your dreams. Have you had any interesting ones?"

"I dreamed I was shut up in the Glaine gardens. Someone locked the door while I was inside."

This seemed a good way of bringing the talk back to Glaine. But Cousin Alice countered with another dream of her own, which returned them to Wolfering. The minutes were passing and Maud grew reckless.

"Oliver is coming down again tomorrow," she said, at the first break in the flow of interesting dreams.

Cousin Alice seemed faintly surprised.

"But you told us, at high tea," she said.

"Did I? Oh, yes—I'm sorry. And old M. is going to be away at a sale, all day. And Charles told me that he and Oliver used to spend a lot of time hunting for buried treasure."

Cousin Alice looked at her thoughtfully; it could almost be said that she looked at her like an aunt. With three Fenistons to choose from, three items of news to assess, her comment was rather slow in coming. But when it came it was satisfactory.

"Charles was always very fond of Glaine," she said.

"Then why did he quarrel with his uncle?"

"I have no idea," Cousin Alice answered repressively. Then, either regretting her abruptness or unable to resist a postscript, she added a few meagre details.

"It was after he had leased the gardens," she said, "and that was after the war. Of course they'd been neglected during the war, and when Charles came back and wanted to start a market garden it seemed a very good plan. But—well, anyway, they quarrelled. And they're both so obstinate. It would be better if Charles gave up the gardens and went away, because then they might make it up. Old M. is probably the kind of man who gets on quite well with his relatives, so long as they keep their distance."

Maud thought this was true. Old M. had a good many relatives and dictated letters to them in very friendly terms, but he never seemed to want to see them.

"I feel rather like that about my relatives," she said; and then added hastily, "I don't mean you."

When Cousin Alice smiled her whole expression changed and one saw a different person, the gay ghost of a light-hearted girl.

"I should hope not," she said. "But when I was your age I felt the same. I was simply *smothered* in relatives—droves of aunts and cousins used to come to Wolfering and stay for weeks, and the nastier they were the longer they stayed—because, of course, no one else would have them. My mother was kind to them because she was a remarkably charitable woman. But it's hardly surprising, really, that my father became a recluse."

"I suppose not."

"Still, when you get older you generally feel more conscious of the ties of blood. Your family seems more important to you and its folklore more interesting. When I first broke away from mine I hardly cared what happened to them—except the few I really liked—but now I find myself wanting to repair the links. I even find myself thinking—"

The thought remained unuttered, for the door burst open to reveal Miss Conway, rather dishevelled but triumphantly clutching the bicycle lamps.

"Where I thought!" she exclaimed, adding honestly, "Well, more or less."

Perhaps there was too long a pause before they congratulated her; or perhaps the sight of them sitting cosily together in the firelight was like an illustration of Cousin Alice's theme. Maud even wondered afterwards whether from long association Alice and Con had become telepathically sensitive to each other's thoughts. For Miss Conway's sulks could have been prompted by the fear that her friend, with a blood relation under the same roof, was less her friend than before.

"Oh, I don't suppose they'll work," she said, brusquely rejecting Maud's thanks. "They're all rusty, anyhow."

"They're not nearly so rusty as the bicycle."

"Some people are lucky to *get* a bicycle—for nothing."

"Yes, and the lamps too. It's awfully kind of you."

"I lit the fire because it was cold," Cousin Alice said apologetically.

"It was much colder last night. No, Alice, don't move—this room seems quite stuffy to me, so I'll sit by the window."

There was a period of uneasy silence. Miss Conway dragged her great work out of its corner and settled down to dogged stitching, refusing all aids to comfort such as a cushion, a lamp, or a softer chair. Cousin Alice opened her book, and closed it, and opened it again, and talked to Wilbraham, and tactfully refrained from talking to Maud. It was as if she perfectly understood why Miss Conway was sulking, and freely forgave her, but did not quite know how to bring her round.

Maud's sympathies at first were with Cousin Alice because she thought Miss Conway was making a silly fuss about nothing. But presently, behind this confident judgment, there stirred a faint, reluctant pity. She realized that her arrival must have made a great difference to Miss Conway; for she represented a link in that family chain which Cousin Alice was seeking to repair.

"We've been talking about Charles Feniston," she said casually. "While you were looking for the lamps."

This half-truth was intended to be reassuring; it was intended to convince Miss Conway that they hadn't been talking about Wolfering and Cousin Alice's family. But as it evoked no immediate response Maud was obliged to continue.

"I was asking about the gardens. I thought he'd had them for a long time, but Cousin Alice says he only came back after the war."

"A pity he did!"

Miss Conway spoke with extreme violence, and then seemed to make an effort to control herself.

"Because it makes things so awkward," she added, omitting the violence and sounding almost plaintive.

Cousin Alice pointed out that they hardly ever saw Charles, but Miss Conway contradicted her and said she sometimes met him in the lane.

"And he *will* say good morning," she complained.

"Well, naturally. It would be strange if he didn't."

"I suppose so."

They exchanged glances, and Maud was almost sure that something was being left unsaid.

"It makes everything so awkward," Miss Conway repeated loudly, as if to dispel the significant silence. "His being here, and—and knowing us and quarrelling with his uncle and making us take sides."

"Does anyone take Charles's side?" Maud asked, after sorting this out.

Cousin Alice answered hurriedly, as if she wanted to forestall Miss Conway.

"It isn't a question of taking sides," she said. "But it's difficult for us because we've been here a long time and we know them all. The Martins and the Woodfidleys are tenants too, but old M. doesn't regard them as personal friends. We don't have to take sides, but, as Con says, we don't want to get involved. That is why I can't ask Charles here."

It wasn't enough for Miss Conway. "We don't *want* him here," she declared.

"Why not?"

"A married man," said Miss Conway, slurring the three words into one dark mutter.

"He *was* a married man," Cousin Alice said softly.

"Utterly disgraceful."

"Con."

A battle of wills raged over Maud's head, and Cousin Alice emerged the victor.

"It's Puppy's bedtime," Miss Conway announced. "Come along, Puppy."

Cousin Alice rose too; but her methods were less abrupt than Miss Conway's.

"Oliver isn't married," she remarked in her postscript manner. "I don't know why. He must be over thirty."

"Perhaps he thinks marriage would be too great an extravagance," Maud said coldly.

CHAPTER NINE

MAUD SUPPOSED Charles must be divorced, and she guessed that the divorce might have led to the quarrel; for old M. would be likely to disapprove strongly of a nephew who brought disgrace on the family name. She wondered if Charles's marriage had ended in some lurid scandal, which would account for his divorce being what her aunts called "a hush"—mysteriously awful and unmentionable. It was certainly unmentionable; Miss Conway had spoken as she did only because she was in a temper, and her remorse at having mentioned it had been plain enough afterwards. It had been a shock to learn that Charles was divorced; but somehow the aura of mystery which now enveloped him, the hint of wickedness and dissipation, did not detract from his charm.

On the contrary, it rather added to it.

She told herself, however, that the divorce was less important than the quarrel. The divorce was in the past, the quarrel still continued, and as old M.'s secretary she would certainly be expected to take sides. Or, as Cousin Alice put it, not to get involved; although this seemed to Maud a mere quibble, because if one shunned Charles's company and did not ask him to the house one *was* taking sides.

She thought about it while she wrote to old M.'s cousin Noel Humby. The letter had been dictated by old M. in a great hurry before he drove off to the sale, and hardly any of her shorthand was legible. But she had taken down more than one letter to Noel Humby and she knew the kind of thing old M. would say: generalisations about the weather and the government, enquiries after the health of Ruth and Lucas and Adeline (Noel Humby's offspring and wife), veiled praise of Oliver. Poor Noel, as she thought of him, was by no means a favourite cousin and it was only in his rôle of patriarch that old M. corresponded with him. He had been feeling uneasy that morning, about abandoning Oliver, and as an act of contrition he had dictated letters to several of the relatives he liked least.

Maud, too, felt uneasy. She had been ordered to receive Oliver and to break the news to him that his father had gone to a sale; it wasn't feasible to suppress this news because old M. hoped to bring back several bulky bargains and Oliver would be sure to notice them. "You must approach him the right way," old M. had said, but she did not trust herself to find it; if, indeed, a right way existed.

She thought she would go upstairs to the long gallery and watch for Oliver's car in the lane; then she could be at the front door to greet him and this would at least show him that his coming hadn't been forgotten. It would also be a good idea to visit her prinking room first and make herself as tidy—as efficient-looking—as possible.

When this had been done she still had time to spare. It was too early to expect him just yet; she wandered slowly through the silent house, pausing to look at the sporting prints on the passage wall, the Minton china in the glass-fronted cabinets (but where was the Spode Miss Goose had broken?), the row of brass cans with wide spouts and hinged lids, on the bathroom shelf, which conjured up a vision of busy housemaids carrying hot water to all the bedrooms now empty and forlorn.

Which had been Charles's bedroom, and which Oliver's, when they were boys? She knew Oliver now slept in what had been the best spare room, and she imagined that his former bedroom had been one of those in the north wing, which was no longer, even in theory, dusted and swept. The north wing had been shut up when the servants left, old M. had told her; and by servants he apparently meant an adequate and fully trained staff, which Glaine had certainly not possessed since the war.

As soon as she thought of this Maud was seized with a desire to visit the north wing. She gave herself ten minutes for the venture and hurried back past the head of the stairs to the locked door which must lead to it.

The key was in the lock and the door opened easily. She looked down another passage, indescribably dismal, with doors on one side and windows on the other. The windows were so coated with grime and cobwebs that hardly any light could penetrate, but what there was showed dirty boards, peeling walls, and patches of plaster that had fallen from the ceiling. She opened a door, and saw that the room within had been a nursery; there were bars across the lower half of the window and a high, rusty guard before the fireplace. In one corner stood a rocking-horse, and in another a square, battered table. But except for these the room was bare, and the thought of its former warmth and happy security—the cheerful fire, the nursery tea on the table, the rocking-horse galloping tirelessly towards the rosebud wallpaper in front of its nose—made the present desolation all the more poignant.

"Oh, how sad!" she exclaimed, much affected.

She supposed that old M., as well as Oliver, had once inhabited the nursery. She walked the length of the passage, opening other doors and looking at the small, dark rooms in which the children of Glaine had grown up. The rooms had been cleared of most of their furniture, but some of their late owners' possessions still remained: tattered books, a rusty carpentry set, a coloured lithograph of a fat baby in a nightgown, clutching a kitten. The last door in the passage led to a back staircase; it was while she was peering down it, wondering where it came out, that she heard Oliver's voice calling querulously from somewhere fairly near at hand.

She shot back through the door into the passage. Oliver was standing at its other end, looking annoyed. Even in the dim light his annoyance was visible—or perhaps perceptible, for it came towards her in waves as she walked back.

"Oh—Maud!" he exclaimed. Evidently he had expected to see his father. His annoyance did not diminish but was forcibly restrained; she was reminded of a small volcano which was longing to erupt. "What on earth are you looking for?" he demanded.

"Nothing. I mean, I was just looking. At the nursery, and the other rooms. I had nothing to do—and really I was waiting for you to arrive. Mr. Feniston asked me . . ."

She stopped herself, realizing that it was not the right moment to tell Oliver that his father had gone to a sale.

"The nursery made me feel terribly sad," she said quickly. "Especially the poor rocking-horse."

"I've been here a good quarter of an hour. There's not a soul about. I looked everywhere. Then I came upstairs and saw the landing door open. I thought my father must have thought up some mad scheme—!"

The short, staccato sentences were like the eruption's preliminary puffs of smoke. Maud's apologies for not being at the front door fell on deaf ears, but something she had said earlier seemed belatedly audible. "What poor rocking-horse?" he asked, interrupting her suggestion that he might like some tea.

"That one."

She opened the nursery door. He looked distastefully at the rocking-horse and muttered something about useless junk.

"It seems to me pathetic," Maud said. "And if this was your nursery I should have expected *you* to feel a little sad, at seeing it like this."

"Sad!" Oliver gave a hollow—and affected—laugh. "Sad, my dear Maud, is an understatement. I feel inexpressibly *triste*. I feel morbidly dejected and at the same time furious. The idiocy of it. The senseless waste. Where *is* my father? If I stay here I shall burst into tears. Oh yes, I feel sad all right."

Maud hurriedly shut the door.

"Hatball is in the stableyard," she said. "He's doing something to his autocycle. I'll tell him you're here. I'll tell him to get you some tea. At once."

Oliver's staccato style was catching, but luckily he hadn't noticed the parody. He was looking down the passage, where her walk had left footmarks in the dust.

"An anachronism," he said. "No, worse than that. A picturesque lunatic asylum. Picturesque is the *mot juste*, is it not?"

"No, it isn't. Romantic, perhaps. Or haunted—but that sounds spooky and Glaine isn't. It's rather melancholy, especially here, but so enchanting that I simply cannot understand why you're blind to it."

Perhaps Oliver's question had been rhetorical, not needing an answer and robbed of its effect by getting one. Certainly she had done nothing to lessen the danger of an eruption. He turned away and strode back to the main staircase. She followed him, locking the north wing's door behind her and barely restraining her impulse to put the key in her pocket. The sight of the north wing had had such alarming results that she felt it would be kinder to prevent his going there again.

At the foot of the stairs she slipped away to find Hatball. When she returned Oliver was waiting for her in the hall, his suitcase at his feet and some letters in his hand. These he held out to her, remarking kindly, "The postman brought them."

"You surprise me," she said tartly.

At once she remembered that this was not the way to address her employer's son, maddening though he was. But it was too late; to Oliver's morbid dejection was now added a feeling of offended dignity, and the cause of it stood in front of him.

"I beg your pardon. I thought it might be one of your duties to deal with the post," he said, pointedly withdrawing the letters and laying them on a chest.

She guessed he would have preferred to say, "Don't speak to me like that," and that the substituted sarcasm hadn't really relieved his feelings. She thought of old M., perhaps even now driving happily homeward with his carload of bargains, and her heart smote her. She had been singularly maladroit. She had utterly failed to find the right way of approaching Oliver.

Nevertheless, the explanation must be given. With a sinking heart she followed him into the drawing room, to which he had retired to lick his wounds. He had just had time to establish himself on the spindly sofa and to appear absorbed in a book; she noticed that it was a Keepsake Annual which he must have snatched up from the what-not by the door as he entered the room.

"You must be wondering where Mr. Feniston is," she said meekly.

Oliver looked up with a start. He recalled his mind from its intellectual task; he gave his polite attention to what his father's secretary was saying.

"You must be wondering where he is," she repeated, to save him the trouble of asking for a repetition. "I should have told you before—it was most remiss of me. Mr. Feniston asked me to explain—and I'm *very* sorry I wasn't there to meet you; it was wrong of me to start exploring the house, but I'd meant to be at the look-out and I thought I had plenty of time—Well, you must be wondering—" Oliver showed signs of controlled impatience, which caused her to omit several phrases of the prepared explanation. "As a matter of fact, he has gone to a sale at a house the other side of Yeo—"

The volcano erupted.

"I knew it!" cried Oliver, springing to his feet and forgetting all about the Keepsake Annual, which crashed to the ground with a broken spine. "I knew it! Good God—as if being a miser weren't enough. As if it wasn't enough to grudge every penny that's needed to keep the house from falling down about his ears. But no—he has to go to sales!"

Maud stared at him. "A miser?" she faltered, hardly able to believe she had really heard this epithet—which, if it belonged anywhere, belonged to Oliver himself.

"A skinflint! When I think of it—when I come here and see it! A ridiculous parsimony, an absolutely unnecessary and false economy over the basic essentials, a completely antisocial outlook—quite terrifying disregard of the future—complete indifference, of course, to any interests but his own!"

This must be what people meant when they talked of someone "foaming at the mouth." Though not literally foaming Oliver made the metaphor come alive for Maud; she spared a thought for the possible remedies if he should suddenly fall down in a fit. This was the Feniston temper, all the more alarming and violent for being so long pent up in Oliver's civilised breast. She realized that he had quite forgotten whom he was addressing, had perhaps even forgotten that there was anyone else in the room.

"I know it's hopeless to look for any co-operation," Oliver was saying. "He doesn't know the meaning of the word. But I find it intolerable that he should not only refuse to spend money when it's needed, but *waste* it—throw it away—on the acquisition of utterly worthless rubbish. These sales! That so-called library!—a home for mice and the less discriminating bookworms."

His voice ceased suddenly. Maud turned round and saw Hatball framed in the doorway, bearing the tea tray but apparently rooted to the spot by Oliver's eloquence. Oliver had seen him too, and his embarrassment was great.

He gave an awkward laugh, as if he were trying to show that he had been joking; he retrieved the Keepsake Annual the carpet and examined its injuries with concern; finally it occurred to him to speak to Hatball, who had entered the room and was setting out the tea, and to ask with a show of interest after Mrs. Hatball's health.

Maud was sure her own presence would also be an embarrassment to Oliver when his temper subsided. She slipped away while Hatball was describing his wife's peculiar rheumatism and its supposed cause (with a wealth of physical detail for which Oliver clearly had not bargained), and returned to the study. She did not linger there; after putting things away and giving it a superficial appearance of tidiness she crept quietly out of the house.

She hoped old M. would return fairly soon while Oliver was still feeling subdued, but she did not meet him during her ride back to Combe Cottage. Miss Conway was surprised to see her back so early; and Maud was rather surprised to find Miss Conway there alone. But it appeared that Cousin Alice had taken Wilbraham for a walk and that Miss Conway had had to stay at home because they were expecting the coke.

"Puppy is so disappointed if he doesn't get his walk," Miss Conway said. "So Alice said she would take him down to the cliffs and come back by the Home Farm and along the lane. She wanted to go to the Farm to see if they're selling chickens for Christmas this year."

Maud said she would walk back along the lane to meet Cousin Alice. She felt that Miss Conway would have liked her to stay and receive the coke; there was a note of grievance in her voice when she said that it was a nice afternoon for a walk, but Maud ignored it.

It was indeed a nice afternoon, but its beauties were wasted on Maud. She walked slowly, waiting for old M. to overtake her, wondering whether he would stop and what she should tell him if he did. Now that her vexation had subsided she rather regretted leaving Oliver so abruptly. It would have been interesting to see how he behaved if she had stayed to pour out tea.

Oliver, she decided, was self-conscious, except when his temper got the better of him. At other times he tried to present himself in the right light, rather as if he feared that the wrong light might reveal too much of him. And he didn't quite know how to treat her; he wavered between treating her as Father's-new-secretary and as the-cousin-of-Father's-old-friend. She thought the distinctions Oliver drew were a kind of defence, that he was not so much a snob as a man who was unsure of himself and anxious not to make mistakes. She thought that his career as an economist had encouraged him to think of people as mere groups, and that being inherently shy he was at a disadvantage when the groups dissolved into individuals.

Having analysed Oliver's character she felt quite kindly disposed towards him. She even wondered if he was justified in calling his father a miser. It was, of course, an exaggeration, but there might be a grain of truth in it; she had been shocked when he said it, yet now she could not help remembering how old M. had grumbled about Hat's wages and the bills for cattle food and the estimate for new electric wiring at the farm. She had thought of him as being desperately hard up—landowners were always said to be—but could it be true that he grudged spending *money* and preferred to hoard it?

This new possibility took her to the gate of Pixie Cot. Ensie was standing just inside it and greeted her appearance with cries of pleasure.

"Better late than never! I've been wondering when you were going to drop in, and it's awfully nice you've come now when I'm on my ownsome! Mind the wet paint. I've just been giving the gate a doing over. I'll leave it propped open—like this—so that Father won't have to touch it when he comes in."

The gate was now bright purple, to match the water-butt. Maud followed Ensie up the steps to the front door, curious to see if purple carpets or chair covers were to be found inside. But the small sitting room was furnished in muddy tones of beige; not even a purple cushion to brighten it up. And Ensie herself, in her working clothes, seemed more subdued, in every sense, than she had seemed at the Woodfidley party.

"Sit down," she said. "No, not there—that's Father's chair—of course he isn't here but he might come back. He's gone to

Yeomouth to buy a collar for Pixie, with a little bell on it. I don't suppose he'll be able to get one."

She sighed. Maud looked at the empty, sacrosanct chair, standing between them exactly opposite the fire, and thought it would be easier to make friends with Ensie if they could sit in the kitchen, or her bedroom; in some place not dominated by her Papa. She asked why Pixie had to wear a collar with a bell, and Ensie explained that the cat was always getting lost.

"So is Wilbraham. I mean, he would get lost, if they didn't watch him all the time."

"He's a dear little dog, isn't he?" Ensie said gushingly.

"No, he isn't. He's a sly little dog. He exploits them."

Ensie looked puzzled. But Maud did not want to go on talking about dogs—she had quite enough of that at home. So she asked Ensie whether she had enjoyed the party. Ensie did not seem to have enjoyed it very much, but it gave them something to talk about; Maud learned that the very old clergyman was the Rector of Yeomouth and that his curate was called Don and generally took the services at the chapel-of-ease on the top of the hill, this side of Yeomouth, which Ensie and her Papa attended. It was too far to go to the parish church, Ensie explained, although Father . . . She sighed again, and murmured something about Don not doing things the way Father liked them.

"What is Don's full name?" Maud asked.

Ensie blushed brightly and said it was Donald Crouch. So stupid of her—but of course everyone called him Don and she had got into the habit of it. And he was—well, awfully nice. It was a shame Maud hadn't had a chance to talk to him at the party.

Maud walked home thinking that Ensie wasn't so bad after all, and that anyway talking about Don would be a change from the subjects they discussed at Combe Cottage. At the party she hadn't paid much attention to Don, but it was clear that Ensie thought the world of him; and she would probably make an excellent wife for a clergyman, having been, so to speak, educated for the part.

Of course she needed taking in hand; her taste for bright purple must be curbed and her powers of self-defence developed. Naturally one would have to find out whether Don really liked her; it would be cruel to encourage her if her love was sustained by nothing but listening to his sermons or gazing at him across a crowded room. It was a pity that Don had looked so much younger than Ensie, but perhaps her top-heavy hair and depressing clothes made her look older than she was. . . .

It was quite a shock to find that she had reached Combe Cottage without giving a single thought to the troubles of Oliver and old M.

CHAPTER TEN

"DID YOU CRY?" Ensie asked. "I cried so much that I used up both my handkerchiefs, and I brought two on purpose. Quick, there's Annabel Woodfidley, I mean Curtis! Quick, quick, before she sees us!"

She seized Maud's arm and propelled her up a narrow alley between the cinema and the next building. It turned at right angles and led them to safety in what looked like Yeomouth's slums.

"What an escape," she said.

"Why don't you like her?" asked Maud.

At once Ensie drooped. She drooped against a dirty railing, her attitude symbolizing a sudden return to being what Maud called "Papa's Ensie." The visit to the cinema on a Saturday afternoon had been planned by Maud as the first step towards liberating Ensie from her Papa, and she dealt with the relapse firmly. "Stand up," she said. "I don't mind whether you like Annabel or not. But don't droop."

"It seems horrid to run away from her, when she's always so—well, so nice to us. After all, one ought to try and see the good in people."

This was Papa's Ensie speaking; but the Ensie who had cried a warning and fled had been a different person. Ignoring Papa's Ensie, Maud announced that she was dying for a cup of tea and suggested the café called The Golden Kettle. But Annabel would be sure to go there, Ensie muttered, wavering between her two selves. Very well, they would go somewhere else, said Maud. Ensie, being difficult, said there wasn't any other nice place, and anyway she didn't know where this alley would bring them out.

To be lost in Yeomouth did not dismay Maud, who took charge and marched Ensie off, past the back gardens of crumbling cottages, down a long flight of steps to the river, and along the lane which bordered it. "We shall come out in the square," she prophesied, and Ensie said she was awfully clever. But the lane turned away from the river and went uphill; a warehouse and then a high wall interposed themselves between Maud and her objective; Ensie said plaintively that they were going in the wrong direction.

"There must be a turning," Maud said. She found one, but it led to a square she had never seen, not the square with shops in it but a small, shabby one enclosed by terraced dwelling houses. It was a charming bit of old Yeomouth, but it offered neither tea nor guidance.

"Now we're lost," said Ensie. "What a pity you didn't ask someone the way." Maud prided herself on being able to find the way without asking, but Ensie clearly believed in standing still and waiting for help.

She did it now, and much to Maud's surprise it worked. Ensie stood still and looked lost, and almost at once someone drove into the square and stopped beside her. That he should be an acquaintance, not a stranger, was an additional stroke of good fortune, but Ensie seemed to accept it as her due.

"I'm afraid we're lost," she said. "But I expect you can tell us how to get back."

Charles Feniston asked where they wanted to get back to. Ensie said they were looking for a nice café and Maud said not The Golden Kettle because there was someone in it they wanted to dodge. Ensie said perversely that there was really nowhere else, and added that there wouldn't be much time for tea anyway, it was getting so late. Charles said it wasn't too late, and invited them to get into the car.

If it hadn't been for Ensie I shouldn't be here, Maud thought, sitting beside Charles and listening quite kindly to Ensie's mutters, from the back seat, about missing the bus if they sat long over tea.

The hotel to which Charles took them was on the other side of the town from Glaine, and was larger and more imposing than the hotels along the Marine Parade. Too grand and gaudy for Yeomouth, Maud thought; it was more like the hotels at Eastbourne and Folkestone where her stepmother stayed, and she was rather surprised that Charles should have chosen it. The inmates looked grand too, and she agreed with Ensie that they had better go and tidy themselves, while Charles parked the car.

In the ladies' room Ensie drooped terribly; the full-length mirrors and pinkish fluorescent lights seemed utterly to discourage her. "I feel awful," she complained. "My eyes are red with weeping and just look at my hair! I'd have worn my best coat, and a hat, if I'd dreamed we were coming here."

"Well, you couldn't be expected to dream it."

"Fancy Charles Feniston taking us out to tea. I do wish I'd worn my other coat. But of course anything's good enough for the cinema."

Or for a female friend, Maud thought, perceiving that Ensie was one who dressed to please the opposite sex. And a born worrier too; for now that her fears about missing the bus had been removed by Charles's promise to drive them home she had found several new worries—her hair, her eyes, her second-best coat—to keep her from enjoying herself. The process of tidying-up took so long that at last Maud said it was a pity Charles hadn't taken them to The Golden Kettle, where old coats wouldn't have mattered or at least wouldn't have been so noticeable.

"It's a good thing you didn't tell him who it was we wanted to dodge," Ensie said, as they walked back to the lounge, "or he'd have gone there. And of course this *is* a nice change. I mean, it's not the sort of place we'd come to on our ownsomes."

"Do you mean he'd have gone if he'd known Annabel was there?"

"We don't even know she *was* there," Ensie temporised.

"Oh, don't be silly—that's not the point. Why should he want to—to see Annabel?"

"Oh, I just thought . . ." Ensie muttered. Then, meeting Maud's steely glance, she added hurriedly, "Well, I've sometimes thought he's—well, keen on her."

"But Annabel is married," Maud said austerely.

"Divorced," said Ensie, in a shocked whisper. "Look, there's Charles over there. I expect we're going to have tea in that glass sun-lounge place."

The sun-lounge aimed at being Moorish. There were palms in brass pots, and a life-like oasis painted on the end wall. It was rather late for tea, but a few visitors were still sitting at the Moorishly low tables and gazing somnolently out at the magnificent view of the bay. Charles looked more of an eagle than ever, among the plump doves and bald-headed coots at the other tables, Maud thought dreamily; and she wondered whether Ensie knew that Charles, like Annabel, was divorced. She had sounded so shocked about Annabel. Would she be taking so much trouble to find out exactly how he liked his tea, if she knew about his lurid past? Or were Ensie's moral judgments, like her clothes, different for different sexes?

Ensie, presiding over the tea-pot, assumed that it was her duty to converse, and told Charles the whole story of the film from the beginning in the Liverpool slum to the end when the heroine jumped into the wintry Atlantic.

"I cried and cried," she said. "I enjoyed it so much. I'd simply love to see it again."

"Did you cry?" Charles asked Maud.

"A little. Not as much as Ensie."

"You must be lacking in feeling. Or has Ensie got too much?"

"Far too much, I'm afraid," Ensie said bravely. "Only sometimes it seems—well, a kind of luxury to cry over other people's troubles. Haven't you ever felt that yourself?"

"No," said Charles with decision.

Then, as if he had heard quite enough about the fictitious troubles of imaginary characters, he turned to Maud and asked what she and old M. had done to frighten Oliver away.

Maud was considerably startled; for how had Charles known about Oliver's fleeting visit and his abrupt departure?

"We didn't frighten him," she protested. "He—he couldn't stay as long as he meant to."

"Not like Oliver to change his plans," Charles said blandly.

"I didn't know he was here," said Ensie.

"He isn't. He arrived on Thursday afternoon and left first thing on Friday morning."

"He left because he had to go and see a friend in Bristol," Maud said. This had been Oliver's excuse to the Hatballs, and she thought it would do equally well for Ensie and Charles.

"He could have done that in the day, and come back," Ensie told them. "It isn't really so far, if you have a car."

"He fled," said Charles.

"He didn't."

"Very well, he didn't. He removed himself in a huff."

Meeting Charles's eye Maud tried hard to look noncommittal, but in fact he had so exactly described Oliver's behaviour that it seemed a waste of time to deny it. She was grateful to Ensie, who turned back into being a clergyman's daughter with a duty to defend the absent. Oliver had never struck *her*, said Ensie, as the sort of man to go off in a huff. He had never seemed hasty or irritable; in fact, she had always felt a little sorry for him because he was the kind of mild, well-meaning man who got—well, pushed around. . . .

"So he was," said Charles. "Old M. and Maud between them pushed him around. And naturally the poor chap resented it—and, being Oliver, he pretended he was urgently needed elsewhere. But I'm interested to know what sort of pushes they gave him."

He looked at Maud, commanding her to tell him. Ensie decided to treat it as a joke and broke into a nervous laugh; but for a moment Charles and Maud measured each other's obstinacy. If they had been alone Maud might have yielded, but she wasn't going to reveal old M.'s family troubles to Ensie. Indeed, she hoped she would have refused to reveal them to Charles alone, because there was no doubt that he was the enemy at the gates, the undeserving nephew, the relative whom old M. (with a wide choice) liked least.

Still, he was a Feniston; he loved Glaine and would understand; and he had blue eyes. With an effort she reminded herself of his utter unsuitability as a confidant, and felt thankful that Ensie was there.

Not only was she there, but she was tactfully ready to keep the talk going, to pour oil on waters which she dimly suspected of being troubled, and to remind Charles that she mustn't be too late or Father would be wondering where she had got to. "Besides, we mustn't make *you* late," Ensie said thoughtfully "Were you on your way out to Glaine when we first met you?"

No, Charles had been on his way back to his lodgings in Monmouth Square, which was the square where Maud's bump of locality had seemed to fail her. She no longer regretted this failure, even when Ensie told Charles that she had known they were walking away from the centre of the town but hadn't liked to say so because Maud seemed so certain of the way.

"And yet I felt sure, all the time, that the parish church was *behind* us," Ensie stated.

Charles wasn't impressed, but Maud remembered Don and wondered if he had been inside the parish church and acting as a kind of magnetic north to Ensie's emotional compass.

At Combe Cottage Maud found her high tea awaiting her, the scrambled egg toughened by a sojourn at the back of the stove. Cousin Alice told her to make herself a fresh pot of tea, and Miss Conway explained that they had had their meal rather earlier than usual because they were hungry.

Maud thought that was no wonder; lunch had been a disaster and even Wilbraham had rejected the burnt potatoes. If it hadn't been for Charles's hospitality she would have been hungry herself, but as it was she did not want tough scrambled egg and dried-up bread-and-butter. She felt thankful, too, for the tin of biscuits she had secretly acquired and hidden in her wardrobe to prevent night starvation. The earliness and meagreness of the meal sometimes made it difficult for her to keep her vow about not grumbling, but the thought of the biscuits was a decided comfort. Tonight, sustained by Charles's tea, she could afford to leave most of her evening meal untouched; and this was easy because Cousin Alice and Miss Conway had retired to the sitting room.

She had just hidden the distasteful remains in the hen-bucket when Cousin Alice came into the kitchen and asked if she had had enough.

"Oh yes, thank you—and now I'm just washing up," Maud replied guiltily, hoping Cousin Alice had not seen what she was doing.

Cousin Alice lingered. Presently she took a biscuit from the tin on the table and munched it absent-mindedly. Then she offered one to Maud. They were known as the go-to-bed biscuits and their rather gritty texture concealed a wealth of vitamins or calories (Maud could not remember which), but they really needed the go-to-bed hot drink to wash them down. She refused, and wished she could offer Cousin Alice one of her own superior biscuits from the tin upstairs; but naturally the existence of this tin had to be kept secret. To explain her refusal she said:

"I'm not a bit hungry. Ensie and I had a huge tea in Yeomouth. And of course I've just had high tea as well."

"Was it a good tea?" Cousin Alice asked, taking another biscuit.

"Yes, lovely. We met Charles Feniston, and we went to the East Cliff Hotel."

"And did Charles pay for it?"

"Yes," said Maud. "I'm sorry, if that counts as fraternizing with the enemy, but you see Ensie was there, and she . . . Well, I suppose—"

"You think he thought of it as taking Ensie and her friend out to tea?" Cousin Alice paused, and the postscript took Maud by surprise. "It's a bad mistake to attribute your own unsatisfactory thoughts to other people."

"What?"

"You can't be sure, you know. You may be only projecting something you dislike thinking yourself."

Maud nodded agreement; with Cousin Alice she felt sure of nothing. "Ensie is a chameleon," she said, changing the subject.

"What do you mean?"

Maud told her about Papa's Ensie, and Ensie the girl-friend, and the Ensie who presided over tea-pots and entertained the opposite sex. But she did not mention Don's Ensie, partly out of loyalty to her own generation and partly because she did not want to discuss affairs of the heart with Cousin Alice. Except in the reference to the parish church Don's Ensie had not appeared that afternoon, but Maud knew she was at least as real as the others.

"We are all chameleons in a way," Cousin Alice said. "I am one person with you and a rather different person with Con." She pondered. "But I suppose that poor girl has to be Papa's Ensie, whether she likes it or not. She has been drilled in the part. I don't believe it's natural to her."

Maud nodded her agreement. "He's a domineering parent," she said with youthful certainty. "And of course she's a bit weak, and she's got no one to encourage her. She needs—well—"

"A strong-minded friend? But I hope you won't rush to the rescue, Maud. I used to believe in rescuing people," Cousin Alice admitted, "but I've come to the conclusion that it's generally a mistake. Too often one only unsettles them; and then they suffer. Or, if you set out to rescue a man, there's a great danger that you may fall in love with him while you're doing it. And then *you* suffer."

Maud hardly realized that this good advice might apply to her, for she heard it as an oblique reference to Cousin Alice's long-dead husband. Had he needed rescuing and become beloved in the process? She wished she had paid more attention to family history, but she could only remember that the late Mr. Grayson was always alluded to as "poor Anthony." Wondering about poor Cousin Anthony, she looked up to meet Cousin Alice's gaze and was disconcerted by its likeness to the gaze of an admonitory aunt.

"Of course you're very young," Cousin Alice said. "And Ensie is older than you, and not as weak-willed as you think, so I suppose I oughtn't to be a wet blanket about your trying to rescue her. I don't really think you'll hurt her, or she you.—Yes, perhaps it would be better if you stuck to Ensie."

The words did not match her expression, and Maud waited for the postscript.

"But not the Fenistons," said Cousin Alice pleadingly.

"They don't need rescuing! I mean, *I* couldn't rescue old M., and anyway I don't want to because he is quite happy as he is. And Oliver can rescue himself," Maud declared, repudiating the idea of holding out even a finger tip, let alone a helping hand, to Oliver. "He only has to sit stagnating in the Midlands until his father dies. He said so!"

"Oh dear."

"Yes, wasn't it horrid of him? But I didn't mean to tell you."

"No, you'd better not tell me any more. Old M. wouldn't like it," said Cousin Alice.

In spite of this high-minded reply Maud felt that Cousin Alice was not unwilling to be told more. But at that moment Miss Conway thrust her head round the door to ask what they were up to. It was an interruption which Maud had come to expect whenever she and Cousin Alice found themselves alone together, and she only wondered that it hadn't happened sooner. She was sorry, however, that Con should have caught Alice eating biscuits, since the reflection this cast on her cooking depressed them both for the rest of the evening.

CHAPTER ELEVEN

"WINTER'S THE BEST time of year," old M. asserted. "Nice and quiet. None of these tourists about. And you can see the branches."

It was certainly quiet. Since their party, the Woodfidleys seemed to have settled down to hibernate. Maud's only recreation was going out with Ensie or having tea with her at weekends, at Pixie Cot, and once having her to tea at Combe Cottage. This hadn't been a great success because Ensie had tried to please Cousin Alice by praising everything fulsomely, and had offended Miss Conway by crumbling up her cake and leaving half of it, and had hurt Wilbraham most of all by stepping on him as she walked over to inspect the great work. Unnerved by this, she then became inaudible and almost justified Miss Conway's description of her as "practically a moron." Cousin Alice had been more forbearing, but neither of them suggested that she should be asked again.

Winter might be the best time of year for old M., but if the cold weather acted on him as a tonic Maud could only hope for a countering sedative of warm, muggy days. His energy was no less remarkable than his restlessness; but his restlessness ensured that no task should ever be finished. He was for ever thinking of new schemes and new ways of carrying them out. He had begun to catalogue the library on an entirely different system, and had abandoned that to catalogue the pictures. But before they could be catalogued they had to be rehung; and before they could be rehung the girl in the pink muslin dress had to be identified. If she was Benjaminina Potts she must hang next to her husband Thos. Feniston III; but if she was Benjaminina's cousin Charity she ought to hang on the stairs and not in the long gallery. For the long gallery was reserved for Fenistons (and their lawful wedded wives), and poor Charity had just failed to secure one.

"An artful puss," old M. said, surveying her. "Tried for Thomas III first, but he preferred her cousin. Then she set her cap at his uncle. And it was all settled—banns called and everything—when he fell out of a window or down some steps or something, and broke his neck. So she didn't get either of them."

"How sad. Still, we aren't sure this is Charity. It may be Benjaminina."

"Make a note to look for the old list. It's probably in the library. We can't do much till we find it. Put this picture down as Charity question mark Benjaminina Potts."

Maud added another problem to the many already awaiting research, and followed her employer on his zig-zag progress down the gallery.

"There's Oliver," he said. "Not very like him, is it?"

He had asked her this question before, but she could not answer it because the charcoal sketch of Oliver had been done when he was a small child, anonymously chubby and curly-headed. "It's an attractive drawing," she said, and old M. remarked helpfully that of course Oliver looked different now he wore spectacles.

"Not that he needs to," he added. "The Fenistons all have good eyesight. Still, I suppose he has to, being a professor. Make himself look older, I mean. Oliver's a clever feller, you know, but people might think he was too young for the job."

Maud found it both comic and touching that old M. should be so proud of his son, and she would not have dreamed of pointing out that Oliver wasn't a professor. Watching him as he stared at the charcoal drawing, and hearing him sigh as he turned away, she suddenly wondered if it was the quarrel with Oliver that was making him so restless and difficult. At the time, the quarrel had seemed no more than another heated dispute—though perhaps more violent than its predecessors—about thrift and extravagance, but it occurred to her now that old M. was taking it seriously. Or that he was worried because Oliver was taking it seriously.

"Will Oliver be coming for Christmas?" she asked.

"He hasn't said so. Shouldn't be surprised if he went to Switzerland. Funny thing how people like *snow*."

"Why don't you write and ask him?"

Old M. swung round to glare at her. But even in his first, indignant "Hey!" she detected more than anger.

"I shall do as I please," he added, on a note of dying fury. "Lot of nonsense about Christmas anyway. Sentimental hypocrisy to send cards to people you never want to see again. And as for presents—!" He seemed to transfer the glare from Maud to his absent relatives. "Hoping to get something out of the legacy," he grumbled to himself. "Sending me jujubes and expecting champagne in return. As if I'd come in for a fortune!"

She wondered what he was talking about, until she remembered the aunts, the three little owls, who had left him their books and "a tidy sum." Had it been, in fact, a fortune? That would account for Oliver's despairing rage when he looked at his crumbling home, as well as for the hopeful despatch of jujube-sprats to catch a champagne-mackerel.

Two days later old M. told her to write to Oliver and find out if he was coming for Christmas. She could do it that afternoon while he was out; yes, write the letter herself, he hadn't time to dictate one and it had better go today. Time was getting on.

It was nearly a month to Christmas, and Maud understood perfectly why she was to write the letter. But it took her some time to compose it, and no carbon copy was kept to show old M. that it had been longer and more friendly than the mere enquiry he had sanctioned. Cousin Alice's good advice had fallen on deaf ears; but if Maud had remembered it she would have argued that this was not the same thing as rushing, uninvited, to the rescue, since old M. had asked for her help. If help was requested, even the most cautious knight errant could not be expected to "stick to Ensie."

Not that she neglected Ensie. Their friendship had reached the stage of confidences, at least on Ensie's side, and Maud knew she kept a photograph of Don hidden in her *Oxford Book of English Verse*, and a short note, about buns for last year's Church Fête, in the recesses of her desk. The photograph had been cut out of the *Western Gazette* and included a few Boy Scouts and was a poor likeness; the note was formally phrased and was signed Yrs. sincerely, Donald Crouch. Neither, therefore, offered any proof that Don returned Ensie's affection, and Maud had confined herself to showing sympathy and interest—which wasn't difficult, since Ensie was a great talker.

"These men," she began, greeting Maud at the door. "It's all right, Father's out and there's a nice fire. You look quite perished."

"I can't come in or I'll be late for high tea. I only brought the library book—"

"Oh, come in, do. Really Father is very tiresome sometimes. Would you believe it, he's thinking of unretiring for Christmas! Coming out of retirement, I mean, and he's gone off to Yeomouth to see the Rector about being invited to preach on Christmas Day at little St. Alfred's. And I'd been looking forward to Don. At little St. Alfred's, I mean."

Ensie's sad wails drew Maud inside the door, and the waves of cosy warmth lured her into the sitting room. (At Combe Cottage there would be damp logs smouldering in the grate and rugs to wrap round one's knees as the frost grew keener.) "These men," she echoed sympathetically, wondering why Ensie always dwelt on the littleness of St. Alfred's, which was by no means a dwarf among chapels. These men, for Maud, included Oliver, whose reply to her letter had arrived that morning, and Hatball, who had infuriated old M. by demanding a rise.

Even Hatball seemed more of a problem than Ensie's Papa, who could surely be kept from preaching by fair means or foul. "Tell him he's looking ill, just before Christmas," she suggested. "Say you're afraid he's starting influenza."

"Then he will start it. And I shall get it too!"

Maud had forgotten that Ensie, like her Papa, had a tendency to hypochondria. "Oh well, we'll think of something," she said confidently. "There's plenty of time before Christmas."

"But—"

"Listen, Ensie. Do you know Oliver Feniston? Well, of course you do. He's coming here for Christmas, and we must entertain him. Keep him amused. It's only for four days so it shouldn't be too difficult, if you'll help. You could ask him here, couldn't you?"

"Yes, but why?"

"Oh, he gets bored," Maud said quickly.

"But does that matter, if it's only for four days?"

"Well, yes. I do want this Christmas to be a success, and I think the only thing is for. Oliver to be out as much as possible. Not to spend all his time at home, being bored."

"I do see," said Ensie. "And of course I'll do my best. Actually, I thought you'd be going home for Christmas, but I suppose you're glad you're not, now. And I can see it's awfully difficult for you—I mean, about asking him to Combe Cottage. Even Father—"

The door bell rang. When Ensie had dashed off to answer it, Maud knelt down by the fire, telling herself that she must hurry back to Combe Cottage and wishing she could absorb enough heat to last her the rest of the evening. She continued to think about Oliver; his stiff letter, hinting at the sacrifices he was making by spending four days under his father's roof, lay crumpled in her pocket, and the plans for his entertainment included a wholly impracticable one of telling him just what she thought of him. But this would defeat her object, which was to keep Oliver in a good temper so that old M.'s Christmas should pass off smoothly.

The voice outside, replying to Ensie's, was certainly masculine. For an instant Maud wondered if Charles had called on his way home, then she remembered that it was dark and the Glaine gardens had been shut an hour ago. It was odd, and tiresome, that she never seemed to meet Charles nowadays; for of course he could be of the greatest help, he could tell her how to deal with Oliver or even assist in the non-stop entertainment which was to keep him under old M.'s roof but out of his way. No, he couldn't, because they had quarrelled and he was the Enemy at the Gates and must not be consulted.

"Oh dear!" she said, aloud.

The sitting-room door opened, and she hoped they had not overheard her. But Ensie was listening raptly to the new visitor, who was continuing a remark begun outside. In fact he had not even noticed Maud's presence.

". . . so we must remember that there are compensations," he said, "and we must look forward—"

He looked forward, extending his arm in a confident gesture, and was momentarily disconcerted to find Maud in front of him. But with remarkable dexterity he turned the gesture into a handshake, while the sternly encouraging expression softened into a boyish smile.

"We have met before," he said. "But your name—I'm most terribly sorry—"

Ensie supplied the names, though Maud did not need to be told that this was Donald Crouch. While he recalled the circumstances of their previous meeting and told her what an awfully jolly party it had been, she was able to study his appearance. At the party she had not looked at him particularly, for she did not then know so much about Ensie's feelings; and the newspaper photograph did him decidedly less than justice. But it was a pity—a great pity—that he looked so young.

He wasn't the weedy, pale young curate of the comic papers. His hair was thick, brown and curly, and his eyebrows were almost shaggy and would one day be the beetling eyebrows of a bishop. He had already acquired some clerical mannerisms: an exuberantly friendly approach, a tendency to speak with authority even on trivial, non-religious matters, and a broad-minded laugh. But as if aware of his calling's dangers he strove to avoid pomposity by using everyday language. Or so Maud assumed, listening to the stream of "awfully's" and "frightfully's" and all the jolly slang idioms they qualified. She had heard him speaking in another strain when he entered the room; and she hoped this meant that Ensie was more to him than a mere parishioner.

"Combe Cottage?" he echoed. "That's that little duck of a place at the corner of the lane? You know, you're frightfully lucky to have an aunt handy—"

"A cousin," Maud murmured, on principle.

"—instead of being in digs in Yeomouth. Now, my land lady—well, bless her, the poor old dear means terribly well, but . . ."

"Oh, Don, how uncomfortable for you," Ensie said, at the appropriate moment and with more than appropriate sympathy.

The anecdotes flowed on. Maud remembered how Oliver had talked about *his* landlady, and thought how fussy men were about lodgings, and wondered how Oliver (or Don) would endure living at Combe Cottage. But if Don found a lodger's life so uncomfortable it might encourage him to think of getting married; a dear little wife to look after him, to cook hot suppers and iron his surplices without scorching them, would be an investment, not a handicap. And how lucky that Ensie had not fallen in love with the lantern-jawed type of clergyman who believes in celibacy even if it condemns him to a lifetime of dismal lodgings.

"Ensie is a very good cook," she said, having worked the conversation round to meals.

Ensie looked rather surprised (her cakes were the only thing Maud had tasted), but to Maud's keen eye Don looked unmistakably interested.

"I wish *I* were," he said. "My landlady gives me the run of the place—she's always popping off to the flicks—but I'm frightfully stupid. I can't even boil an egg properly."

"There are two hundred and eighty-three ways of cooking eggs," Maud observed. "You should get Ensie to give you some lessons."

She rose to go. Don rose too, explaining that he had really dropped up to see Mr. Martin about the services on Christmas Day at little St. Alfred's—not knowing, of course, that Mr. Martin had popped off to fix it up with the Rector—and he really ought to be getting along. But Ensie, assisted by Maud, soon persuaded him to wait a little longer. Father would be back at any moment, and would love to see him, Ensie said nervously, and it would be, well, *awfully* nice if he could stay for supper.

Maud knew why Ensie was nervous; she hoped the supper dish would be good enough to sustain her reputation as a cook, and large enough to go round. She had done her best for Ensie, and her final good deed was to remove herself and leave them to a tête-à-tête. She did this as quickly as possible.

Unfortunately Ensie had been right about the imminence of her Papa's return, and Maud met him in the lane outside Pixie Cot. Behind him, just visible in the light of the young moon, she saw his car drawn up against the hedge, and her first thought was that he was coming to fetch Ensie out to help him in garaging it. She knew that Mr. Martin was not a very good driver and that he seldom drove after dark. In fact, he seldom drove at all, for in wet weather he would not take the car out lest its immaculate paint-work should suffer, and on hot, dry days he would not take it out for fear that its frail old tyres would expand and explode. It lived in a small wooden garage a short distance down the lane, swathed in dust sheets and protected from thieves by a heavy padlock and chain across the garage doors. But as it was a very old two-seater of an obsolete make, car-thieves were unlikely to fancy it.

"Good evening," said Maud. "Can I help you to garage the car? I've got a torch in my bicycle-basket, if you want a light for backing in."

Mr. Martin, who evidently suffered from night-blindness, peered suspiciously in her direction. Maud identified herself, and repeated her offer of help.

"Oh no," he said, decisively. "I don't think it's going to rain or freeze. I think the car will be none the worse—on this single occasion—for a sojourn in the open. A rug under the bonnet, and a mackintosh sheet to cover it—Ensie will bring one out—"

The note of self-confidence was absent. Maud judged that the drive home had frightened Mr. Martin considerably and that he did not feel capable of steering his car into its garage. Ensie could not drive, and although Maud had occasionally driven her stepmother's car she thought it would be rash to offer to drive Mr. Martin's. But she stood firmly between Mr. Martin and his front gate, bent on delaying him.

In the dark Mr. Martin was at a disadvantage; his bland, patronizing look could not quench foolish chatter, nor could he see well enough to outflank Maud and get the gate open. With the minimum of civility he answered her questions about his health and the health of his cat Pixie, and to her remarks about the weather and the pretty moon he replied with impatient grunts. At last, changing his tactics, he lengthened the grunts into coughs and interrupted her to say hoarsely that the night air was—ar-hum—regrettably unkind to a man with a delicate throat, and that he had to be particularly careful at this time of year.

"And so, my dear young lady, I must—ar-hum—hasten indoors. Good night."

Sympathizing at some length, Maud gave ground. Mr. Martin moved forward alertly, helped by a faint beam of light which rapidly grew brighter—the headlights of an approaching car. The car was coming across the combe from Chestnut Lodge or Glaine, and travelling fairly fast, and Maud and Mr. Martin instinctively stepped closer to the hedge for safety. But the driver of the car had seen them, and swerved out, as far as the width of the lane permitted, to give them room. Then, as he passed them, he swerved back again.

Perhaps it was the swerve that did it; or perhaps their figures had hidden Mr. Martin's car, which was parked without lights just beyond them. Certainly it was parked close to the hedge, but the lane was narrow and the pretty moon had gone behind a cloud. There was a squeal of brakes and a splintering crash as the moving car stopped. It was all too plainly a collision; and the thing that surprised Maud most was that neither Ensie nor Don came rushing out to see what had happened. For even if they had thought that loud metallic noises did not concern them they surely could not have failed to hear and respond to the loud human noise, the anguished and outraged bellow, that immediately followed.

CHAPTER TWELVE

"Aaah!" bellowed Mr. Martin. "My car! You oaf!"

"Are you hurt?" cried Maud.

She peered at the other car, while Mr. Martin peered at his own. It had been a head-on collision, but Mr. Martin's car had been pushed against the hedge and the other one leant against it at an oblique angle. Both cars had suffered, but Mr. Martin's seemed to have come off worst; and to Maud's great relief the occupants of the other car had escaped injury. Slowly they emerged, through the doors on the undamaged side, and revealed themselves as Mr. and Mrs. Woodfidley and their daughter Annabel Curtis.

"We are shaken," said Mrs. Woodfidley. "Badly shaken. And bruised."

"It's a miracle we're not dead," said Annabel.

They continued to say these things over and over again, with minor variations, during the quarrel that followed, and Maud continued to congratulate them on their lucky escape. But she did it automatically (while listening enthralled to Mr. Martin and Mr. Woodfidley), and their civil trio was often drowned by the denunciatory duet. Mr. Martin bellowed, but Mr. Woodfidley kept up a steady flow on a high-pitched note which was as penetrating as the bellow. Unlike the clergyman, he was not handicapped by having to refrain from swearing.

"My car! Smashed to pieces! Look at it!"

"How the devil could I, when you left it standing there without lights?" Mr. Woodfidley retorted.

"You come tearing up the lane like an incompetent maniac—"

"It's a danger to the public when you're inside it, but a damned worse danger when you get out and leave it—just leave it sitting there, in the darkest part of the lane! And as for accusing *me* of incompetence—well, all I can say is—"

All he said was enlarged and underlined by full-blooded adjectives. Maud feared she would not be able to remember all of them.

"You shall pay for it," Mr. Martin declared. "I shall make a full report to the police. I shall demand restitution. I shall expose you. I belong to the Road Safety Society, and I shall not hesitate to—"

"Road Safety!" said Mr. Woodfidley, qualifying it. "Old Fools' Society is what you ought to belong to."

"I have been driving for fifty years and I have never seen a—a more glaring example of utter carelessness and lack of control. Straight into my car!"

"Your car is worth about twopence ha'penny, and I only hope it is a total loss so that you won't be able to drive it out on another dark night and cause another accident. I might have been killed. And my wife and daughter too," Mr. Woodfidley added, suddenly remembering them.

"You deserve to be killed—driving like that! My car wasn't even *moving*."

"Nor—as I keep telling you—had it got its lights on."

For the first time Mr. Martin faltered in his attack.

"There's a moon," he said, pointing to it.

"A moon up there isn't the same as sidelights down here," Mr. Woodfidley argued shrilly. "You won't get away with that! More than an hour after sunset—don't forget to say so in your report to the police. *I* shan't."

Maud thought it must also be more than an hour after high tea, and she hoped Cousin Alice was not worrying about her non-return. Mentally endowing her cousin with the adjective "sensible" (and therefore not a foolish worrier), she abandoned the thought of high tea. After all, she had a tin of biscuits; and anyway the dramatic events of the evening were well worth a few pangs of hunger.

"Yes, you were awfully lucky," she assured Mrs. Woodfidley, while Mr. Martin, breathing deeply, returned to the attack with a scathing comment on his opponent's lack of common decency.

"Not a word of apology! Not a glance at the damage! Not a thought for the—the shock I have suffered! I am not a young

man, Woodfidley—in fact, I am an elderly and a *delicate* man—
and to be run down on my own doorstep . . ."

"I'm freezing to death," said Annabel. "And we're going to be
terribly late. Why doesn't Ensie come out and take him away?"

Maud wondered too. The lack of interest shown by Ensie and
Don was puzzling; though of course it might be interpreted as
favourable, implying that each was too interested in the other
to heed the clamour outside. But the next moment Mr. Martin
(who had perhaps heard the name "Ensie" through his own bel-
lows) felt the need for reinforcements.

"Ensie!" he called loudly over the gate. "Ensie, come here
at once!"

Dramatically, he leaned back against the gate; the indirect
light from the Woodfidley car's lamps showed him to be sagging
slightly, as befitted an elderly and delicate clergyman suffering
from delayed shock. Mrs. Woodfidley said, "Oh, Ernest," to her
husband, and the resourceful Annabel went to the car and put
her finger on the horn-button and kept it there. The continuous
blare of a powerful electric horn made even more noise than
the angry voices, and it must have reached every corner of Pixie
Cot. Mr. Woodfidley, who had been pressing home his advantage with unchivalrous triumph, was silenced; and when the
front door of Pixie Cot opened and Annabel took her finger off
the horn there was not a sound to be heard. Maud looked up
and saw Ensie and Don silhouetted against the interior light.
Mr. Martin also looked up, and the sight of two figures where he
had expected only one seemed to strike him dumb. The silence
was broken by the feminine voices of Maud, Annabel, and Mrs.
Woodfidley, who announced in an incoherent chorus that there
had been an accident, not a bad one, no one hurt, a collision
but the car was empty, your father is here, perhaps you'd better
come down.

It was Don who came first, leaping down the steep steps in
the bank like a well-intentioned mountain goat. He had missed
the reassuring clause in the chorus and was eager to render
first aid. At the foot of the bank he stopped and called to Ensie
to go back for a torch; then he advanced to the gate and found
Mr. Martin propped against it. In an instant Mr. Martin had

been removed from his temporary support and tenderly seated on the lowest of the stone steps, where, from sheer surprise, he remained. Don ran to the Woodfidley car, delved inside it and pulled out a sumptuous fur rug which he brought back and wrapped round Mr. Martin, murmuring to himself, "Treat first for shock—keep warm and reassure." Having reassured Mr. Martin by patting him on the shoulder and telling him he was all right, Don looked for other victims; he seemed quite disappointed that there were none.

"Quite sure you're all accounted for?" he asked anxiously, staring about him as if a body or two might have been hurled out of the car and escaped their notice.

"It's a miracle we weren't all killed," said Annabel.

Maud hoped it did not strike Don as a superfluous miracle, depriving him of a glorious chance to practise his first aid; though of course it would have been equally galling if the victims had all been dead before he got to them. But there was still Mr. Martin, who for lack of other victims now came in for a great deal of attention. He was reassured all over again, and as soon as Ensie had brought the torch he was carefully examined and his arms and legs felt to see if they were fractured; the pupils of his eyes were scrutinized, and he was begged to state if he had any pain. Mr. Martin accepted his new rôle of victim without a demur; but the Woodfidleys, and even Maud, muttered disconsolately that he did not deserve it.

"Why, he wasn't *in* the car," said Mrs. Woodfidley.

"I never touched him—did I?" Mr. Woodfidley demanded of Maud.

"No. You didn't touch either of us."

"Of course it's utterly ridiculous," said Annabel. "But now he's inside the gate and being fussed over, couldn't we go?"

At an earlier stage retreat would have been unthinkable for Mr. Woodfidley; he had proclaimed his intention of getting the police out so that they could see for themselves. But his opponent was now in a much stronger position; with another clergyman fussing over him and his daughter uttering anxious cries he had become an object of sympathy, and he was quite cunning enough to sustain this character with the police, who unfortunately would remember Mr. Woodfidley himself as a man who had twice been fined recently for exceeding the speed limit in built-up areas. It was monstrously unjust, but still—

In four sentences Mr. Woodfidley thought his way round to agreeing with his daughter.

"Of course I shall report the accident immediately. No point in staying here all night arguing. Anyway, the insurance companies will sort it out. Let's see if the car will still move."

Quietly, almost furtively, the Woodfidleys got into their car, and as soon as Mr. Woodfidley had started the engine they were off. There was a loud metallic clatter as the car disengaged itself from Mr. Martin's, which momentarily distracted him from his rôle of injured victim. But the speed of the Woodfidleys' departure gave him no time to take action and he wisely reverted to his helpless, badly shocked state. It was Ensie who tactlessly exclaimed:

"Oh, we've still got their rug!"

A cluck of displeasure came from the rug's occupant. Maud said they wouldn't miss it—the night was quite warm. Don struck the right note by saying that the thing now was to get Mr. Martin into the house, and by anxiously asking him if he could manage to walk.

"I'll try," Mr. Martin responded bravely.

Supported by Don, with Ensie and Maud as a rearguard, he slowly ascended the steps. In the sitting room he was helped to the sofa; Ensie took off his shoes, Don sent Maud back to fetch the rug, and tucked it round him, and then commanded Ensie to make a pot of tea.

Mr. Martin raised his head. "No," he said. "Fetch the whisky."

Don said persuasively, "Tea is what you need, sir. Just you try it. It won't take a moment, and—"

"No, I need whisky. I keep whisky in the house for medicinal purposes—for emergencies, you understand. Get the whisky, Ensie."

"But honestly, sir, tea is what you *need*. It says so in the manual. Warm, sweet tea."

Mr. Martin shuddered. "Are you a teetotaller?" he demanded.

"No, no! Only I'm pretty keen on first aid, and as a matter of fact I do know what I'm talking about. Warm, sweet—"

"I know what I'm talking about too. I have a far better knowledge of my own system than you can possibly have. Ensie, the whisky."

"But it says in the manual—!"

Ensie stood irresolute, torn between love and filial duty, but Maud felt impelled to intervene; for a quarrel between Don and Mr. Martin must certainly be avoided, "*I'll* put the kettle on," she cried, and rushed off to do it, leaving Ensie to get the whisky and placate her Papa.

The kettle took its time, and presently Don thrust his head round the door to tell her it would not be wanted.

"He's having a second glass of whisky, and I must say he seems to be getting over the shock nicely. But it's jolly risky, you know. The first-aid manual is absolutely against alcoholic stimulants."

"You did all you could," Maud assured him. "But Ensie couldn't refuse to get the whisky, though I'm sure she agreed with you about tea being best. Mr. Martin is a harsh parent."

"Is he?"

"Oh yes. Poor Ensie is rather afraid of him. He treats her like a domestic slave."

"What a frightful shame," said Don, shutting the door behind him and showing a satisfactory desire to hear more.

By nine o'clock Alice and Con had discussed all the mishaps that could possibly account for Maud's absence and it was evident to them that something must be done about it. An imaginative sortie down every avenue had enabled them to postpone taking any actual steps, such as ringing up old M. or the police, although they had, of course, debated the wisdom of doing these things; but the time had come when action could no longer be postponed. Even Con felt it would be wrong to go to bed as usual.

"Where is the torch?" Alice asked, getting up reluctantly.

"Here. But it's rather dim. You're not going *out*?"

"I'll take Wilbraham."

"The telephone?"

"But what's the good? Old M. won't answer it and Mrs. Hat is deaf and her husband doesn't listen properly. Last time I telephoned to Glaine he thought I was the grocer."

It was no more than an excuse; Con knew that the telephone was only for real emergencies: fire, floods, or a severe and sudden illness. She was glad to see that Alice wasn't really, seriously worried, but at the same time she half hoped that something might have happened to Maud, something vaguely disabling (not painful, of course, and not permanent like death or lunacy) which would remove her to the Yeomouth hospital and subsequently to her own home, far away from Combe Cottage. Well, why not? thought Con, consciously dwelling on her hope as she watched the dim torch disappear round the corner of the lane. Maud was a nuisance. Of course one had nothing against her personally, only she was in the way. It would be far better if she returned to Surrey, thought Con, her thoughts gaining momentum like a runaway car now that the brake—or Alice's restraining influence—was no longer working. If nothing *had* happened to Maud, couldn't something be made to happen? After all, it was one's duty to look after Alice. And Alice had once had a nervous breakdown (though admittedly it was years ago), which was entirely due to family troubles; and Maud had brought the family back again, reviving old memories, encouraging Alice to talk about Wolfering, reminding her of another world far bigger than Glaine. If one wasn't careful, poor Alice might be in for another breakdown.

Shrill barks in the distance suggested that Puppy was chasing something. He never ran mute—nor did he bark when he was on the lead. Con wondered if Alice had dropped his lead while she stooped over an unconscious Maud; but the loss of Puppy ranked higher in her list of disasters than any injury to Maud. Puppy was precious, he was Con's own darling, he must be rescued at once.

She stepped back into the house to get her coat and another torch and the little dish of minced liver which was to have been Puppy's treat for tomorrow. (He would smell the liver and come for it.) It took her a few minutes to find the torch, which was underneath everything else at the back of a drawer, and when she had found it she wasted more time fiddling with it before she could make it work. Without a light she could not go scrambling about in the Glaine woods, following the sound of Puppy's chase; already the barks were getting fainter, as if he was far away at the head of the combe. Trembling with anxiety for her darling, Miss Conway told herself that it was all Maud's fault—and serve her right if she had fallen off her bicycle and knocked her head on a stone. One wouldn't lift a finger to help her. But one must, somehow, recapture Puppy.

There was Puppy, coming back down the hill, heading this way; his barks grew louder, stopped, and then broke out again in a crescendo of excitement. Just short of Pixie Cot Miss Conway climbed over a field gate and took the direct way up the hill, stumbling through tussocky grass and twice missing her footing and falling heavily. At the top of the field was a rough stone wall; it was an obstacle she would have shunned in daylight, but now, in the dark, impeded by the basket which held the minced liver and breathless from her scramble up the steep field, she tackled it without hesitation. In the wood on the other side, and apparently quite near, Puppy was having hysterics.

And there were other voices, human, male and female; a gang of poachers perhaps, who in lieu of pheasants would steal Puppy and hold him up to ransom. She remembered that Elizabeth Barrett Browning's dog had been stolen by thieves; the story was in one of her dog books, but the poetess had been an invalid and naturally she had not been able to rescue her dog by force so she had had to pay the ransom. It would be different with Puppy. What a good thing she had brought a stick.

Confused, excited, and breathless, Miss Conway at last surmounted the wall. She jumped down and fell again, heavily, partly in a patch of brambles. There were lights in the wood, two torches which swung round to dazzle her as she searched for her stick and the basket, and one of the torch-bearers came hurrying towards her, uttering reassurances which in her confusion she mistook for threats.

"Don't try to get up! Lie still. I'll be with you in a jiffy."

The trailing brambles delayed him, and Miss Conway had time to reply.

"You leave my dog alone," she shouted. "Puppy, come here at once. Poor little Wuzzums!"

"Miss Conway!"

"Oh, Don, please come back. I think Pixie's up that tree, and Maud nearly had the dog that time. Poor little Pixie!"

"It's Miss *Conway*, Ensie. In that bramble patch. Lots of first aid for Don!"

"But she wasn't with us when we started," said Ensie's voice, sceptically.

CHAPTER THIRTEEN

EXPLANATIONS MUST wait till the morning, Cousin Alice had insisted. As it was they had been up half the night, calming Miss Conway, removing thorns from her person and sponging her scratches, and persuading her to accept a hot-water bottle, a glass of hot milk, and three aspirins.

"I'm perfectly all right," Miss Conway had repeated frequently, though even to Maud's eyes she looked all wrong. She looked even worse the next morning, with a large bruise adding to her facial disfigurement, and a badly swollen ankle, and a general air of being too stiff to move. It was really noble of her (and also exasperating) to drag herself downstairs at nearly the usual time. Maud, who was just about to start for Glaine, joined with Alice in beseeching her to go back to bed or at least to lie on the sofa and have her breakfast on a tray.

"Can't do that. Got my work to do," said Miss Conway, hobbling across the kitchen.

"I've done the chores. And Cousin Alice is getting your breakfasts."

It was clear that Miss Conway was not pleased to find herself forestalled. "You're using the wrong pan," she told Alice. "And you'll be late, Maud, if that clock's right. I suppose you overslept."

"No, I didn't. I got up extra early to do the stove, but—"

Maud became aware that Cousin Alice wished her to go; or at least, not to argue.

"—but I suppose I wasted time, talking," she ended, and hurried off to fetch her bicycle from the shed. Cycling down the lane, she realized she had said the wrong thing; for Miss Conway at all times resented tête-à-têtes at which she was not present and this morning she already looked brimful of grievances. She really ought to rest that ankle, Maud thought, but obviously she wouldn't; she would stump about being brave and exacting sympathy. Never mind, perhaps Don would call to see how she was; it would give him a good reason for coming to Glaine again, and he could go on and visit Ensie.

Maud considered that the events of last night had been truly fortunate for Ensie, since they had established Don as a close friend of the family. First he had succoured Mr. Martin. Secondly, when Cousin Alice appeared just as Maud was leaving, he had saved the cat Pixie from sudden death. Pixie had strolled along the path and Wilbraham had seen her and had wrenched the lead out of Cousin Alice's hand; he would have slain Pixie if Don had not grabbed him as he rushed forward. Unluckily Wilbraham had quickly wriggled free of Don's grasp, but the delay had given Pixie time to fly. Then Don had taken command again, leading Maud and Ensie in a search party to rescue Pixie and capture Wilbraham, and detailing Cousin Alice to console Mr. Martin. Finally, he had won general esteem by extricating Miss Conway from the brambles, re-uniting her with Wilbraham, coaxing Pixie down from a tree, bringing them all safely back to Pixie Cot, and escorting the Combe Cottage party home.

Moreover it was now clear to Maud that Don admired Ensie and had been longing to know her better. He had been distressed to learn of her enslavement to a harsh papa, and he had shown a very proper wish to help her. Maud was still prepared to play the part of knight-errant but she felt it would no longer be necessary; she could safely leave it to Don, and resign herself to becoming the female confidante.

All this was satisfactory; except that she would have preferred a more active role. She was conscious of a marked contrast between her life and the lives of Ensie and her other neighbours. Things happened to them: they fell in love, had dramatic accidents, maintained feuds or started new ones; their lives, even when outwardly tranquil, seemed to enclose hidden re-serves of strong feeling (look at Con and Cousin Alice), or else, like the Woodfidleys, they presented intriguing problems. (What on earth had induced the Woodfidleys to settle in Glaine?) But nothing happened to her, nor could she endow herself with strong feelings or a mysterious past. It was unsatisfactory; it was even—after a sleepless night—rather depressing.

At the back drive she left her bicycle and took the short cut across the lawn, for Miss Conway had been right and she was already late. She was too late to see old M., who had set off at an early hour to visit a distant auction room, but a note on her desk commanded her to "have another look in the library." She obeyed reluctantly; the library was cold and damp, and "a look" meant searching for the missing list of the Feniston portraits, which was just as likely to be upstairs in the attics or mouldering in the cellars. She lit the oil stove (one of old M.'s less success-ful bargains), and it filled the library with the fumes of paraffin but made little difference to the temperature. It was a relief to get outside, where the winter sunlight dazzled her after the li-brary's gloom, and to run across the sodden lawn and through the encircling shrubbery. She thrust the last branches aside and bounded into the back drive with more speed than elegance. And there, watching her arrival with interest, stood Charles.

"Good morning," he said. "Are you still under doctor's or-ders?"

"What?"

"If I remember, he ordered you to take plenty of exercise. I suppose he's increased the dose."

It was bad enough when one saw oneself as a mere confidante, but it was much worse when other people—well, Charles—saw one as a child to be teased. Maud drew herself up and looked him sternly in the face.

"I was running to get warm," she said. "Also, I am rather late, and it isn't a good day to keep them waiting."

Charles pointed out that it was barely a quarter past twelve. She looked at her watch again and maintained that it was a quarter to one.

"Your watch is wrong," he said.

"Well, it isn't very reliable. I forgot to set it by the kitchen clock this morning. And the clocks at Glaine are never right. I needn't have run after all."

"Except to get warm," he reminded her. "Why isn't it a good day to keep them waiting?"

With twenty minutes to spare Maud had time to do justice to the excitements and alarms of last night, culminating in the sudden appearance of Miss Conway on top of the wall and her headlong descent into the brambles.

"I saw her looming up as she climbed over, and then I recognised her voice. But Don thought she was Mr. Martin come to spur us on, and Ensie kept saying she couldn't be there because she hadn't been with us when we started. It was a scene of dramatic misunderstandings, but it seems funnier now, because at the time I thought she might have broken her leg and I was wondering how we would get her out of the wood. Still, I suppose Don would have coped."

"Is he so good at coping?"

"Oh yes, he's wonderful," she declared. "Quite wasted on little St. Alfred's. He ought to be a missionary."

She wondered if Ensie would enjoy being a missionary's wife, and kindly provided her with an imaginary alternative.

"—Or else the vicar of a crowded industrial parish with lots of factory explosions and street accidents. It must be so dull for him here."

"You all seem to have done your best to mitigate his boredom," Charles said drily. He looked down at her. "Don't you find it dull yourself?"

"Oh no. I'm very happy."

Indeed, she was. Meeting Charles had quite dispelled the feeling of depression, and she looked back with tolerant wonder on the Maud who had bicycled to work.

"Of course, you're lucky," Charles said. "You've got the run of the house."

Obviously he meant Glaine, but for a moment Maud didn't understand why she should be dubbed fortune's favourite just because she worked at Glaine. And Charles himself seemed to think his statement needed clarifying.

"It means quite a lot to me," he explained. "Though naturally I don't want to go back there—as things are."

She waited, hoping that if she had to be a confidante she could be one for Charles and learn something about his mysterious past. But Charles skipped the immediate past and went right back to his boyhood, telling her a longish and rather dull anecdote about how he had once dressed up as a ghost and frightened the cook, and describing in detail the upper landing where this had taken place.

It was the detail, loving and exact, that redeemed the anecdote from total dullness. She saw Charles as a prodigal son, his thoughts turning homeward after a life of wickedness and dissipation—but with the sad difference that his home was barred to him. She saw herself as a link between Charles and Glaine; or even as a heroine who would risk the world's scorn by standing up for him when everyone else was against him.

It was a satisfying vision, but it lay well in the future; she would not be able to stand up for Charles with any hope of success until her own position was assured. At present she was a newcomer, still on approval, and her advocacy would have no effect.

In the pause which followed Charles's anecdote she remembered how important it was not to be late today. A certain quality of desperation had loomed in Cousin Alice's mute appeal, which suggested that more than a tiff could be expected if Miss Conway were not appeased. Maud had grown fond of Cousin Alice and she did not wish to make things difficult for her; moreover there was a danger, remote but not impossible, that Cousin Alice might decide to manage without a paying guest if she upset Miss Conway. The mere thought of it was enough to take her across to her bicycle.

"I really must go," she said. "But I hope I shall see you again soon. It's odd I haven't seen you for so long, when I come here every day."

"But I don't," said Charles.

She couldn't wait to find out why, nor did it really matter, for it was clear that his heart was in Glaine, just as the hearts of the Jacobite exiles were in the Highlands. She pedalled away at her usual reckless speed and reached Combe Cottage on the stroke of one.

The need for punctuality seemed just as important at the end of the afternoon, because the luncheon session had been decidedly sticky. Maud was pleased to see another bicycle propped against the porch of Combe Cottage, a bicycle whose low handlebars and gaudy colour were misleadingly secular, but which she nevertheless guessed to belong to Mr. Crouch. His coming would surely have made a good impression on Miss Conway, and his presence would unlock her lips. She could hardly sit silent, as she had done through lunch, without ruining the reputation for cheery grit she had acquired last night.

It might have been wiser not to join them, she thought afterwards. The strain of behaving coldly to Maud and amiably to Mr. Crouch was bad for Miss Conway's nerves, and Cousin Alice was not in the room. An awkward three-cornered conversation dragged on between Maud in the window, Miss Conway on the sofa, and Don by the fire; the events of last night were discussed with desperation. Maud put in a good word for Ensie and Miss Conway received it with an unfriendly grunt. Don said he hoped the Martins' cat was recovering from its fright, and Miss Conway managed to reply that it was a pretty little cat in its way. Maud looked round for Wilbraham, who generally barked if cats were mentioned, but he was not there either. She wondered if Cousin Alice had had the temerity to take him out for another walk.

"I do hope you've been to a doctor about that ankle," Don said with concern.

"No, I haven't. I don't believe in doctors." Miss Conway gave a sharp glance at Maud (a doctor's daughter) and added that most tonics were just pink water and only fools believed they did any good.

"But this is a different thing from needing a tonic. Honestly, you ought to have it X-rayed. One of my Scouts—jolly little chap called Podge—wrenched his ankle in camp last summer, and when we took him to hospital—"

"I'm not going to hospital! Ghastly places. Never know how long they'll keep you. It's kind of you to bother," said Miss Conway, calming herself with an effort, "but I'm perfectly all right. Got to keep going, you know. Can't afford to lie up."

"Are you going on to see Mr. Martin and Ensie?" Maud intervened.

"—Podge had *broken* his ankle. The X rays showed it. Yes— and I must jolly well rush."

"Mrs. Grayson will be sorry to have missed you," Miss Conway said graciously. She got up, disregarding protests, and limped out into the hall to see him off. Maud could not help wondering if this action was meant to define the difference between Miss Conway and herself: the one a resident and acting-hostess, the other a lodger with no proprietary rights. But she told herself not to be fanciful; and after giving them two minutes' start she slipped out of the room and went to the kitchen. As she crossed the hall she could hear Miss Conway in the porch, sounding twice as affable as she had appeared earlier.

In the kitchen was Cousin Alice, sitting at the table and reading a book which she shut with guilty haste as Maud entered.

"Oh—it's you! I thought it was Con. Has Mr. Crouch gone? Do you think you could take that bone away from Wilbraham before . . . well, now?"

Wilbraham was being kept quiet by an outsize bribe which he was chewing on the spotless tiled floor. Maud did not have to use force, because Cousin Alice produced a biscuit as an alternative bribe and while Wilbraham was begging for it she was able to snatch up the bone and hide it, as directed, in a bowl at the back of the larder.

"Con doesn't think bones are very good for him," Alice said. "But I find they last so much longer than biscuits."

"Is it—surely we didn't have—"

"No, dear. We didn't have the joint . . . only the bone. The butcher's van comes to Glaine today and I lay in wait for it, and luckily he had some bones for soup and he let me buy one. I thought it would make up to Wilbraham for not getting his usual walk. I often think it's rather hard on him having to be a semi-vegetarian just because we are. After all, his views on diet may be quite different from ours."

"I daresay they are."

"Where is Con?"

"Saying good-bye to Mr. Crouch. Why didn't you come and talk to him? I thought you must be out."

"I saw him approaching. It seemed a little awkward, considering that I never go to church. Though I don't feel at all awkward with Mr. Martin—but then, a clergyman without a parish doesn't carry the same weight. He's as unreal as a man without a shadow."

"Not if he's a bishop."

"Don't quibble, Maud. Anyway I knew Mr. Crouch had come to enquire after Con, so I thought it better to leave them to it. And Con does sometimes go to church. . . . There! He must have gone."

The front door shut with a bang. Alice and Maud instinctively stood up and moved apart, Alice to the sink, Maud to the dresser, and busied themselves in vague preparations for supper. Maud assembled plates and cups; Alice filled the kettle. They waited for Miss Conway to join them, but she did not come.

"Con must be resting," Alice said presently.

To Maud this seemed highly improbable, after Miss Conway's brave words about carrying on and her observed dislike of being left alone. Perhaps Alice thought so too, for after another short interval she said she would go and draw the curtains upstairs. It was now quite dark and the curtains were usually drawn at dusk; but of course she had been lying low in the kitchen ever since Don's arrival. Maud did not offer to draw the curtains, because she feared Miss Conway might have retired to rest in her bedroom and she did not want to intrude. Instead, she laid the table, cut the bread-and-butter, and put the vegetable pie in the oven to warm up. She wiped the tiles where Wilbraham had chewed his bone, and thought about the big, juicy joints of meat other people had, which provided sustenance for themselves as well as bones for their dogs.

"She is not here," Cousin Alice said, standing in the doorway and looking less serene than usual.

"But she must be."

"She must be but she isn't. I've looked everywhere, even in your bathroom."

Maud did not see why Miss Conway should have taken refuge there, but it seemed equally unlikely that she should have accompanied Don to visit the Martins.

"Could she have gone for a walk?" she suggested.

"In the dark? With a swollen ankle?"

"Well, can she be hiding?"

"Why should she hide? Anyway, there aren't any hiding-places."

"I don't see why she should go out, either."

The right answer might have occurred to them if they had stopped to think. But Miss Conway's behaviour during the day lent colour to the dramatic conclusion that she had stumped off in a fury and was now limping to Yeomouth or preparing to sleep under a hedge. At least, these notions were vivid to Alice, whose dismay infected Maud. Con was so impulsive, Alice explained . . . and not quite herself today. But Con could not have gone far; she must be overtaken and persuaded to return. She herself would go one way, towards Yeomouth, and Maud the other—just in case. They would put on their warm coats. No, Wilbraham must stay in the kitchen, they would get on quicker without him. Here was Maud's coat, and here was Alice's. But where was the torch?

The absence of the torch might have recalled to them its everyday uses, but it did not. At the gate they parted and Maud set off towards Glaine, walking at a brisk, conscientious speed but hoping she would not be the one to overtake Miss Conway.

CHAPTER FOURTEEN

". . . AND WE NEVER thought about the hens! There she was, stumping about in the orchard, trying to round them up by herself in the dark. And I walked all the way to Glaine and back, looking for her!"

"How frightful," said Ensie.

"Oh well, it was worse for Cousin Alice. She'd forgotten to shut up the hens at tea time, so it was 'all her fault.'"

"I don't see that it was."

"Of course it wasn't! I mean that Miss Conway implied that she'd had to go out, broken ankle and all, to remedy Cousin Alice's neglect. She remembered them as soon as Don left and went to see if they'd been shut up—instead of asking us. Some of them had gone to roost in the trees, stupid creatures, and she was out there for hours. At least, it seemed like hours."

"While you were looking for her?"

"Yes, and before that. Wondering where she was, wondering what to do, and then setting out on the search—it seemed to go on and on. But the worst time was when we got back and found her. I am thankful—truly thankful," said Maud, "that Cousin Alice got back just before I did. You see, I'd done this awful thing. Goodness knows what would have happened if Cousin Alice hadn't been there to be reproached for not shutting up the hens. It did at least take Con's mind off the pie."

"What happened to the pie?"

"I left it in the oven and it was burnt to a cinder."

Ensie looked shocked. "How could you?" she exclaimed.

"But, Ensie, anybody could. In times of crisis one doesn't think of pies."

"I should have thought of it, if I'd put it in the oven. But then I'm really interested in cooking."

Maud sat up and gazed at Ensie, who blushed becomingly.

"Don says my cooking is delicious," she confided. "And I tell him it's because I'm interested enough to take trouble. He's coming to supper again on Monday night."

"Oh," said Maud. She saw the Good Cook Ensie as her own creation, and felt quite awestruck.

"What a pity Miss Conway didn't ask Don to help her," Ensie remarked. "But I suppose she didn't think about the hens till after he'd left."

"I suppose not," said Maud.

She realized that Ensie herself would be incapable of thinking about hens while Don was present, but she could not believe he had the same effect on Miss Conway. Still, it would be unkind to tease Ensie, who was now putting on her scarf and coat and showing a touching anxiety about her appearance. "Does my hair look all right?" she asked, frowning at her face in the look-

ing glass. Maud assured her that it did, and watched with interest while Ensie applied a layer of pale lipstick and then wiped
most of it off. Ensie's bedroom, usually so tidy, was littered with
scarves, jerseys and skirts which had been considered and rejected, and her best hat had been taken out of its box and laid on the
bed in readiness. But she had already changed her mind about
wearing a hat, and Maud kept her from changing it back again.

"No, Ensie, you don't need it. I know you wear one to go to
church on Sundays, but it's different when we're only going to
do the flowers."

"Father doesn't approve of hatless women in church."

"I'm sure Don doesn't mind."

Ensie's frown lifted. "Oh, Don doesn't mind! In fact he thinks
it's wrong to be fussy. Last summer he used to tell the people
from the caravan site to come just as they were."

Maud thought that must have brightened up little St. Alfred's considerably. "Well, that's all right, then," she said. "And
your hat would be a great nuisance, bicycling in this wind. We'll
have a job to keep the flowers from being spoilt. Have you got a
deep basket?"

"Oh, we're not bicycling after all. I forgot to tell you. Charles
Feniston is taking us."

For an instant Maud experienced the indecision and anxiety
which had been Ensie's, sharpened by regret at being in Ensie's
bedroom and not in her own. "You might have told me yesterday," she said.

"I didn't see you yesterday."

"No, you didn't. But I saw Charles, at lunch time. He didn't
say—"

"He didn't know, then," Ensie explained patiently, exam-
ining and rejecting one spotless handkerchief after another.
"I went along to Glaine Gardens in the afternoon, to buy some
chrysanthemums. You see, ours weren't as good as I should
have liked. I thought there were plenty, but when I came to look
at them some were too much out and others weren't out enough.
You see, the rain had spoilt the ones I was really counting on—"

"Yes," said Maud. She saw that none but the best would do
for little St. Alfred's. "So you went to buy some."

She had to hear which chrysanthemums Ensie had chosen, and why the pink ones wouldn't do, and all about the quite cheap greenery which Charles had produced instead of the expensive stuff Ensie had wanted at first. At last she learned that Ensie had said she would take the flowers home and keep them in buckets, and that Charles had offered to deliver them at the chapel in the morning, on his way to Yeomouth—which was a much better plan because they would have been difficult to transport on bicycles.

"So then I said we'd be there at eleven, and he said he might just as well take us, too. Of course we shall have to walk back but it really isn't far along the cliffs."

She hesitated and then said something else, in a mumble which Maud did not hear because she had already turned to peep through the muslin curtains.

"He's arrived. Come along, Ensie!"

"I must just say good-bye to Father, and remind him about getting his lunch."

Ensie and Maud had planned to have lunch in Yeomouth after doing the flowers; or rather, Maud had planned it and Ensie had agreed with misgivings. Mr. Martin did not like his daughter to be out for meals, even if she left everything prepared and did the washing-up when she got back. But Maud had decided that Mr. Martin must be trained to do without his daughter and had easily persuaded Ensie that she "ought to have more free time"—though without mentioning the ultimate reason for it. Ensie, of course, did not need to be told the reason, but although she had agreed in theory it had been difficult to persuade her to start the actual training of her Papa by going out as often as possible. Maud had had to appeal to her kind heart by making out that she herself was anxious to have an excuse for escaping from Combe Cottage cookery and that a Saturday expedition to Yeomouth with Ensie would provide it. Fortified by the knowledge that she was doing a good deed, Ensie had finally agreed to come. The fact that it was the Saturday when she was responsible for the flowers at the chapel had not only helped to ease her conscience (two good deeds were better than one), but had also made it an outing to which no clergyman could reasonably object.

Maud had been pleased with the success of her planning; yet now, descending the steps to the gate, she wished the plan had never occurred to her. If Ensie had been returning to Pixie Cot after doing the flowers then she, Maud, would have been free to lunch with Charles. That was, if by any chance he asked her to lunch with him . . . but of course she couldn't, now, because she was lunching with Ensie. Of course, she owed it to Ensie that Charles was driving them to the chapel. Nevertheless, one could not help feeling that Fate was being uncommonly perverse, snatching back with one hand what it gave with the other.

"I hope we haven't kept you waiting," she said to Charles. "Ensie will be here in a minute, she is just mollifying her Papa."

"I hope you have been able to mollify Carrie Conway," he replied.

"How on earth did you know?"

"Know what? You'd better get into the van or you'll be wet through."

"This is new," Maud said, standing back to gaze at the shiny new van and hoping it was a sign of prosperity.

"Yes. More useful than the car for delivering plants. But I miss old Thomasina."

"This is very comfortable. And roomy," she said politely. She exerted herself to praise the van's interior, until Charles laughed and told her not to bother.

"It's a utilitarian job, but it's what I need for my business," he said. "No point in pretending it isn't a come-down, after Thomasina. Still, it was about time I came down to earth."

Through the van's open window she looked out at Charles standing in the rain and saw him again as an eagle—but not a soaring eagle. Down to earth. The phrase had tragic implications undreamed of by Charles. How different, how very different from Oliver, she thought; and was at once confounded by an unmistakable Feniston gesture of impatience as he turned round quickly to stare at the closed door of Pixie Cot. The differences between the Fenistons were less striking than the resemblances, when they were kept waiting.

"She won't be a moment, I'm sure. I expect he's being awkward. Shall I go and see?"

"Wouldn't it be awkward to intrude on awkwardness? No, don't go." He shut the van door which Maud had impetuously opened. A silence, broken only by the increasing noise of rain and wind, spread damply over the scene; a silence in which she rejected trivial remarks as rapidly as Ensie had rejected clean handkerchiefs. But at last, in sheer desperation, a triviality had to be uttered.

"I suppose the grape-vine told you about Miss Conway running away, but how did you know her name was Carrie?"

"What?" said Charles.

"*Not* running away, I mean. I mean, we thought she had, and of course the grape-vine is sure she did. Ensie had heard it before I got here this morning. But that was an unfortunate misunderstanding, and what I really would like to know is—"

"Running away!"

"No, *no*. She didn't."

"It beats me why you should think of anything so improbable," he said. "And as for Alice . . ."

"Well, we panicked, I suppose. It had been a—a difficult day."

"That's what I meant, when I asked if you had mollified her. The grape-vine hadn't reached me."

The signs of suppressed impatience had vanished, but Maud feared he was thinking about Miss Conway and not about herself. His next words confirmed it.

"She'll never run away. She'll see it through."

"How did you know her name was Carrie? I didn't."

Charles stared down at her. She had all his attention now, but he looked oddly perplexed, as if it were a question he had not expected.

"But didn't she tell you—?" he began.

"If she had done, I should know," Maud retorted. "But why *should* she tell me her name? Even Cousin Alice never calls her anything but Con. That's why I wondered how you knew it."

"Well," said Charles. "Yes. I didn't realize. I suppose Alice stopped her. Yes. . . . And I can guess the reason for it."

He made these comments slowly and audibly, but they seemed to refer to something else; Maud could see no reason why Cousin Alice should have stopped Con from revealing her Christian name.

"I am most terribly sorry," cried Ensie, flinging open the garden gate. "I got delayed. Oh dear, I've kept you waiting ages! Father wanted . . ."

Compelled to hear what Father wanted, Maud could not concentrate on unravelling the tangled threads of her talk with Charles, nor could she ask him—with Ensie sitting bodkin—to explain the confusion. Confusion there must have been, at some point, though she could not imagine how it had started. . . .

Of course, one could always ask Cousin Alice. But if it wasn't a mere misunderstanding—if Cousin Alice had deliberately stopped Miss Conway from revealing something that Charles had expected her to reveal—then, of course, one was not likely to get from Cousin Alice a satisfactory answer.

"Here we are," Ensie announced. "And look—there's Don waiting for us."

St. Alfred's, a chapel-of-ease attached to Yeomouth parish church, stood at the top of the long hill leading down to the town. It had been built about 1890 when Yeomouth was enjoying a wave of prosperity and expansion, but it marked the limit of the wave's advance; beyond it on the hill-top there was only a thin fringe of bungalows, a pair of old cottages where the lane from the combe joined the main road, and the windswept caravan site. The chapel was equally exposed to the wind, which was now blowing strongly, and Maud could see Don Crouch sheltering in the porch.

She got out of the van and Ensie jumped out after her and hurried up the path calling apologies and explanations for the delay. Don advanced to meet her (he wasn't the man to stand sheltering while women struggled through wind and rain) and ordered both of them to run along and keep dry. He would bring the flowers in a jiffy—no, he didn't need any help.

"Good-bye," said Maud, turning to Charles. But Charles had gone round to the back of the van, where he was stopping Don from unloading a lot of potted plants which were going on somewhere else. Her farewell was cut short by Don's repeat-

ed command to run along out of the rain; and anyway Charles
wasn't listening.

"Don't ram it in like that," he said to Don. "You'll have the
whole lot over. Good-bye, Maud—steady on, you're bending that
leader."

Don stepped back and collided with one of the azaleas he
had unloaded before Charles reached him. It reeled sideways
to the ground and there was a crunch of breaking pot. Maud
already knew what the Fenistons were like when roused and she
did not wait to see whether Charles would restrain his temper
out of respect for the cloth. It seemed better not to be associated
with another incident of wanton destruction; for she supposed
he still thought of her-—if he ever did—as the girl who had torn
up handfuls of his Michaelmas daisies on the occasion of their
first meeting.

She followed Ensie to the, porch, and soon Don joined them
bearing the chrysanthemums and the cheap greenery, and quot-
ing the appropriate verse from the psalm about bringing his
sheaves with him. It made a transition passage, Maud supposed,
between his secular and his professional manner, and was exactly the right remark to utter in a church porch.

The remarks which followed, about the whereabouts of the
vases and the water tap, she recognised as mere excuses for lin-
gering, because Ensie had her place in the rota of flower-providers and must know where everything was to be found. An
appointment with the Rector made it impossible for Don to stay
and assist Ensie with the flowers as he had hoped to do, and
Maud kindly retired to look round the chapel while they said
good-bye. She reflected on the difference between her behaviour and Don's; but the circumstances, too, were different. It
was ridiculous to suppose that Charles would have welcomed
the chance of a few words alone.

"They don't go far, do they?" Ensie said, when the flowers
had been arranged and the vases carried to their places. "I wish
there had been enough for another bowl, to hide that ugly little
bookcase by the door."

Maud thought there was much else in St. Alfred's that needed hiding, but she pointed out that this was just an ordinary

Sunday and that Ensie could look forward to doing wonders at Christmas.

"December belongs to Mrs. Peveril and Mrs. Manchett-Jones," said Ensie, referring to the flower-providers' rota. "Of course everyone helps to decorate for Christmas Day, but *they* decide who's to do what. Last year they gave me the awkward window with the sloping sill above the vestry door, and the ledge of the Penwortham tablet."

It will be different when you're a vicar's wife, Maud thought, She hoped Ensie would develop enough strength of mind to claim the chancel, the pulpit, and the lectern for herself—especially the lectern, whose convoluted brasswork lent itself to schemes of intricate floral decoration. Then she remembered that Don's preferment, when it came, would remove him from little St. Alfred's and this particular lectern. It seemed a pity for Ensie to miss her chance.

"Perhaps they'll give you something better, this year," she said. "If you turn up with some specially striking flowers—poinsettias or those scarlet African lilies—"

"It should be holly and evergreens, at Christmas," Ensie said rebukingly. Nevertheless, she had listened. "Anyway, I couldn't afford them," she added, on a note of distinct regret. She looked longingly at the intricate lectern. "I don't think one can buy those exotic sorts of flowers down here. Of course, they'd look wonderfully effective."

"A patch of strong colour," said Maud. "That's what this chapel needs, to warm it up. And I need warming up too. Shall I race you down the hill, all the way to the square?"

It would be too far, Ensie said, and anyway they would look silly. There was a half-hourly bus service along this road and the next bus was due in ten minutes. They had better walk along to the bus stop now, in case it came before its time.

"I wonder if Charles will have any very bright, showy flowers ready at Christmas," Maud said, while they waited for the bus.

"I do wish Father wasn't going to preach at matins. It's bound to spoil it," Ensie said gloomily.

"It's a pity Charles hasn't got more greenhouses. There must be a lot of profit in forced flowers at this time of year. But there isn't any room for more greenhouses at Glaine."

"His greenhouses are at Cheriton. If only I could think of some way of stopping Father, I mean something that wouldn't be wrong. For Don's sake, really."

"What do you mean?" Maud exclaimed.

"Well, Don is a wonderful preacher, and Father—"

"No, no! About the greenhouses."

Ensie looked at her with mild surprise. "The greenhouses are at Cheriton," she repeated. "That's the other side of Yeomouth and about as far as Glaine. I mean, as far in the other direction. It's just beyond the fork where the main road divides, and you take the right-hand one—no, sorry, the left-hand one. Charles has quite a big market-garden over there, bigger than Glaine, and whole rows of greenhouses. Didn't you know?"

"How could I know?" Maud said crossly. "No one ever tells me anything."

"Well, I'm telling you now. Oh look—here's the bus coming at last."

CHAPTER FIFTEEN

THERE WERE at least twelve clocks at Glaine and they were all kept going. Old M. wound them up on Tuesdays, and the gift clock in the drawing room got an extra winding on Fridays because its spring was damaged and would not carry it through the week. He hated to see a silent, stopped clock, which he morbidly likened to having a corpse in the room; but it was their ticking, not their time-keeping, that mattered. On Tuesdays he put the hands of the clocks to approximately the right time and after that they could go as they pleased. Some went fast, and others very slowly.

Maud thought that time in Glaine combe was as varied, as irregular, as the time recorded by the clocks. Days and weeks passed slowly, keeping pace with the lagging gilt clock, and then everything speeded up as if Galloping Grandfather had suddenly taken command. Thursday sped by and it was Friday, the weekend shrank to a few hours, Monday was over almost before it was begun. And all too rapidly, with Galloping Grandfather's mad contempt for the busy world outside his mahogany case, Christmas rushed towards them; the week before Christmas slipped into the past tense; the days of preparation for Oliver's arrival became the frantic hour of hoping he would be delayed by the traffic.

"The chimney's cold—that's all," old M. said, when the newly lit fire filled Oliver's bedroom with smoke. "Leave the windows open and it'll soon clear. And tell Who's-it to put a hot-bottle in the bed, and remind Hat about those cereals for breakfast."

"Who's-it" was a young female relative of the Hatballs who was staying with them for Christmas. Old M. regarded her as an acting unpaid under-housemaid and ordered her about in a way which no present-day English housemaid would have put up with, but luckily she was an inexperienced foreigner and seemed rather to enjoy it. She ran about with dusters and brooms and furniture polish, doing what she could to make home beautiful for Oliver; if she had come a week sooner, Maud thought, the results would have pleased and surprised him. But she had had only a day's start and her labours were constantly interrupted by old M.'s shouted commands. Even if the matter was not urgent he shouted on principle, because she was a foreigner.

Maud was as busy as Who's-it. She helped old M. to hide things he did not want Oliver to see: the estate account-books, the mass of notes relating to the library, the second-hand bargain buy of a dozen double-bed-size blankets, which had turned out to be full of moth, and—as a final precaution—the key of the library door.

"Oliver's bound to notice we've been working on it, if he should stick his nose in. Now, where shall I put the key?"

"On your key ring," she suggested.

"Don't be stupid. Thing is, I must hide it somewhere where it might have got by accident. Don't want Oliver guessing I've deliberately locked him out, because then he'd soon guess why. Feller isn't a fool, you know."

"I know, but—"

"Now think quickly. He'll be here any moment."

"Under the door mat."

"But that's the very first place he'd look for it. I've just told you, Maud—feller's no fool. *Think!*" cried old M., towering over her and contriving to look both impatient and pathetically anxious.

He was indeed anxious; anxious that the Christmas visit should be a success and that it should erase the memory of the last one. He was fond of Oliver and proud of him, and he did not wish to carry on the Feniston tradition of dramatic, violent quarrels between fathers and sons. True, he and Oliver had always bickered a bit; but on his last visit the bickering had nearly ended in a full-scale quarrel, and Oliver's abrupt departure had been frighteningly like a traditional exit. Everything must be different this time, everything must be as Oliver liked it. And the things he obstinately refused to like must be kept out of sight.

All this was quite clear to Maud because old M. did much of his thinking aloud, and she shared his wish that all should go well. But the bustle of preparation, the last-minute disasters such as the smoke-filled bedroom, had exhausted her; she simply could not suggest a hiding-place that fulfilled her employer's requirements.

"Think!"

"There—on top of the picture frame behind you."

"How could it have got there by accident?" old M. objected.

"But—oh dear, he's arriving! I heard a car hooting in the lane. Look, put it under the door mat and then slide it under the bottom of the door, so that he won't see it if he picks up the mat."

Maud picked up the mat as she spoke and old M. dropped the key on the floor. Hurriedly (for he must be in the hall to welcome Oliver) he kicked it under the door. He kicked harder than was necessary and the key slid away at speed and could be heard scudding across the boards inside the room.

"Put the mat back. Come along and meet Oliver. Just tell Hat we'll be ready for tea in ten minutes," old M. commanded.

Maud wondered how they were going to get the key out again.

At Combe Cottage Miss Conway bided her time. Maud's stepmother was wintering in Africa with her husband so one could not suggest that the girl should go home for Christmas; and anyway Christmas wasn't the right season for scheming to get rid of her. "Peace and goodwill and all the rest of it" was Miss Conway's reason for calling a truce; but the armistice was to be limited to the period during which these principles were consciously borne in mind, a period which lasted, for Miss Conway, from the arrival of the first Christmas card till Twelfth Night.

Apart from feeling vaguely pacific she took little account of Christmas even in its secular aspects. In other years she and Alice had celebrated it with the minimum of fuss, exchanging simple, useful presents, eschewing holly and mistletoe, drinking each other's health in home-made cordials, and refusing invitations to parties.

"But I don't think we can refuse this one," Alice had said yesterday. "And it's sure to be a good dinner."

Con had agreed with her that it would be awkward to refuse old M.'s invitation to dine with him on Christmas Day, and accordingly they had accepted. It was the first sign that things were going to be different this Christmas, but only now did she realize its significance. Facing Alice, in a room quite transformed by holly, she wished she had taken a strong line from the start.

"I thought I'd better do a little decorating," Alice explained. "Did you get the things you wanted? Is your ankle all right?"

Con had just returned from an exhausting day in Yeomouth, but she even forgot to limp. "What's all this for?" she asked, and with foreboding she added, "Surely we—you're not having a party!"

"Only the Martins, and Oliver Feniston. They are coming for sherry at six o'clock tomorrow. I asked Mr. Crouch the curate, but he doesn't think he can manage it . . . and Maud thought it better not to ask old M."

"We haven't got any sherry."

"I ordered some," Alice said. "The van brought it today while you were out."

The Christmas cards strung on a silver ribbon across the looking glass reminded Con that the season of peace and goodwill had begun. "Um . . . It looks quite festive," she commented. "Did you get the holly out of our hedge?"

"Yes, Maud helped me to cut it at lunch time. Do you think you could make some of those little cheese biscuits? I think they'd be nice with the sherry."

It was a long time since Alice had praised her cooking or asked for a particular dish, and Con was not sure whether this was an order (to be resented) or a request (to be granted).

"Well, I'll see," she replied cautiously.

The Combe Cottage sherry party was the first item in Maud's list of distractions for Oliver. She wished the list had been longer, but she did not worry much about the success of the party because its real purpose was to get Oliver away from old M. for an hour or two; though it would be advantageous if he were also amused and kept in a good temper. Nevertheless she could not help feeling, though in no spirit of captious criticism, that a sherry party at Combe Cottage was strikingly different from her stepmother's well-organized parties at home.

One difference was that the sherry and the guests were separated, the sherry being in the dining room while the guests were in the sitting room. Maud thought it would have been better if they had all been in the same place, but Alice—or Con—had thought otherwise. The dining room was tiny and was now crowded out with things that had been banished from the sitting room (among them Miss Conway's great work) so that it wasn't possible for the party to change its ground and join the refreshments. Every time a drink or biscuits were wanted, Con went and fetched them.

The Martins had brought an aunt; or rather, Ensie's aunt and Mr. Martin's sister, who was staying with them till the New Year. She was a placid-looking aunt who had spent a lot of her life in New Zealand and was amiably ready to talk about it if other subjects failed. They had also brought Don, who could only stay for ten minutes but for whom the minutes seemed to slip by unnoticed. He had come on urgent business; it had been frightfully important to catch Mr. Martin before he set out for Combe Cottage; Ensie had persuaded him to look in, since Mrs. Grayson had been good enough to invite him and he was, by sheer chance, right on the spot; but now he must jolly well fly. So saying, he looked across the room at Ensie and waited for her to respond to the magnetic lodestone and turn away from Oliver.

"Is the Rector seriously ill?" Maud asked.

"Well, the doctor says it's nothing to worry about," Don replied. "Just a touch of gastric 'flu—but of course he has to be careful, at his age. Jolly bad luck, just before Christmas."

Maud suppressed the unworthy thought that Ensie and Don had ill-wished the Rector. But his sudden illness had meant a re-organization of the Christmas services and Don had come to beg Mr. Martin to assist the Rector's recently ordained grandson at the parish church instead of preaching at St. Alfred's chapel. Jolly lucky that the grandson was staying with the Rector, of course, but he didn't feel quite equal to managing on his own. Very young; and just a shade unsure of himself. But Mr. Martin had very sportingly stepped into the breach.

"How will he get there?" Maud asked.

"Colonel Cathcart, the Rector's warden, has got transport laid on. It's a bit complicated but I think it will work out all right. I thought I'd better come and see him, because he's not frightfully good on the telephone."

"How frightfully thoughtful of you."

"Oh well, one does what one can. I'm jolly glad Miss Conway's ankle is mending so well. I was really a bit worried, that day. . . ."

Ensie had left Oliver and was coming towards them; but she looked less happy than Maud had expected, considering that she was to have the pleasure of listening to Don's sermon tomorrow and that the pulpit from which he would preach had been decorated by herself. Maud had heard her telling Con about the church decorations earlier in the evening and it had all sounded utterly satisfactory. With Mrs. Peveril in quarantine for her grandchildren's measles and Mrs. Manchett-Jones unable to stay long because of a burst boiler at home, Ensie seemed to have had things all her own way and to have decorated the chapel single-handed. But she hardly looked like a person whom Fortune had so singularly favoured.

And there by the fireplace was Oliver, with no one to talk to and nothing to drink. He had an unsettled air, as if he were about to take wing; but it was important that he should stay as long as possible. Abandoning Don and Ensie, Maud hastened across the room.

"Let me get you another drink," she said, risking Miss Conway's displeasure. Miss Conway, the official dispenser of sherry, was rather slow to provide it and moreover she was deep in conversation with Mr. Martin and not even looking to see if glasses were empty. Without waiting for Oliver's reply Maud picked up his glass and hurried to the dining room, where she found one empty sherry bottle and two others which had not been uncorked. But it was no time to ask permission; she seized the corkscrew and set to work.

"Let me do that for you," Oliver said helpfully. "Or was I supposed to stay put in the other room?"

He was standing in the doorway, and Maud thought he looked both owlish and more human than usual; an owl that would have liked to join in the simple human pleasures of a sherry party if it had known how to stop being an owl. She wished she could tell Oliver to remove his horn-rimmed spectacles (because if old M. was right he didn't need them, and it would be interesting to see what he looked like without them), but instead she gratefully handed over the bottle and the corkscrew, and said:

"I think we were both supposed to stay in the other room, but it doesn't matter. Miss Conway is in charge of the drinks but I expect she can't break away from Mr. Martin."

"I find your aunts rather alarming," Oliver said. "The last time I came here—"

"They are not my aunts. Cousin Alice is my father's first cousin. And Miss Conway is no relation."

"I'm sorry. But you did talk about your aunts, the first time I met you."

"If you had listened you would have known that they didn't live here," she replied coldly.

"I am sorry," Oliver repeated. The cork came out with a faint pop. "I *do* listen," he went on, staring at the bottle as if it and not

Maud had accused him of inattention. "I remember now; you told me before that Mrs. Grayson was your cousin, and I can't think why I forgot it."

He sounded truly perturbed, and Maud said it didn't matter, she sometimes forgot things herself and one simply couldn't account for it.

"I shouldn't think you often forget things. My father says you're a wonderful secretary. Indeed, one realizes that oneself."

Old M.'s reported remark sounded quite unlike him; nor had she expected to win praise, even in so impersonal a form, from Oliver. But he had filled his glass and was holding it up. "Your health, Maud, and long may you continue to watch over Glaine."

"Oh—thank you." The owl was trying very hard, she thought, though it was difficult not to laugh at his solemnity. "I am—er—deeply attached to Glaine," she said, matching her manner to Oliver's.

"One realizes that, too." Quite suddenly Oliver broke through the bounds of owlishness and became human. "I didn't, at first. I thought you were very young and inexperienced and would just give in all along the line, even if you stayed here. I even thought—it was stupid of me—that you had a romantic penchant for cobwebs. A sort of Gothic hang-over; a sentimental attachment to ruins. I see now that I didn't give you time. It was all new—you hadn't got things sorted out—you hadn't begun to make any impression. Of course it's a positively Herculean task. But already, I mean on this visit, I can see a real difference. It's absolutely astonishing!"

"What astonishes you most?" she asked, hoping her own astonishment was not visible.

"Hot bath-water. A clean bedroom—not a cobweb in sight. The hole in the stair carpet mended." He started ticking off the improvements on his fingers, and then spread out his hands in a gesture which embraced a whole new era. "Oh, it's everything! Not so much the visible arrest of decay as the feeling that there's someone in control. Someone who can stand up to my father and stop the rot."

"I am very fond of him, you know."

"I can see that. If you didn't like him you'd never have stuck it. Though mind you, I'm fond of him myself. If he wasn't so—"

Oliver stopped abruptly. Perhaps he remembered it was Christmas Eve. "I'm glad that I came," he went on, slowly. "I'm glad you wrote to me. It was a pity—about my last visit. One doesn't want to quarrel. . . . Too many quarrels in the family, as it is."

It was a sentiment with which she entirely agreed. Moreover she saw that Oliver was as anxious as his father that the Christmas visit should be a success and that he too disliked the tradition of quarrelsome fathers and sons. Even with goodwill on both sides the Feniston temper might break out if two Fenistons were left alone together for long, but at least the visit had had an auspicious beginning.

"I feel I've done nothing, really," she said.

This was true, because it was Who's-it who had swept away the cobwebs and mended the stair carpet and who presumably was responsible for the hot bath-water. It was wrong to take the credit for Who's-it's labours, but she did not want to provoke Oliver by disclaiming any intention to reform old M. or restore Glaine. For the four days of his visit he must be kept in a good humour.

He was in a good humour now; a wonderful good humour, which expressed itself in a beaming smile and a friendly pat on her shoulder.

"No, no, Maud, don't say that. You've done wonders."

"Oh—there you are. Couldn't think where you'd got to," Miss Conway exclaimed. She advanced into the room and her eyes went at once to the sherry bottle, as if she suspected Maud and Oliver of carousing in secret. "Mr. Crouch left some time ago," she announced, "and the Martins are just going."

Oliver took the hint and said he must be going too. Maud congratulated herself on his having stayed till the end of the party. Miss Conway shepherded them back to the sitting room, but in the hall they were waylaid by Ensie who turned back from the front door to grasp Maud's hand and say forlornly, "Happy Christmas!"

"It isn't Christmas yet," Miss Conway protested.

"I don't suppose I shall see Maud tomorrow. Or any of you. I'd better wish you *all* a happy Christmas," Ensie said, in a muted voice that made happiness a mockery.

"But we shall see you at St. Alfred's in the morning," Maud reminded her. "Are you going to bicycle?—because if you are I'll come with you. What time are you starting?"

Ensie's drooping figure drooped still further.

"I shall have to go to the parish church with Father," she muttered. "They're sending a car and he says I should be silly not to take advantage of it."

Maud had not thought of that, and for a moment she was nonplussed. But with surprising helpfulness Oliver suggested that if Ensie preferred to go to St. Alfred's (and it must have been plain to him that she did) she could tell her father there would be a car going there, too; he would be delighted to give Ensie and Maud a lift. And Mr. Martin would have his sister with him, Maud pointed out; it wasn't as if he would be all alone.

Ensie needed little persuasion; the new offer of transport seemed to counterbalance the transport already arranged, and she hardly needed convincing that a sister's companionship would do as well as a daughter's. Flushed, grateful, erect, she quickly settled on a time for starting and then hurried off to join her father and her aunt.

Maud returned from the door to hear Oliver assuring Miss Conway that there would be room for her as well; and she detected a note of relief when he learned that Cousin Alice was not a churchgoer. His car could probably have held them all, she thought, but it would have been a squash and Oliver was not a man who would take kindly to squashes, even in a good cause and on Christmas Day.

CHAPTER SIXTEEN

"RELATIVES ARE a good thing," old M. said dogmatically. "Especially when you're getting older. Should hate it myself, if I hadn't any. They give you an interest in life."

He raised his glass, drawing fresh eloquence from the vintage port.

"Relatives are the ancestors of the future."

No one knew exactly what he meant, but after a minute Cousin Alice remarked that photography had put an end to the cult of one's ancestors. A collection of fading photographs had none of the dignity of a long gallery hung with portraits, and it did not give one the feeling of being mysteriously part of the past.

Maud looked sideways at Miss Conway, wondering if she would resent the implied link with Wolfering and a past she could not share. But Miss Conway had eaten and drunk much more than she was accustomed to and the port was making her soporific rather than combative. She sat back in her chair, massively inert, and let the talk eddy round her like ripples round a jutting rock.

"Relatives are excellent, if they keep their distance," Oliver said. "They're an essential background to one's landscape. It would look very bleak and empty if they weren't there."

He spoke quietly to Maud, who was sitting on his right hand. But old M., at the other end of the table, heard him and joined in.

"You're too young to understand. Wait till you're my age—they won't be just figures in a landscape then. You'll be attached to them, really interested and sorry for 'em. You'll write to them in turns every week. I do, don't I, Maud?"

"Yes. Yes, you do."

"And they write back," old M. said. "Nice, long letters. Tell me all their difficulties." He gave his sudden, crowing laugh. "Keeping in touch!"

"Does he really write to them?" Oliver asked, when old M. had returned to his gossip with Alice.

"Well—I type the letters, of course."

He nodded and began to speak of something else; the ambiguity of her reply went unnoticed. In fact, she not only typed them but composed them, thereby ensuring for old M. a constant inflow of nice, long letters without his being burdened by having to dictate replies. He liked getting letters but he did not like answering them, and it was several weeks since he had done more than scribble his signature at the foot of the last page.

"You'll be able to start tomorrow, I expect," Miss Conway said suddenly.

The remark was addressed to Maud, who for a moment could not think what was to be started. Then, with dismay, she remembered.

"Perhaps not tomorrow, because it's Boxing Day and I have to write my thank-you letters. But I shall certainly start it as soon as I can."

What else could one say? Gratitude and enthusiasm were obligatory when referring to a Yuletide gift.

"The frame is included," Miss Conway assured her. "It's all yours. So you'll be able to do more tapestries when you've finished this one."

Maud lived again the moment of horror that morning when she had seen the label tied to the great work and realized that Con had given it to her.

"It's a beautiful frame," she said.

"And the tapestry will look lovely when it's finished. All the wools and everything, you know. It's all yours."

Con settled back in her chair again, and looked as if she were going to sleep. Perhaps old M. noticed it, because he announced almost at once that they would have coffee in the drawing room, and Con was forced to jerk herself wide awake and begin a surreptitious pawing under the table for her missing shoe. Alice saw what she was about and kindly delayed her own rising until the shoe had been located.

Glaine looked quite different tonight, Maud thought; different, but no less enchanting. Who's-it's ministrations had removed the worst of the dirt from the ground-floor rooms, and the rather inefficient lighting did not reveal the broken cornices, the damp-stained ceilings, or the threadbare state of curtains and carpets. A blazing fire dispelled the taint of mildew which till now had pervaded the drawing room, and even the spindly sofa seemed to have recovered some of its former elegance. The dinner party had brought the house to life again and given her a glimpse of what it must have been like when it was fully inhabited and cared for.

Alice and Con, sitting side by side on the sofa, were less appealing than the three little owls but just as necessary to the scene. They sipped their coffee and talked and sometimes laughed; the coffee had roused Con from her torpor, and Alice was enjoying to the full the almost-forgotten pleasures of dining out. Old M. was manifestly delighted by the success of his Christmas party and seemed ready to go on talking till midnight. Oliver had less to say but his silences held no hint of sulkiness; he listened with apparent interest, and at times showed a capacity for self-restraint which Maud found truly surprising.

Everything was going splendidly; it was almost too good to be true, she thought, watching Oliver and wondering if his docility would last the evening. Perhaps he felt the strain himself, or perhaps he merely found it tedious to listen to a discussion of sermons and those who preached them; returning Maud's gaze he leant towards her and suggested that she should come up to the long gallery and tell him which ancestor was which.

"The ones I don't know apart," he reminded her.

"Hey—where are you going?" old M. demanded. But the reply pleased him; he commended Oliver's wish to renew acquaintance with his ancestors and told him Maud would be an excellent guide.

"I only know a few of them," she protested, feeling that Oliver might dislike the public exposure of his ignorance.

"Better find the catalogue, then," said old M. "Not complete—but it'll help. Can't remember offhand where it is—"

"It's in the library," Oliver said. "Or at least, it used to be."

There was a guilt-laden pause, in which Maud and old M. ostentatiously avoided catching each other's eye. Old M. had been speaking of the new catalogue in the making and Oliver was thinking of the old one, the list that couldn't be found, but what really startled Maud was that he should refer so calmly to the library. Of course it was Christmas, the season of peace and goodwill, but one hardly expected that to count when a man had a bee in his bonnet.

"Don't suppose it's there now," old M, said hastily. "Doesn't matter anyway—Maud will tell you who's who. Off you go!"

Off they went. But to Maud's alarm Oliver walked straight across the hall towards the passage that led to the library.

"I shouldn't bother," she said, hurrying after him. "It's getting late—we shall have to go home soon—"

"It won't take a moment. I know exactly where that list used to be. And it's highly unlikely that anyone has even dusted it for the last five years, so it's probably still there."

"But I'm afraid—"

"It won't take a moment," he replied. She recognised the Feniston obstinacy in his voice and said no more. A locked door might keep Oliver out of the library, but nothing else would.

After rattling the door several times and assuring himself it really was locked Oliver started looking for the key. As old M. had predicted, he looked first under the door mat; then he felt along the top of the lintel and searched the drawers of the table that stood in the passage. He peered into the Chinese porcelain jars which stood on the table, and opened the glass front of the Dutch wall clock to inspect the ledge within. "Might have put it anywhere," he muttered. "Probably doesn't remember himself." Maud did not dare to commit herself in words, but she gave vague exclamations indicating regret, sympathy and unhelpful bewilderment.

They did not work. Abruptly, Oliver abandoned the search and turned to face her.

"You knew it was locked," he said.

"Wh-what?"

"So perhaps you'll tell me where the key is."

"Oh dear, Oliver, I'm terribly sorry but the key is unobtainable. Even if I wanted you to go into the library it couldn't be done. The key was more mobile than we expected and it went before we could stop it. In the twinkling of an eye," she added graphically.

The picture was by no means clear to Oliver. "Went where?" he demanded.

"Under the door. It slid away when—when your father gave it a push. It's inside. He—we—it had dropped to the ground—"

"Oh no, it hadn't. You'd put it there."

She trembled. "An *accidental* push, I mean. Please don't tell him I told you. It was all an accident."

"It was not. You didn't want me to go into the library. Or more likely, he didn't want it. You were trying to hide the key.—Just like him to bungle it," Oliver said angrily but, as it were, in parenthesis. "I had a feeling that something was up, in the drawing room, but I couldn't spot what it was. And again, when you tried to stop me coming here. Stupid of me to waste time looking for the key, you're thinking, but I couldn't guess that you—*you*—"

He paused to draw a deep breath of revulsion and fury.

"Then, suddenly, I saw it all. You gave yourself away. I realized that the door had been locked and the key hidden, to keep me out, and that you were just standing there watching me make a fool of myself. You'd known from the beginning that I shouldn't be able to get in."

"Yes," said Maud, "I did know. But what was I to do? I didn't *want* you to waste your valuable time looking for a key which wasn't there. I tried to stop you but you wouldn't let yourself be stopped. Because you're so obstinate. I couldn't tell you that the key had been hidden, because it would have been betraying your father. You're quite right about that. He didn't want you to go into the library."

"Obstinate!" Oliver cried. He drew another deep breath, but Maud did not wait for it to revive him.

"Yes, obstinate—like all the Fenistons. Or at least like the ones I've met and the ones I've seen in the portrait gallery. You 'had a feeling' that we were trying to head you off the library, and that made you absolutely determined to go there. And now you've found out about the key and I suppose you'll make a fuss about it and your father's Christmas will be spoiled. It's a shame! He only tried to keep you out of the library for your own good."

"Well—really!" He raised his hand—not to strike her, but, to signify ironic bewilderment. The light at the other end of the passage threw his shadow on the locked door and the shadow's gesture reminded Maud of the way Oliver had raised his glass last night to drink to her health. But the shadow's owner had clearly forgotten ever expressing such sentiments.

"Please tell me why it is good for me to be kept out of the library," he said coldly.

"Because it upsets you. Your father wanted this visit to be a success—surely you can see how hard he is trying to please you. And he thought—"

"He thinks of me as a child—and so do you! I assure you that I don't need to go into the library, it is sufficiently upsetting to know that it exists—behind a locked door. Of all the futile, incompetent things to do!" Bearing out Maud's and old M.'s alleged opinion of him, Oliver turned furiously on the door and kicked it.

It did not budge; and there was no magic formula of *Open Sesame!* which would override futile incompetence. But in the distance another door must have opened, for a low murmur of conversation showed that the rest of the party was now in the hall. There were faint feminine cries for Maud, followed by a loud bellow for Oliver. Maud looked at the clock; even by Dutch-wall-time standards it was getting late. "I must go," she said, and walked away without a backward glance. If Oliver had not been behaving so violently she would have begged him to spare his father's feelings and keep silent, but one might as well plead with a volcano as with a man who kicked doors.

Old M. and his companions were standing at the foot of the stairs, looking up and trying to make their voices heard in the long gallery where they supposed Maud and Oliver to be. As she came out of the passage she realized that old M. would guess at once that they had been to the library (or at least, to its door), and she wished she could warn him that Oliver knew about the key. But there was no time; for Oliver must have noticed the withdrawal of his audience and desisted from door-kicking, and he caught up with her as they crossed the hall.

"Thought you were upstairs," said Con, the first to observe their approach. "Quite startled me, you coming from there. Time to go home, Maud—that's why we were calling you. Been a wonderful party."

Very amiable Con looked; her face was florid, and little rushes of words—hardly sentences—kept bubbling up from the reserves of peace and goodwill within. But Cousin Alice, as if aware that amiability wasn't enough, drew Oliver a little to one side and began to talk to him, explaining that there was no need for him to drive them back to Combe Cottage because it was a fine night and they would enjoy the walk and it was no distance at all. She kept it up steadily, while old M. talked to Maud.

"Didn't you go to look at the portraits? Thought you were going to tell Oliver who was who."

"We were going—I mean, we started to go—"

"Pictures everywhere," Con remarked. "Very fine pictures."

"Well, what stopped you—hey? Nothing wrong with the lights. I was up there myself last week and I thought they looked better with the lights on. Some of 'em, anyway."

"Yes, I expect they do. But we thought—Oliver thought he would just look for the list, first. So we went to look for it. In the library."

It seemed to Maud that every word she spoke was echoing round the hall, while Cousin Alice's diversionary politeness was practically inaudible. She felt that Oliver was simply waiting for the right moment to launch his thunderbolts.

"And did you find it?" asked old M.

"We couldn't get in, because the door was locked."

How stupid—how useless! Why hadn't she contrived to utter a word of warning? But before she could add one old M. was registering dramatic surprise; the surprise proper to a man who had just been told that his library was inaccessible.

"Locked—hey!" he exclaimed. "And the key missing? That's damned odd—begging your pardon, Maud. Wonder where that key can have got to." He brooded for a moment on the perversity of inanimate objects. "Must have a hunt for it tomorrow," he decided.

He could not restrain himself from darting a quick look at Maud—a look of sly triumph, which invited her to applaud his foresight in hiding the key. But she did not respond to it. She looked instead at Oliver, who had turned away from Cousin Alice and was about to join in.

"I expect that silly man Hatball has taken it," Oliver said. "I'm fond of foreigners myself, but there's something disconcertingly unpredictable about Hat. For all one knows he may be collecting keys and writing a monograph about them. Are any of the others missing?"

"My bedroom key hasn't worked properly for ages," Miss Conway told them. "But it isn't missing. It won't come out."

"We really must be going," said Cousin Alice.

"I'll get the car," Oliver said. "No, really . . ."

For an instant, before he turned away, he stared meaningly at Maud. But she did not interpret his look as one of forgiveness; he was simply telling her that she had grossly misjudged him, that he was neither obstinate nor unfeeling, and that a Feniston could rise to the occasion without prompting from outsiders. Or despite it.

"Glad you enjoyed yourselves," said old M., while they waited for Oliver to fetch his car. "I enjoyed it too. Good company—good dinner—something to be said for hospitality after all. Enjoyed it much more than I expected to," he added frankly. "Must do it again."

Maud knew that the dinner party had been given to entertain Oliver, and also as a safeguard against bickering on Christmas Day. She could not feel that Oliver would look back on it as a thoroughly successful evening, but she was glad it had been an agreeable one for old M. His only regret, as he was now explaining, was that the dinner table had not been properly balanced; there had been three ladies and only two gentlemen.

"We ought to have got another man," he said. "But it's not so easy. Not so many bachelors about as there used to be—or widowers either, come to that. Couldn't think of one."

Naturally it wasn't to be expected that he should think of Charles—who in any case was not a bachelor or a widower. Maud wondered whether Charles had spent Christmas by himself in his dreary Ycomouth lodgings; and the drabness of this picture was intensified when Cousin Alice said soothingly that it had not mattered about the numbers not balancing this evening because it had been just like a family party.

"No one worries about an extra aunt or two at Christmas," she explained. "It's the season of reunions and they are always overloaded with women. Aunts everywhere, and a sad shortage of uncles. But the aunts simply love it—and so did we, tonight."

This glimpse of the Wolfering past was well received; old M. himself was the head of a family, and he liked to be reminded of it. It was perhaps at that moment that his great idea was born.

"Family party," he said thoughtfully; while Miss Conway wondered aloud what had happened to Oliver and departed to the porch to look out for him. "Hmm—yes. Might have asked one of them to stay, if I'd thought of it. Would have made the numbers right."

"You can do that next time."

Cousin Alice spoke casually, with one eye on Con. Both she and Maud were rather surprised that old M. should toy with the thought of having a relative to stay; for relatives might be a good thing but visitors had always been emphatically discouraged. No one had stayed at Glaine for years, unless one counted Oliver—and even his visits always seemed to last too long.

They could not guess that the great idea was beginning to grow and flourish.

"Here is Oliver," Miss Conway announced. "You'd better sit in front, Alice. Maud sat in front going to church this morning and I sat in front coming back, so it's your turn now."

Maud was thankful that the privilege of sitting in front with Oliver was not to be hers.

CHAPTER SEVENTEEN

AT WOLTERING, Boxing Day had belonged to the servants. The family had spent it quietly, writing thank-you letters and eating cold left-overs and going for a brisk walk in the afternoon, if weather permitted. At Combe Cottage there were no servants to be considered, but the Wolfering customs were still kept up. No Christmas dinner had been needed but the chicken had been ordered before they knew this, so Con had roasted it on Christmas Eve and it served as left-overs for Boxing Day, accompanied by a soggy potato salad and followed by leaden mince pies, which had also been cooked beforehand, and stored in a tin. After eating this chilly midday meal they set off on the brisk walk.

It had not been necessary to plan a diversion for Oliver, since he had arranged one for himself. He was going to lunch with a professor (a real one) who lived on the border of the next county, and this meant that he would be out for most of the day. The respite thus afforded to old M. was also welcomed by Maud, whose waking wish had been that she could avoid seeing Oliver for the rest of his visit.

Unfortunately there seemed no way of avoiding a meeting tomorrow, unless Oliver himself should invent a reason for staying at home. He had readily accepted Ensie's invitation, given on Christmas Eve, but then he had been under a misapprehension, he had seen Maud as a meek but wonderful secretary, a restorer of order, a good influence; she must look quite different now. Perhaps he would cry off, preferring the risk of family bickering to the obvious awkwardness of meeting her. The invitation had been given by Ensie, but he must know that Maud would be there.

True to her promise to provide entertainment, Ensie had asked Oliver to a tea-party at Pixie Cot if the day was cold or wet, or to a tea picnic in Grim's Cave if it was fine and dry. It would be lovely down there, she had said, when Maud protested against picnicking in winter; but the real advantage of having a picnic was that it would exclude her Papa. He did not like picnics—nor did he like the idea of having five people to tea. Still, if it was wet he would have to put up with a tea-party. The words were Ensie's, and they showed that she was no longer Papa's Ensie all the time. Nevertheless, Maud understood why she was hoping and praying for a fine day.

During Boxing Day, and especially during the brisk walk, Maud had plenty of time to think about the painful episode of the library door. A strong wind beat in their faces as they walked and made talking impossible; instead, she listened to an inward repetition of angry exchanges, in which her own voice sounded as loud and as scornful as Oliver's. It had not seemed so at the time; but now, looking back, she had to admit that the faults were not all on one side. She ought not to have called Oliver obstinate, or scolded him for upsetting his father; and of course it had been silly of her to tell him what had happened to the key.

If she hadn't made that impetuous confession . . . if only she had kept calm . . . or if she had told him at the beginning instead of letting him hunt for the key. . . . How differently the scene played itself when the "ifs" were given their head; and how humiliating the difference seemed when one remembered one's actual behaviour.

Naturally, there was also a whole set of "ifs" for Oliver. When one started to look for them—as Maud did now—Oliver's errors outweighed her own. If he hadn't been so obstinate (yes, he deserved to be told about it) and so hot-tempered . . . if he hadn't raised his hand and reminded her of his Christmas Eve toast . . . if he hadn't said this, or that. . . . How easily she could have coped with a different Oliver; and how comforting to forget one's humiliation by dwelling on Oliver's faults.

"It will be a breezy picnic," Cousin Alice said, when they reached the comparative calm of the lane. But Miss Conway predicted that the wind would die away by the evening.

"More likely to be raining tomorrow," she added. "And a good thing too. Then we shall be able to have tea round a table like Christians, instead of huddling in a cave."

"But lots of early Christians lived in caves . . . didn't they?" Cousin Alice hazarded. "Anyway, this won't be a pagan picnic. The curate will be there."

Ensie had generous ideas about the amount six people would eat for tea; of course she had to sustain her reputation as housekeeper and cook. The only disadvantage was that everything had to be carried, since Grim's Cave could only be reached by a footpath across the fields to the cliff wherein it was situated, and it was also necessary to carry rugs and cushions and blankets, as a protection against the cold and the discomfort of sitting on rocks. The departing picnickers, walking in single file on the narrow path, reminded Mr. Martin of laden porters setting out for Everest, and he called his sister to join him at the window and see what he meant. Bowed down, probably tired out already, he pronounced, though they were only halfway across the combe. And to think that they were doing it for pleasure—

setting off on a winter afternoon to picnic in a damp cave among dead seagulls! He could only say—

He had said it at lunch and his sister wasn't disposed to hear it again. "Who are the other two?" she interrupted. "—Yes, James, of course there are eight. Can't you count?"

She was a sister, not a daughter, and she could not be told to look for his binoculars. By the time Mr. Martin had found them the picnickers were out of sight. This was just as well, for his peaceful afternoon would have been spoilt if he had known that the picnic party now included the daughter of his enemy Mr. Woodfidley, the destroyer of motor cars, and that dubious character Charles Feniston, whose market-garden made it so easy for Ensie to waste her money on flowers.

The path across the fields skirted the Woodfidleys' orchard, where Charles was advising Annabel on what should be done for some sickly-looking young apple trees. Maud was at the end of the single file, following Ensie and Don (as far removed as possible from Oliver, who was leading the way), and she could not see what happened when Oliver first observed his outcast cousin. Had he walked by in silence—was it Cousin Alice who had so tactlessly stopped to speak to Charles and Annabel, and thus compelled the rest of the file to stop too?

Whoever started the conversation, it was Don who prolonged it; and it was Don who, to Maud's alarm, suggested that Annabel and Charles should join the party. Of course she quickly guessed why; he was trying to heal the breach, to draw Annabel and Ensie together as a prelude to reconciling their respective papas, which was a proper and laudable task for a clergyman to undertake. But while he brought all his tactful jollity to bear on Ensie and Annabel he totally ignored—or perhaps was quite ignorant of—the existence of the other feud. Now he was helping Annabel to climb the orchard railing, now he was shouting explanation to Mrs. Woodfidley, who was keeping well out of range, now he was redistributing the picnickers' burdens, giving a man's load to Charles and a ladylike portion (one cushion, with a handle for carrying it) to Annabel.

He was a splendid organizer, an experienced tender of olive branches and healer of breaches; he knew that the great thing was to keep things moving and not give people time to protest. He knew this, he knew that, his reassurances to Ensie were wafted back to Maud but they did not console her; for who knew what would happen to a picnic party that contained both Oliver and Charles? She followed apprehensively, waiting for the time when the safe single-file formation would give place to a group.

The cave was at the foot of the cliff and the way down to it was rough and steep. Oliver offered assistance to Cousin Alice and Miss Conway, Charles guided Annabel, and Don fussed round Ensie, giving unnecessary advice and physical support—which was also unnecessary, but understandable. Maud scrambled down unaided till she reached the last turn of the zig-zag track, where she was surprised to meet Oliver coming back to help her.

"It's very slippery on this last bit," he said, almost apologetically.

"I expect I can manage."

"I expect you can."

Maud stared. Oliver stared back, in his most owl-like manner. But her first suspicion was confirmed; the owl was laughing at her.

If he had been a real owl she could not have been more startled. "I *can* manage. Why shouldn't I?" she demanded.

"Of course you can," Oliver said, still outwardly solemn. "I knew you would. I could hear you saying so as I came up."

"But—"

"Or rather, I apprehended your unspoken thoughts. You don't like to be helped, by me. You want to do it all on your own. Shall I go down first, or give you a start?"

The question Maud had determined not to ask sprang from her lips.

"Why are you laughing at me?"

"My dear Maud, I wouldn't dream of laughing. I'm admiring you; your independence, your resolution, your determination to have nothing to do with me. Think of us walking across all those fields, one at each end of a long, long file. Think of that extra basket you insisted on carrying because I had offered to take it. Picture yourself now, a beautifully intrepid mountain goat spurning my clumsy hand. And all because I spoke sharply to you on Christmas night, after considerable provocation."

Oliver's view of that episode would have taken her breath away had there been any left to take; but she had listened to him with the increasingly breathless sensations of an explorer sighting oceans, hills and forests where he had expected nothing but desert—the desert of blank imperceptivity and obtuseness. Like stout Cortez she could only stand silent on her peak, staring at the newly discovered Pacific. But Oliver, naturally unaware of ever having been a desert, mistook her surprise for annoyance.

"Well—I'll leave it at that," he said, with a return to his earlier manner.

"Oh no—please don't. That is, please don't think—I mean, I was acting for the best, in keeping away from you; only I didn't expect you to notice it."

"You must have thought me remarkably unobservant," he retorted. "And now, we had better descend or that curate be bounding up to rescue us."

Maud had disregarded the shouts from the beach, but now she looked down and saw Don at the foot of the cliff. A short distance away Charles and Annabel were collecting driftwood, a task which apparently required the closest attention. At once she remembered the dangers that lay ahead, and as they descended the track she anxiously debated how Charles and Oliver could be kept apart. But as soon as they reached the beach it became clear that the management of the picnic was not her business.

You go and help Ensie to unpack, Don told her; and you walk along there under the foot of the cliff and find some dry stuff, really dry and small, for starting the fire. With the critical eye of a good scoutmaster he watched Oliver set off, and then hurried back to his own task of building a hearth which would contain the fire and support the kettle. The beach was strewn with stones and there was also plenty of driftwood, but Oliver must have had difficulty in finding enough small and really dry stuff; everything was ready, and the whole party assembled, before he returned.

His inadequate bundle of kindling was at once put to use, and while Don and Ensie fanned the flames Oliver walked over to Charles and said amiably that it was a long time since he'd seen him. Must be a year ago, Charles replied, and Oliver said surely not as long as that—what about that time in Yeomouth? The question of exactly when this meeting took place seemed of absorbing interest; and while they discussed it Maud had time to reorganize her ideas about outcast cousins and family feuds.

It had never occurred to her that Oliver wasn't involved in the feud, for somehow one could not imagine a Feniston remaining neutral. It was true that Charles had shown no marked hostility when alluding to Oliver, but then he also talked quite tolerantly about old M., and she knew old M. went out of his way to avoid the enemy at his gates. (He shunned the back drive; he had drawn an invisible line round Charles's territory and he never crossed it.) Moreover she had discerned in Charles a touch of the injured victim: he spoke tolerantly but not humbly, he contrived to make it clear that he was in the right and old M. in the wrong, and he had never suggested that Oliver was less blameworthy than his father or a secret sympathizer.

She had expected therefore a coldness, or even an outburst of Feniston tempers, instead of the exchange of family news which was now taking place. While they waited for the kettle to boil Charles and Oliver strolled up and down, and references to Noel Humby and other relatives could be heard as they passed. Don tended the fire and Ensie handed him the driftwood as it was needed; Cousin Alice helped Miss Conway to dry Wilbraham, who had insisted on paddling. Maud was presently enlisted as an audience for Annabel.

"Frankly, I never expected to be asked," Annabel said. She drew Maud a little apart and told her about the progress of the new feud between her father and Ensie's father, and said in a worldly way that they were both old enough to know better.

"That's the worst of living in a small place like this," she added. "If you quarrel with someone it sort of goes on and on. Just look at the Fenistons."

Maud looked at them, and Annabel said she didn't mean those two but Charles and his mad uncle. Of course Oliver didn't count because he didn't live here.

"He's absolutely negative anyway," she said.

"He isn't!"

"Oh well, he's what I call rather dull. Bookish, you know and nothing to say for himself. Charles is much more of a real fact."

Bookish Oliver might be, but no one who had argued with him could think of him as inarticulate. Maud wondered why she had bothered to defend him; and then she wondered how Charles manifested his factual qualities.

"They were brought up together," she said.

"I know. Terribly bad luck on poor Charles. He's got a thing about Glaine and he's the eldest and yet he's not the son and heir. That's why he won't give up the gardens, I expect—he still thinks of it as sort of his. It's what I call pathetic," Annabel remarked soulfully.

"But I call it silly, if Charles thinks like that. He must have known for years that he wasn't really the son and heir. It's time he grew up."

Maud was surprised by her own reactions to Annabel's soulful sympathy; and Annabel was surprised too.

"I suppose he does rather go on about it," she said. "But all the same he's terribly attractive."

Then she changed the subject and began telling Maud how much nicer picnics were abroad, where the sun was simply blazing and one did not have to hang about waiting for the kettle to boil.

But even in England, and in winter, a picnic could be successful. The sun shone on Ensie's, and although it did not blaze they were kept warm by the fire and by the sheltering walls of the cave. They sat just inside the cave (for further back it was cold and damp), and even Miss Conway seemed to be enjoying the picnic; certainly she did full justice to Ensie's magnificent tea. So did Cousin Alice—and so did Maud herself. The inhabitants of Combe Cottage, she reflected, must be quite renowned in other households for the amount they ate when Fate threw a good meal in their way.

"It's a pity the days are so short," Ensie said.

Everyone agreed with her. They had had tea early, but already it was time to leave; the sky was darkening and a breeze ruffled the sea, the sun had vanished behind the cliff-top and it would be dusk before they got home. But Maud thought the brevity of the picnic was perhaps a good thing; it had been harmonious and agreeable but the harmony might not have lasted. Even now, she was aware of discordant elements.

It wasn't Charles and Oliver who had to be kept apart; it was Charles and Miss Conway, and, to a lesser degree; Ensie and Annabel. The small gulf between Ensie and Annabel had been bridged by Don, who sat there talking to each in turn with a curate's practised gaiety. But between Charles and Miss Conway Alice had judged it wise to set up not a bridge but a barrier, several persons thick, and after tea when the barrier dispersed itself she deliberately let Wilbraham escape, so that she and Con could pursue him and then follow the rest of the party at a safe distance. Miss Conway walked quickly and the gap lessened, but Cousin Alice lengthened it again by sitting down on a rock and taking off her shoe.

"Just a stone. Don't wait for us," she called.

Of course Don waited, to help them up the steep track, and at the top of the cliff Maud, Ensie and Oliver waited too. Maud could not tell whether Charles would have waited, if Annabel had not suddenly felt extremely cold and insisted on walking on; but naturally he had to accompany her.

"So silly of me," Annabel said. "It's been a lovely picnic, Ensie—absolutely marvellous. But you don't mind if we rush away now, do you?"

Maud had scarcely spoken to Charles, and she had been dismayed by his coming—although, as it turned out, unnecessarily. But his going dismayed her for a different reason; she felt that she ought to have enjoyed the afternoon much more because Charles had been there. Her interest in Cousin Alice's manoeuvres, in Oliver's perceptiveness, and in Ensie's revolt from daughterhood, seemed a kind of disloyalty and she felt quite angry with herself for being so easily diverted. It was as if she had, inexplicably failed to produce the right emotions.

The sense of guilty failure was still with her when she said good-bye to Oliver, who was leaving Glaine early the next morning after a visit which he described as "extremely satisfactory." The reason for his satisfaction was not stated, but she supposed he still thought of her as the annihilator of spiders and the provider of hot bath-water. Moreover, he had shown his goodwill towards her by getting up early and prising open one of the library windows and pushing the key under the door, where it could be retrieved from the other side.

"And you'd better be the one to retrieve it," he suggested. "Then you needn't make it seem too easy."

"I will. And thank you for—for thinking of it."

"Don't mention it. I'm sorry I upset you. Of course I realized afterwards that you'd had just about enough of the library, with my father. He can be extraordinarily difficult. But another time, please don't treat me as an untouchable—because I'm not really deaf and blind. I notice it."

"No," said Maud. "Of course not. All the same—"

"That's all right, then. You know, I really enjoyed this afternoon."

"Did you?"

"Nice to see Charles again."

"Yes, I suppose it was."

"If only he wasn't so pigheaded," said Oliver, becoming chatty. "And so stupid. Hanging on to hit Naboth's vineyard just to be awkward, when it doesn't pay and never will pay—and when he has the chance of more land out at Cheriton. Of course he's a Feniston through and through, blue eyes and blatant good looks and all the rest of it. But he'll come another cropper if he isn't careful."

Maud's guilty remorse, coupled with her annoyance at being described as "upset" by a man whose fury vented itself on doors, hardened into a conviction that Oliver was being grossly unfair.

"Charles isn't the only pigheaded Feniston," she said sharply. "And he isn't stupid either. He *loves* Glaine—but you don't understand that, you only think of it in terms of profit and loss. I suppose you would pull it down and sell the land for building and think you were being awfully clever!"

"Hey?" Oliver cried, like a faint, startled echo of old M.

"I must go—Cousin Alice is waiting for me, and I haven't said good-night to Ensie. I hope you have a good journey tomorrow."

"But—"

"Good-night," she said, retreating in haste.

CHAPTER EIGHTEEN

APRIL MIGHT BE the cruellest month, Cousin Alice said, but January was the least bearable. It was a month devoted to minor disasters, to streaming colds and household breakages and frozen pipes and toothache. One couldn't fall in love in January, or write poetry.

"Not that I still do, at my age," she added. "But it's how I feel about January."

Maud agreed that it was a horrid month.

"I don't mind it at all," said Miss Conway. "It can be quite exhilarating."

What exhilarated her was the sight of the tidy room, holly and Christmas cards banished, the season for armistices at an end, the season for campaigning stretching before her. Casually, more for fun than for practice, she fired a ranging shot.

"You left your bathroom tap dripping last night, Maud. Mustn't do that in this weather, you know. If the waste pipe had frozen we might have had a flood."

"I'm sorry. I didn't notice it was dripping."

The dripping was still, so to speak, in the future; for having uttered her warning Miss Conway intended to visit the bathroom on a frosty night after Maud had gone to bed and arrange for her prediction to come true. What was a flood compared with Alice's ultimate well-being? For Con the end justified the means, and she had now convinced herself that it was her sacred duty, as friend and ministering angel, to get rid of Maud.

But she mustn't rush it; that would upset Alice, who felt quite sentimental about Maud because of her being one of the family. Maud's eviction must be managed so that the final decision came from her; she must be goaded into going, and in the meantime she must be treated firmly but kindly. To show open hostility at this stage might easily make her suspicious. She was a sly little thing, Con thought, thinking too of legacies, expectations, the undue influence exerted by ties of blood, and the lease of Combe Cottage. Alice had been saying for years that the lease ought to be in both their names and that Con would be able to afford to stay on, but it seemed rather ominous to Miss Conway that she had not said it during the past two months.

"Can you keep a secret?" Ensie asked coyly.

Maud said she could, but even if her reply had been different Ensie would have told her, for it was obvious that she had to tell someone or burst. The middle of a crowded bus was not the best place for telling secrets but she put her mouth close to Maud's ear and spoke in a throaty whisper.

"It'll be a tremendous surprise to you, I know. I can hardly believe it myself, and you must promise not to reveal it to a soul because of Father. Of course he should be the first to know, but he can't be told just yet because of Mr. Woodfidley. Oh, Maud, just think—Don and I are engaged! Isn't it wonderful? Aren't you frightfully surprised? I simply had to tell you!"

"Oh, Ensie, how exciting! I do congratulate you. I'm sure you'll be awfully happy, and of course you'll be just the right wife for a—for Don."

When they reached Yeomouth they sat on the Marine Parade, which was deserted because of a chilly wind and threatening rain, and Ensie was able to speak in her normal voice and to tell Maud the whole story of how Don had proposed and been accepted. They had met by pure chance, she had been to the dentist (a providential January toothache, Maud thought) and on the way home she had popped into little St. Alfred's to rub up the candlesticks, and naturally Don had had no idea she was coming because she didn't know it herself, but by an extraordinary coincidence he had been there collecting some sermon notes he had left in the vestry, and he had said he would walk home with her because—well, said Ensie, blushing happily, because he wanted to, she supposed now; but at the time he had said because it was. getting dark. And he had seemed rather silent and not like himself and she had been afraid he was starting the influenza. But it wasn't the onset of influenza, but of a proposal. And she had asked him why he wasn't wearing his thick coat (thinking of the influenza turning into pneumonia) and he said it had got wet through and his landlady hadn't dried it—and then he said how much he longed for a home instead of lodgings—and then he said "a home, and a wife to welcome me." Then, having said so much, he begged her to be his wife, and she had said she would be, and they were engaged. And she had not got over the surprise—the wonderful surprise—of finding herself engaged to Don.

Maud was delighted but she found it difficult to feel as surprised as Ensie did, for she had already come to think of Ensie's marriage to Don as a settled fact. It was hard to remember that the proposal had only just been made and accepted, when one had settled their future and decided on a suitable parish and provisionally endowed them with two children and arranged for them to keep a Siamese cat. (Its dog-qualities would please Don, and its cat-qualities Ensie.) Luckily it was hardly necessary to say anything; Ensie talked and talked, and the wind grew stronger and the tide came in and slapped at the base of the Marine Parade, and behind them in the town the cinema was showing the film they had come to see, and presently the café would be serving, to other customers, the tea they had planned to eat. Maud did not mind missing the film but at the thought of the tea she experienced a typical Combe Cottager's pang.

"Do you think your Papa will object?" she asked, after Ensie had reiterated the need for absolute secrecy.

"Why do you say 'Papa'? I always call him Father."

"I know. But I think of him as your Papa. It's a Victorian word that seems to suit him, though it's a pity he hasn't got a large Victorian family as well as a Victorian personality, for then he wouldn't miss you. As it is, he's probably counting on you to minister to his declining years."

"Oh, Maud, don't be so gloomy. Of course I'm very fond of him," Ensie added quickly, "and I daresay I've spoilt him a bit. Given in too much, you know, and sacrificed my own life to his."

"I daresay you have."

"Don says I've been almost *too* unselfish. He says we shall have to be very careful about telling Father or he may be really hurt. And Don is most anxious to get him to forgive Mr. Woodfidley, first, because he says that he won't be able to do any more about that, about healing the breach I mean, if Father hears about our engagement and—and doesn't take it very well."

Maud thought what a good clergyman Don was, and how wise of him to tackle one breach at a time; for a second one was almost bound to open when Mr. Martin learned that his daughter intended to leave him. She thought he would take it very ill indeed.

"Of course it will be ages before we can be married," Ensie continued. "But that's a good thing in a way, because it will give Father time to get used to the idea of having a housekeeper or living in an hotel."

"Leaving Pixie Cot! But would he like that?"

"Well, he can have a housekeeper. I'd thought of Aunt, but she is going back to New Zealand. Anyway, I don't think Aunt would make him comfortable. She's a very bad cook."

It was Papa's Ensie speaking, perhaps for the last time, Maud thought; she was fading away like a ghost at sunrise, and the sunrise was appropriately rosy-pink and hopeful, the dawn of a new life for Don's Ensie who already looked confident and robust, like the best kind of clergyman's wife.

"I don't want Father to suffer," said Papa's Ensie, in the detached voice of a thinning ghost.

"Of course not."

"But, as I said to Don, he'll simply have to get used to the idea. Oh, Maud, this time yesterday I didn't *know*! It's been such a complete surprise—I can hardly get used to it myself!"

Did proposals always come on one like that, Maud wondered; a complete surprise, a bolt from the blue, not of course a painful or lethal one but still bolt-like in its stunning unexpectedness? Could Ensie have failed to notice what was so clear to everyone else, or had she forbidden herself to look forward to a proposal for fear of being disappointed? Or perhaps she thought it wrong to dream about being proposed to, conceited or indecorous or simply unlucky like counting one's chickens before they were hatched. How awkward a totally unexpected proposal might be, if one had not seen it coming and decided whether to accept or refuse it. But in Ensie's case the answer could never have been in doubt.

Maud thought a lot about Ensie. It was Sunday, the day after she had sat on the Marine Parade and heard all about the proposal, and as it was a miserable January Sunday she spent most of the day indoors. Con had the January streaming cold and stayed in bed to get rid of it, and Cousin Alice produced a large piece of rump steak which she had bought off the butcher's van yesterday, and she and Maud ate it for lunch.

"Con had promised me she would stay in bed today if she wasn't better," she said. "And I knew she wouldn't be—her colds always take a week—so I went out and waylaid him. She only wants porridge and Herb-Soma, that's what she always takes for her colds, and I thought this would be nice and easy for us to cook."

"Very nice," said Maud, sniffing the beautiful aroma of grilling steak.

"Shut the kitchen door, dear, or the smell will get all over the house. I thought we'd have luncheon here in the kitchen, as it's just ourselves."

Alice and Maud ate slowly, savouring the delicious taste of juicy steak. Maud wondered whether the butcher's van habitually carried large slabs of steak on the chance of being waylaid or whether Cousin Alice had telephoned the shop and ordered it in advance. Wilbraham whimpered and slobbered until he was given a bone, which the van had also provided. Upstairs, in her bedroom over the dining room, Miss Conway lay and pondered on the reason for the lack of sound from below.

"One understands what cannibals go through when missionaries convert them," Alice said thoughtfully. "One does so miss what one's been brought up on, even when one knows that it's quite the wrong diet. And for cannibals, of course, sinful as well."

"But rump steak isn't sinful for Christians."

"Except on Fridays, if you're High. We weren't at all High, at Wolfering, though we did make some concessions to Lent, giving up sweets and reading only serious books."

"Don would be very High indeed, if it wasn't for the Rector," Maud said. "The Rector won't allow it. Ensie says Don says he ought to retire, because he's so old and out of touch with the church of today."

"Curates always seem to adore their superiors or else utterly despise them. Shall we have some coffee? I ordered some this week because I thought it would be a change from all those milk drinks."

Maud put the kettle on and Alice fetched the coffee from its hiding-place. Maud hoped Miss Conway's cold would last longer than a week.

"Of course, it's a father-and-son relationship," Alice remarked. "And I suppose Don can't help thinking what a good Rector he would make, if this one retired."

"Oh no! Don and Ensie don't want to stay in Yeomouth, they think of being missionaries or at least Ensie says—"

Maud stopped short. Cousin Alice asked with interest whether Mr. Martin approved of his daughter's becoming a missionary.

"He doesn't know. It's a secret, and I shouldn't have told you. Please, please promise not to tell anyone else."

"But, Maud, one cannot be a missionary in secret." Cousin Alice thought it over. "Unless one could be a crypto-missionary, cunningly converting people by undermining their atheistic principles. But I don't think Ensie could do that, she's too obviously a clergyman's daughter, or . . . Oh, you mean that they are secretly engaged?"

"Yes," said Maud.

"Well, it won't be a secret for long—engagements never are. But I promise I won't be the one to tell it."

After this assurance Maud felt rather glad that she had accidentally revealed the secret, for now she could discuss with Cousin Alice the reasons for Ensie's being surprised when Don proposed to her. At first Alice said nonsense, Ensie simply must have known it was coming, but presently she admitted that she might be wrong, after all Ensie had until quite recently thought of herself as cherishing an unrequited passion and she might not have dared to revise her ideas.

"Of course Don had admired her for ages—but from afar," Maud said. "And Ensie was so dominated by her Papa that she lacked all initiative. She was stuck."

"Until you gave her a push," Cousin Alice said drily.

"Well, just a tiny little push in the right direction. I turned her round and started her off."

"So long as you are sure it *is* the right direction."

"Of course it is! They are perfectly suited to each other," Maud declared, with all the enthusiasm of a successful match-maker.

Cousin Alice did not dispute it, but she looked worried; or, more precisely, she looked like an aunt. The occasions when she did so were rare and they always took Maud by surprise, as proposals took Ensie, and made her feel more of a niece than she cared to be. Before she had time to conquer this feeling Cousin Alice, in her guise of worried aunt, began to speak.

"One makes mistakes, sometimes," she said. "An unrequited passion is romantic . . . in a way, it's like fancy dress, you feel not quite your everyday self and you begin to act a part, perhaps to exaggerate it a little . . . one does, you know, when one is one's own, and only, audience. But then, the unrequited passion suddenly *is* requited and the man you think you're in love with begins to look your way—well, then you may find he's quite different from the distant, unattainable hero of your dramatic private dream."

"I suppose that would be disillusioning," Maud said politely.

"Disillusionment doesn't hurt anyone," Alice retorted. "It may hurt at the time but it's merely part of growing up and you're all the better for it. No, the danger is that you won't admit to being disillusioned . . . you cannot bear to acknowledge that all that splendid emotion, all the attitudes that went with the fancy dress, were a mistake. So you go on pretending that the real man is like the dream hero . . . and perhaps you get engaged to, and even marry, a man who doesn't exist. That's why it is as well to be certain that one isn't pushing someone, or pushing oneself, in the wrong direction."

"But honestly, Cousin Alice, Ensie will be frightfully happy with Don. She was born to be the wife of a good clergyman."

"Oh—Ensie!"

Cousin Alice sounded impatient and for a moment Maud felt herself to be not only a niece but a rather stupid niece. But the next instant her companion had changed back into a first cousin once removed and was regarding her with a tolerant, cousinly smile.

"Oh yes, I expect they'll be very happy," she conceded. "And I daresay he's an excellent curate, as curates go. But not a missionary, I think. Wouldn't it jeopardise his chances of becoming a bishop?"

"I think he's almost certain to become a bishop, with those eyebrows."

Cousin Alice speculated on the part eyebrows played in securing preferment; she thought that on the whole Maud was right and that one could spot potential winners among curates by their physical characteristics, though eyebrows weren't everything. There were jaws of two types, bull-dog and lantern, which counted, and legs that were designed to wear gaiters and legs that weren't, and limp, flabby hands that would condemn any curate to a poor, rural parish and at the best a rural deanery. It was most unfair and *most* interesting.

The kitchen chairs were hard but the kitchen itself was steamy and warm. They sat on, arguing and laughing, until three heavy knocks sounded directly overhead, followed after a very short pause by three more. The nearness of these knocks showed that Miss Conway must have got out of bed and come along the passage to deliver them.

"Goodness, Con's tray," Cousin Alice exclaimed. She jumped up, knocking over her chair and frightening Wilbraham and perhaps sounding to Miss Conway like an angry return volley.

"No, Maud, I'll go up and fetch it . . . it will be better, I think. You start the washing up. Turn the taps on, that's right, and stack the things on the draining board . . ."

The washing up would explain their presence in the kitchen—although it was rather late in the day. Maud turned the taps on, and stacked and clattered with vigour.

CHAPTER NINETEEN

"I THINK WE should have a fire," Maud had said. "Some of these books are very valuable and they'll be ruined by the damp if they lie here much longer. That oil stove isn't really quite big enough for a room this size."

She had had to say it several times, with slight variations, before old M. had given in. But this morning there was a beautiful fire burning under the hideous marble chimneypiece and the library looked quite transformed. Piles of books still covered the floor but in front of the fire there was an open space, like a clearing in the jungle, where she and old M. could camp out in comparative comfort. It was furnished with two chairs, and a small table, and one of the three typewriters from the estate room, and all these objects as well as the marble chimneypiece and its ornaments and the bit of carpet free from obstructions had been swept and dusted. Looking at this small, neat clearing which had been hacked out of the surrounding jungle, Maud recognised the hand of Who's-it.

"That girl's still here," old M. said, as if he were reading her thoughts.

"Yes, I know."

"She's been here a month. I told Hat she could come here for Christmas and now she says she can't afford to go home. Doesn't want to, I expect, for she says it's all ruins and Russians and her mother's dead and I don't know what. Boo-hoo and all that, when I mention it. Can't get much out of her."

Maud wondered how he got anything, since he and Who's-it spoke different languages. "Well, why not let her stay?" she suggested.

"Stay! Stay here? My dear Maud, think what she eats. This place isn't an orphanage . . ."

Old M. rumbled on, and when he had finished she said calmly, "You'd have to pay her, of course. She has a permit to work in England and she wants to stay, and I think—"

"*Pay* her! Do you think I'm made of money?"

"No. But I think you can afford to pay Who's-it, and you must remember that she'd be a wonderful bargain. She works far harder than the others. She'd be like two housemaids for the price of one."

It was hard for old M. to resist a wonderful bargain, and perhaps like Oliver he had noticed the hot bath-water and the other improvements Who's-it had brought about, and while he was thinking of these things Maud reminded him that Oliver hoped to visit him again before Easter and would certainly be here for the Easter weekend. Old M. retorted that he wasn't going to keep another servant just to wait on Oliver; but he spoke so mildly that she knew he had taken the point.

"And there's the spring-cleaning," she said.

"Glaine hasn't been spring-cleaned for years. Not since before the war."

"Then it needs doing."

Old M. actually laughed. He was in a good mood this morning, and Maud felt sure that the fire in the library, and the hot bath-water, and the clean—or, anyway, cleaner—rooms, were having a beneficial effect, he was more comfortable and therefore better tempered and more amenable to reason. She glanced happily at the fire, thinking what a difference it made to her own comfort, and old M. looked down at her and said:

"You feeling warmer? Or was it the fumes?"

"The fumes?"

"I'm not so easily bamboozled. You wanted the fire for yourself, not for the sake of the books. All nonsense about the books getting damp, this isn't a damp house and you know it. And all nonsense too about the oil stove not being big enough, it's big enough to heat a ballroom and I picked it up for next to nothing. It warmed *me*, and it warmed Miss Goose—not that she stayed long enough to feel cold—and I wondered at first what you had against it. But then I thought of the fumes. Make some people turn quite blue and you did look a bit blue, one or two days last week, when I came to think of it."

"Yes," said Maud. "I expect I did."

"Well, that's understandable. We'll have a fire. Don't try to bamboozle me, though. I'm not such a fool as you think."

"I don't think you're a fool at all."

Old M. laughed again and this time she felt rather uneasy, because his good mood seemed to be overflowing into a dangerous excess of high spirits. And if he had seen through her stratagems for getting a fire, what else had he seen through? The mention of Miss Goose had reminded her of her early days at Glaine when she had been so frightened of him and had hidden the carbon copies of the letters and destroyed other evidence of her own incompetence; perhaps Miss Goose had done likewise, and had been found out, and laughed at, and dismissed. But no—Miss Goose had done worse things, she had had hysterics, and had somehow broken a lot of Spode, and—

"—finished by March," old M. was saying, but he interrupted himself to say loudly, "Wake up!"

"I'm so sorry."

"You weren't listening to me. What were you thinking of—hey?"

"Miss Goose," she replied truthfully.

"Why?"

"Well, I was just thinking—I was wondering whether she was a good secretary, and—and what—"

"Of course she wasn't," old M. said sharply. "If she had been I shouldn't have had to get another one. No initiative, no commonsense, a dreadful whining voice. And she was always patting her hair."

"Oh," said Maud. She had pictured Miss Goose as wispy and heedless, not as a hair patter. But perhaps it was just a nervous trick.

"Mind you, she didn't try to bamboozle me. Hadn't the spirit, for one thing. That's what I liked about you, Maud, when you first came here. I said to myself, well, she's got spirit, anyway. Those weren't the letters I dictated, I said to myself, but at least she's a trier."

To this speech she could find no answer at all. She simply gazed at old M., while he slowly turned and threw another log on the fire and then turned back to face her.

"I found you out the second day you were here," he continued sociably. "I sent you upstairs to wash the oil off your hands and you left those carbons lying on your table, the letters I'd dictated the first day, and I looked at them and they were all quite different from what I'd really said. I knew at once. I've got a good memory."

"But—"

"Now don't try to bamboozle me again. It's a good thing I found you out, because it showed me you had your wits about you and that's the kind of secretary I wanted. Not some timid fool like Miss Goose who daren't put in a comma unless I'd dictated it."

It seemed all wrong to Maud that her initial success with old M. had been due to an act of deception which hadn't come off, but she saw what he meant. Her customary bad luck had turned out to be good luck, at Glaine, and she seemed to have, travelled a long way from the Maud who was so quickly discouraged. For she might easily have been another Miss Goose, she might have wept, or patted her hair, and been sent home before she had really got to know Glaine and hear about the three little owls and meet Oliver.

"Oliver frightened her away, in the end," old M. said. "And I can't really blame him, but it's a pity he made her drop the Spode."

Maud corrected her thought to "Charles"; she had thought of Oliver only because old M. had mentioned him at the same moment. But she was interested to learn that he had been in at the death of the Spode and she wondered if she could ask him about it when he was next at Glaine.

"Trouble about Oliver is, he's bored here," old M. continued. "Makes him jumpy, you know, and irritable. That's why he frightened her. He's as mild as milk, really."

"I'm sure he is. Did he—"

"I've been thinking. Now listen, Maud. I've been thinking I might ask one or two people, when he comes here at Easter. Relatives, you know—people he never sees and ought to. Noel Humby and one or two others.—But not his wife, no, I won't have her in the place. I might have Penelope though, and her sister old Agatha. I've been thinking about what Alice said at Christmas. And it'll be easy enough now that I've decided to keep Who's-it. Can't have a house party without a proper staff, but Who's-it will make all the difference. Two housemaids, and Hat and his wife—how many is that good for?"

Before she had a chance to reply, old M. was off again. His high spirits were given their head; his plans for an Easter house party came bubbling out in a happy torrent. He had been thinking of it for a long time, ever since the successful Christmas dinner party, and the more he talked of it the more excited he got. He strode up and down the jungle clearing, discussing his relatives and assessing their points, debating whether Penelope and Agatha should both be invited and whether Noel Humby would come without his wife (if not, he should not come at all), and who should sleep in which room and what they should be given to eat. He spoke very fast and often interrupted himself to laugh; and in Maud's ears his laughter sounded slightly malicious. It was as if he were thinking of the house party as a kind of practical joke.

He must have planned to tell her about it that morning and been working up to it through all their earlier conversation. It explained the fire (a concession designed to make her co-operative), and his good humour, and his jerky dismissal of subjects which would have lasted the whole morning if he had not had this to look forward to. His disclosure about reading the carbon copies now appeared as a mere parenthesis, inserted while he looked for a way to lead up to his startling decision. For he must have known that it would startle her, and that it might seem, unless carefully explained, a mere whim. He was clearly anxious that she should not think this, and he came back more than once to the theme of Oliver's boredom.

"Do him a lot of good to have people to talk to when he's here. He thinks too much, when he's alone, and naturally it makes him jumpy. When I was his age the house was always full of people and it all looked quite different, and this'll show him what it was—what it could be like."

Maud had often pictured Glaine in the glorious past, but now she could only think of its many drawbacks as the site of a present-day house party—the blankets full of moth, the crumbling furniture, the accumulation of dirt and spiders in the unused bedrooms, the ruined garden and the inefficient pump.

"Do you think Oliver will really like having his relations here?" she asked. "Perhaps he's looking forward to a little peace and quiet,"

"It'll be good for him. That's what I'm *telling* you, Maud. And of course he'll enjoy it, too, once he meets them and gets to know them."

Old M. took another turn across the clearing, while Maud reflected on the curious belief, so strongly held by her companion, that relatives were a tonic.

"I've been thinking," he announced. "I've been thinking it would be better not to tell him about it, until he actually arrives at Easter. He'll be coming before then, but we won't mention it. We'll keep it"—he paused and clutched triumphantly at a convincing phrase—"we'll keep it as a nice surprise for him!"

"But surprises aren't always nice. I mean, they can be disconcerting. I think you should give him time to get used to the idea."

"No, no! You can't tell, with a feller like Oliver—he might feel nervous and cry off, and it would all be wasted. Now promise me you won't say a word to him. Better keep it quite to yourself, in case he hears of it accidentally. I know you're discreet, but this is very important."

Maud was by no means convinced that the surprise would be a nice one for Oliver, but she knew that it was useless to argue. She promised faithfully to tell no one at all.

And just as well, she thought that afternoon, when she saw Charles's van drawn up at the end of the back drive and Charles himself helping to unload bundles of bamboos and other aids to horticulture. For if she had not promised absolute secrecy she might easily have told Charles, who would have been enthralled by the news that several Feniston relatives were being invited to Glaine, and who would have appreciated as no one else could do (except perhaps Oliver) the fantastic oddity of the scheme. But it would be disloyal to tell Charles, and her promise of secrecy helped her to resist the temptation. There was no harm however in finding out more about the proposed guests, and she was glad to see that he had nearly finished the unloading. She pumped up the tyres of her bicycle while the bamboos were stacked on a hand-cart, and when the youngest gardener had wheeled them away through the door of the walled garden she advanced on Charles.

"Hullo," he said. "Do you want a lift home? I can put your bicycle in the back of the van. Unless—"

"Thank you," said Maud, forestalling the joke about her needing exercise. It was tiresome of Charles to repeat the joke every time he met her, but she did not allow herself to dwell on his tiresome qualities.

Charles put the bicycle into the van and Maud settled herself in the front and he got in beside her. Then he explained that he was waiting for a packet of seeds, which Carey would bring from the shed when he had dealt with the bamboos. Maud realized that she would have been back at Combe Cottage sooner if she had bicycled, but naturally she did not mind the delay. She asked Charles if he was related to Noel Humby. Charles said of course he was, and why did she want to know.

"Oh, I just wondered what he was like. Old M. writes to him sometimes."

"Does he?" Charles sounded amused and surprised. "Does Noel Humby write back?"

"Yes, indeed he does. They correspond quite regularly."

"I suppose old Noel is still hoping old M. will see reason.— Well, I haven't met him since the war, but he used to look rather like a white rabbit. Yes, *the* white rabbit. He married late in life and his wife is a bossy woman who sits on the Bench and knows what's best for everybody and believes in straight speaking. A real tartar."

Charles and old M. evidently thought alike about Noel Humby's wife. It crossed Maud's mind that, whatever Oliver felt about the house party, Charles would enjoy it with gusto—just like his uncle. It was a pity they could not be reconciled.

"Old M. seems to have a lot of cousins," she remarked.

"They are mine too," Charles pointed out. "Once removed, of course, but still cousins. My grandfather had nine brothers and sisters."

He began to talk about the cousins, and soon Maud had got them sorted out and had learned quite a lot about them. The gardener came back with the packet of seeds, but Charles seemed in no hurry to start; at last she had to remind him that Alice and Con would be waiting for her, and he drove slowly along the lane, still talking about the Fenistons and about Glaine in his boyhood. All these relatives had apparently looked on it as their family home and had stayed there for long periods, or had dropped in uninvited whenever they were in the neighbourhood and had been welcomed and fed and given all the family news, and at times of crisis they had flocked back like Parliament being recalled to discuss and decide what should be done, and naturally they had rallied round for weddings, and in even greater numbers for funerals (perhaps bringing with them the corpse of some distant, deceased Feniston who was entitled to a place in the family vault), and in spite of the inevitable bickerings it had all been great fun.

"We went in for ancestor worship, in those days," he said, drawing the van to a tactless halt immediately outside the dining-room window of Combe Cottage. Inside, Maud could see Alice and Con already sitting down to high tea. But she ignored their reactions, for she was thinking about Charles with his blue eyes and—what had Oliver said?—blatant good looks, a Feniston through and through, an ancestor come to life, and she was thinking that Annabel had been quite right in saying he had "a thing" about Glaine.

Charles lifted the bicycle out of the van and held it while she opened the gate. "What do you do with yourself at weekends?" he asked.

It was of course the prelude to an invitation, which Maud gladly accepted. It would be enjoyable to lunch with Charles on Saturday and perhaps drive out to Cheriton afterwards; it was a day-dream come true.

But in the day-dreams she had been defiantly siding with the enemy at the gates, she had faced disapproval and calumny and conducted herself like a heroine. A lot of excitement seemed to be missing, now that she was really going out with Charles.

"Thank you," she said firmly. "I'd love to."

And having settled the actual time and place for an actual meeting she said good-bye to Charles and walked into Combe

Cottage, almost hoping that Cousin Alice would restore the heady feeling of heroism by looking aunt-like or insisting on not being involved.

CHAPTER TWENTY

JANUARY WAS the least bearable month, according to Cousin Alice, and February was the wettest, and in March things would begin to improve. Maud hoped she was right, although March would certainly be the busiest month, entirely devoted to spring-cleaning and getting ready for the house party and to persuading old M. to spend money on repairs and on such essential items as towels, electric-light bulbs and crockery.

But she wasn't thinking of these kinds of improvements, when she hoped Cousin Alice was right about March, but of the disasters and discomforts which had overtaken her at Combe Cottage. Whatever happened in March, it could hardly be a more unlucky month than February. Her leaking hot-water bottle was a discomfort, and the broken panes in the greenhouse bathroom, mysteriously caused by a late January frost, were a more prolonged one because it took two weeks to get them replaced. The other breakages, however, were disasters; they were due to her clumsiness and there was a whole run of them, so that she began to feel as nervous and awkward as she had felt at home. The handle of the milk jug, which came off when she was washing it, the two plates which slid off the shelf when she had barely touched them, the pot of hyacinths which crashed to the floor when she passed it (she must have brushed against it as she walked), the triple disaster in her bedroom, when her wardrobe door first jammed and then suddenly yielded to her tugging, and fell off its hinges and tilted sideways, breaking a picture frame and also the Chinese plate Cousin Alice had given her at Christmas—these mishaps and other, more personal ones, laddered stockings, snapping shoelaces, mislaid gloves, continued to occur with alarming frequency. Cousin Alice was quite nice about them, but Miss Conway less so. She said Maud was like a bull in a china shop.

"And I feel like one, too," Maud told Ensie.

Ensie said that must be dreadful. But she said it vaguely, not really listening; she never listened to anything nowadays unless it concerned Don. It was nine in the morning and she was standing at the gate of Pixie Cot waiting for the postman, who was always late on Saturdays.

"If Father gets the letters first he looks at them all," she complained. "He doesn't open mine, but he examines them and wants to know who they're from. And he'd think it funny that Don writes to me every day."

Maud thought it funny too, considering that they met so frequently, but she supposed it was a sign of deep attachment.

"He's getting a bit suspicious, as it is," Ensie continued. "The other day . . ."

It was Maud's turn not to listen, and as soon as Ensie paused she said quickly, "Oliver is arriving today, for the weekend. That's why I'm going to Glaine now. I forgot to tell Who's-it something."

"And I expect you want to see him," Ensie said, rather archly. Maud put this down to her being engaged and thinking continually of love. "Not particularly," she answered. "Anyway he won't be here till this afternoon. There's the postman coming now."

Ensie stepped out into the lane. There was only one letter, which she pocketed after giving it a loving pat. Then, to Maud's surprise, she said, "I think I'll come with you. I want to see Charles Feniston about some flowers and I know he's there now. He drove past about a quarter of an hour ago—I was just coming down to catch the postman. I said I'd do the flowers in little St. Alfred's next week. . . . Have you got your bicycle?"

"No. The back tyre is flat. There's something wrong with the valve."

A flat tyre was just another thing, hardly worthy to count as a disaster and less interesting than Ensie's breakaway from her morning routine.

"What about the beds?" Maud asked, thinking about the routine: washing up, bed-making, dusting the bedrooms. Ensie, walking briskly away from it all, replied, "Oh, I've made *my* bed, and Father wasn't down when I finished breakfast but of course he was being late on purpose so I shan't take any notice. I left his breakfast keeping hot, and he'll have to make his own bed, that's all. I mean, he's coming down late so that I shan't be able to go out. And other things, too, just planned to keep me at home—because he's getting suspicious about me going out so much more than I used to. But I think it's much better not to take any notice."

It was easy for Ensie to ignore things because she was always thinking about Don and the future, but Maud almost felt sorry for Mr. Martin, who after a lifetime of being looked after was probably incapable of looking after himself.

"He'll make his own bed, and then he must lie on it," she said, picturing the lumps and the wrinkles.

"That's right," said Ensie.

From the lane they could see Charles on the upper terrace of the walled garden, and Ensie suggested that Maud should come with her to order the flowers, but Maud said she would rather go and find Who's-it first and then they would be free, So they parted in the back drive, and Maud crept round through the shrubbery in case old M. should see her approaching and think of some new ideas for the note-book labelled "House Party."

She had to find Who's-it because she had forgotten to warn her that the house party was to be a nice surprise and must not be mentioned in Oliver's hearing; for although Who's-it's knowledge of the English language was still sketchy she knew those two words quite well, from hearing them so frequently spoken by her employer, and like an affectionate parrot she was in the habit of saying, "For house party—yes?" whenever old M. gave her an order. It proved impossible to make Who's-it understand the nature of a nice surprise, but in the end she seemed to grasp that the house party was a secret and in the same mixture of language and miming she conveyed to Maud her belief that it was a secret because Oliver would dislike it and would try to stop it, if he found out. It seemed to Maud quite probable that Who's-it was right.

She had entered Glaine through the stable yard and had gone up a back stair to find Who's-it; old M. would be in the dining room by now, or discussing food with Hat, so it was quite safe to linger a few minutes in the gallery, where the morning sunlight fell in long dusty shafts across the floor and the ancestors facing the windows stood out like lime-lit principal actors among a stage crowd. There was Charles's prototype in the blue coat, and an ill-disposed old eagle she had hitherto scarcely noticed; for his portrait was so black with age and varnish that little could be seen of him in ordinary daylight. He was wearing an immense peruke but the likeness to old M. was quite startling; he looked as if he were about to utter that crowing laugh, and it troubled her to acknowledge that this air of secret, malicious triumph was the main reason for the likeness. Old M. did not always look like that, but the laugh was more frequent nowadays.

She turned away and crossed to a window. The view of Glaine combe from the high gallery was enchanting in any weather, and doubly so on a sunny morning after a week of rain. But to her surprise she saw old M. himself striding across the sodden lawn, heading for the wicket gate which was the shortest way to the home farm. He went to the farm nearly every day, but it was surprising that he should be going there at this hour, and she wondered what had taken him out so early.

She left the gallery and walked through the house to the main stairway, because it was not necessary to creep back through the stable yard and the shrubberies now that old M. was out of the way. She looked across the head of the stair and saw the door on the other side standing open, the door that led to the north wing where the children of Glaine had grown up, the door to another region which Oliver must not be allowed to enter, since it had an even worse effect on him than the library.

Who's-it must have unlocked the door, she thought; perhaps Who's-it was planning to clean all those derelict rooms in preparation for the house party. But shc must be stopped, because Oliver was arriving this afternoon and anyway they wouldn't be needed. Hurrying past the head of the stairs Maud entered the north wing and started looking for Who's-it. The passage was empty, but one of the doors leading off it stood ajar and she heard a faint sound within, a melancholy, squeaking sound which suggested that Who's-it was riding the rocking-horse, because that was the door of the nursery and rocking-horses make a sound unmistakable to the ears of those who have ridden them.

She pushed the nursery door wide open and was in time to see the rocking-horse still rocking, though nearly at a standstill. He carried no rider, someone had given him a push and after all these years he had enjoyed a brief, squeaky canter, but it wasn't Who's-it that had done this good deed. It was Oliver.

Oliver was standing by the window. He looked as startled to see Maud as she was to see him; moreover he looked awkward and ashamed, as a man might well be who had been caught being kind to a rocking-horse, especially when he had spoken of this rocking-horse in the past as "useless junk." For some reason Maud remembered his saying this and for some other reason she at once felt warm sympathy for Oliver and she ignored the rocking-horse altogether, pretending she had not noticed its last, slowing movements.

"I thought you weren't coming till today," she said.

"I found I was free yesterday afternoon," said Oliver. "So I got here last night. What are you doing here? I thought you didn't work on Saturdays."

"I just came in to see about something I'd forgotten. . . . And then I saw the open door, and I wondered what Who's-it was doing in the north wing, and I came to find her."

"Oh. I see. I—I was just having a look round."

Maud thought it was taking him a long time to get over the rocking-horse incident; but then, in a flash, she remembered their parting words after his visit at Christmas, when she had accused him of thinking in terms of profit and loss. A fearful suspicion smote her, and without pausing for thought she exclaimed:

"Oh—you're planning to pull it down!"

"What?"

"The north wing. I don't know how you have the heart. Anyway, it's horrid of you—it's like trying on the crown."

"What?"

"In *Henry the Fourth*. But never mind that. I know it's none of my business, but I still think you'd be a vandal to do it. For one thing it would ruin the west front of the house, and for another all these rooms are—could be—beautiful, and this is the oldest part of Glaine, and—"

"As a matter of fact I was wondering whether it could be turned into a flat."

The moment he spoke it was obvious that Oliver regretted it. He looked embarrassed, as if he had given himself away, and before she could speak he added that it was just an idea, which probably would not come to anything. Maud was embarrassed too, because her reproaches now seemed not only unnecessary but also childish and impertinent, and she was surprised that he had listened to them so meekly, especially when he was being misjudged.

"I think it would make a charming flat," she said, and Oliver said, Well, yes, perhaps, and asked after the health of Mrs. Grayson and Miss Conway, whom he was careful not to call her aunts. Maud said they were bearing up, and while she was explaining what they had gone through in the way of breakages and the shock of sudden crashes she and Oliver were walking away from their embarrassment, away from the nursery and the north wing, down the stairs, across the hall, into the safe, sunny garden where no discordant memories lay in wait for them.

"I must go home," she said, thinking how fast the morning had gone.

"I am rather—well, a little—worried about my father," Oliver replied quickly; though it wasn't a relevant reply it seemed to have to do with her going, for he put his hand on her arm as if he would detain her. "He's not ill," she said firmly. "In fact, I think he's in very good spirits." Oliver took his hand away and said it was rather difficult to explain but that was partly it, and he wanted to talk to her. But Maud feared that at any moment old M. might return through the wicket gate, and her glance in that direction seemed to convey her fear to Oliver, who said: "Well, not now, perhaps. But what about this afternoon—or tomorrow? I've got the car—I'll come to Combe Cottage and then we can go to Yeomouth or somewhere."

It was tiresome, Maud thought, that she should be enjoying an outing with Oliver, who had only asked her because he wished to talk about his father, more than she had enjoyed her outings with Charles, who had asked her for her own sake. It was not merely tiresome; it was *wrong*. Sternly righting the wrong, with only the briefest pause while she watched Oliver peering anxiously into the tea-pot, like an owl trying to do the proper thing, she thought of Charles's generosity (lavish hotel lunches instead of café tea), of his blue eyes, and of his romantic lonely existence as the enemy at the gates of the place he loved best in the world. But the last thought did no good, for it reminded her she had spent much of last Sunday listening to reminiscences of Charles's boyhood at Glaine; interesting and entertaining reminiscences but not quite the entertainment one expected when one was asked out for one's own sake. The dreadful thought occurred to her that Charles was just a little bit prosy, when it came to his boyhood at Glaine.

"Is this tea all right?" Oliver asked. "Is it strong enough?—not too strong? Would you rather have had China tea?—or Russian? Or coffee or something?"

"Yes. Yes. No. No. No," Maud said, and to please him she drank a big mouthful of tea, boiling hot, and thought it rather nasty but would not for worlds have said so. Obsessed by his responsibilities as host, Oliver poured a jug of hot water into the tea-pot and stirred it vigorously. He offered her toast, scones, cake, and suggested ordering crumpets or muffins or sandwiches if she preferred them.

So far he had not mentioned his father, but she supposed he was saving the subject for tea. They had driven through Yeomouth along the coast road and had left the car in a farmyard and gone for a walk along the cliffs on the east side of the bay, climbing up to the high point called the Landmark, where they could look back across the bay, and eastward to the faint, shadowy outline of the great headland thirty miles away, and down at the wrinkled sea far below them. It had been a wonderful afternoon of tearing wind and high clouds in a blue sky and outbursts of sunshine that turned the sea to purple and emerald, a spring day which belonged to March rather than February, a perfect afternoon for climbing the Landmark but not for the confiding of filial anxieties, which would have had to be shouted to be heard. It was natural that Oliver should prefer to wait till they were back in Yeomouth, in the quiet (and inferior) café which he liked much better than The Golden Kettle because it was not crowded.

But presently, as Oliver still avoided the subject, Maud began to wonder if she ought to help him by introducing it. He kept relapsing into stiff shyness, between snatches of delightfully human (non-owlish) gaiety; he interrupted himself to scan the menu and offer her everything it listed; he fidgeted with his knife and dropped it, and upset the milk jug, and all but upset the vase of artificial carnations while he was mopping up the milk. It wouldn't have mattered, she said, because the vase had no water in it; but Oliver seemed utterly cast down, and it occurred to her that he wanted to talk about his father and couldn't bring himself to begin.

"Your father is thinking of putting in a new pump," she said, to rouse Oliver from his downcast silence. It certainly did this; he sat up abruptly (knocking over his tea cup, which fortunately was made of plastic and, like the vase, empty), and said, "Good God! That just proves it—he's up to something!"

Maud wished she had not mentioned the pump, but she explained quickly that the present one kept breaking down and the expert who had been summoned said it was worn out.

"It's been worn out for years. So is everything else. Oh, I know you've done wonders, Maud, but I don't believe even you could persuade him to install a new pump as long as the old one worked at all. No, I've felt it very strongly—that's what I meant when I said I was worried. He's up to something. He's got some ulterior motive. And one doesn't know what trouble may be in store for one."

Maud knew only too well but was bound by her promise of secrecy, which she now deeply regretted. She longed to comfort Oliver, who was visualizing such depressing things as Harebrained Schemes and Public Mischief, by telling him that the trouble was merely a house party of his elderly relatives, but of course she couldn't; it was the library-key episode over again, but this time her sympathies were wholly with Oliver and she hated having to deceive him by pretending not to know what old M. was up to.

"I think I'll come down again, before Easter," Oliver said. "I can't do much but at least I can try to keep an eye on him. Do you think that's a good idea?"

"I—well, yes—but . . ." No, no, no, she thought urgently, you will be terribly in the way, we shall be busy spring-cleaning and old M. will be over-excited and ready to bicker with anyone. But another part of her thought it would be nice if he came. "I don't think you need worry," she said slowly. "I'm sure your father isn't going to be—well, difficult."

"And that's a nice change, anyway," another voice said. "But what makes you, dear Olly, think otherwise?"

She looked up, wondering how she could have failed to see Charles approaching.

CHAPTER TWENTY ONE

"YOU'RE VERY LATE," Miss Conway had said. And Cousin Alice had said she was afraid Oliver would be late for dinner at Glaine . . . a pity to think so much about food, but then old M. always had. But these reproaches were mild, mechanical ones and they only swelled into a Fuss when Maud explained that she was late because they had met Charles and gone to have a drink with him. It was odd, but both of them minded drinking-with-Charles much more than lateness, and not on account of teetotal principles but because he had asked them. Miss Conway said, "Charles Feniston!" and snorted like a grampus. Cousin Alice said, "Oh, dear."

They could express themselves freely because Oliver wasn't there, he had dropped Maud at the gate and driven off quickly, to be as little late as possible. But the trouble was that they would not express themselves freely enough, it was a Fuss like a swirling fog rather than Plain Speaking, and although Miss Conway seemed once on the verge of breaking into plain speech Cousin Alice restrained her most effectively by saying, "Slanders cost money, Con," which reduced her to sulky silence.

"Did you meet Charles in Yeomouth?" Cousin Alice asked, when the silence had lasted too long. Maud said, Yes, in a café, he came in while we were having tea, no, not the Kettle, the little one down in the square. A poor little place, Cousin Alice said snobbishly; and Maud remembered with a pang that Charles had said much the same thing, teasing Oliver for choosing it, and had then had to explain his own presence by admitting that he sometimes had a bite there.

Somehow this admission had made her feel very sorry for Charles, condemned to having bites in obscure cafés when he longed to be living at Glaine, and she had felt compelled to work off her pity by listening to him attentively while they had drinks and laughing gaily at his funny stories of himself and Oliver doing foolish things in their youth. Oliver had laughed too, though the anecdotes made him appear more of a fool than Charles, but afterwards, driving her home, he had been rather silent, and when he said good-bye he added that he had changed his mind about coming down again before Easter, it wouldn't be any good because he had absolutely no influence over his father and anyway he was sure she would look after the old man and keep him out of real trouble. But he wished he knew what his father was up to.

Maud wished, more than ever, that she could have told him. He was sure to find out at Easter that the house party was not a last-minute project; he would realize that she had known about it, and perhaps he would accuse her of insincerity and look back on this afternoon as just another occasion when he had been fooled. If it had not been for the library-key episode she would not have worried so much, but this was the same sort of thing, and he might think, as he had thought then, that she was laughing at him when she pretended to sympathize. Worrying about Oliver's reactions she presently remembered how she had laughed at Charles's funny stories, and she realized that this too might have been misunderstood by Oliver, who came out in them as the butt, the booby, the stupid little boy who had had to be rescued by cleverer Charles.

Thinking about the problem only magnified it, and in March she tried to persuade old M. to let her write to Oliver, to tell him that "one or two" of his relatives would be coming for Easter.

"I'm sure he'll enjoy it more if he knows beforehand," she argued. "And I won't call it a house party, if you think that would put him off. Anyway he has said he'll be here for Easter and it's too late now for him to find a good excuse for not coming."

"It's never too late to find a good excuse. Sore throat, summons to sick friend—you've got no imagination, Maud. No, no, I want it to be a nice surprise. Much better that way."

"But you don't think it will be a nice one. You are simply determined to have him here."

Old M. might have glared, but he chose to laugh. "It'll be a surprise, anyway," he said. "Surprise for all of 'em. Answer to prayer, that's what they think." He laughed again, and again she was reminded of the malicious old eagle in the long gallery. "But you're wrong about Oliver," he went on. "He'll enjoy it when he gets here, meeting his relations and seeing what they're like. He's a clever feller, you know, but he needs to meet more people. That's why I'm having the house party."

It wasn't true. He was having a house party to amuse himself, and the amusement would come from the reactions of his guests to something he was keeping up his sleeve. She thought it suspicious that old M. had not dictated the invitations but had written the letters himself, typing them out with two fingers and somehow wrecking one of the typewriters in the process. But she saw the replies, and they were all grateful acceptances. Noel Humby quite understood that there wasn't room for Adeline and sounded fulsomely pleased that there was room for him. Penelope spoke of a past estrangement and welcomed a change of heart as "late, but not too late." Little James (a stripling cousin in his fifties) alluded to Aunt Sybil's wishes and to a voice from beyond the grave, but Little James's letter was so disconnected and so full of Biblical references that Maud could not understand what he was driving at. Yet it seemed clear that they were all peculiarly anxious to see old M., and that nothing short of an earthquake would keep them away from Glaine.

"Have to send 'em all to church on Easter Sunday," old M. said. "Five of them. No, six. I'm going to tell Noel Humby to bring his son or his daughter with him. Can put him in the little dressing room if it's the boy—or the girl can sleep in the ghost's room."

"Won't it seem rather odd to ask them, when you said there wasn't room for his wife?"

"I can't help that," old M. asserted. "Must have one younger one, for Oliver. Lucas and Ruth, they're called, and I'll tell him it doesn't matter which. So that's Lucas—or Ruth—and Noel, and Penelope and Agatha, and Little James and his wife. Six. They can walk to church if it's fine but if it's wet you'll have to hire a car. No room for all of them in mine. Thank goodness."

"Will they go to the parish church?"

"*No.* Why should I spend money sending them all that distance? Send 'em to the chapel-of-ease, St. What's His Name's. By the way, Maud, I'm continually meeting that curate feller prowling about the lane. Saw him only yesterday lurking under the hedge at the corner by Combe Cottage. What's he doing—hey? Does he come to see you?"

"Oh, no. I think—well, he wasn't really lurking—"

"Yes, he was. He's courting someone on the sly, I knew it from the look on his face. If it isn't you, I suppose it's the Martin girl. Come to think of it, I've seen them about together."

So had other people. The engagement could not long have been a secret in Yeomouth, and it must have been Annabel Curtis who heard about it and told her parents. Mrs. Woodfidley told her daily obliger, who was the sister of the farm bailiff's head cowman and a close friend of another obliger who sometimes obliged Ensie by giving the Pixie Cot kitchen an extra good scrubbing. Ensie's obliger ventured to congratulate her; and as a result the news spread back (through the head cowman's sister to Mrs. Woodfidley) that the engagement was a secret because Mr. Martin would be dead against it and might be struck literally dead, by apoplexy or heart failure, if anyone told him. Maud and Ensie supposed that Mrs. Woodfidley passed this interesting news on to Mr. Woodfidley, but of course they could not be certain.

What was certain was that Mr. Woodfidley deliberately lay in wait for Mr. Martin and approached him with the friendly air of a man who wanted bygones to be bygones. They met in the lane, just outside Pixie Cot, and he held out his hand to Mr. Martin and said:

"Congratulations!"

"I do not understand you," Mr. Martin replied, presumably raising Mr. Woodfidley's hopes to the highest level.

"Congratulations," he repeated. "We may have had our differences in the past, but this is an occasion for burying the hatchet. I'd like to give you my very best congratulations on Ensie's engagement to Don Crouch. Of course I know you'll miss her, but I'm sure he'll make you an excellent son-in-law."

("I was just inside the gate," Ensie told Maud. "I heard every word and I simply didn't know what to do. I was turned to stone.")

So, it appeared, was Mr. Martin, though Ensie couldn't see him because she was behind the hedge. But he made no reply, and after a minute Mr. Woodfidley said:

"I hope my congratulations do not come amiss."

Perhaps he sounded a false note, or perhaps Mr. Martin would in any case have refused to admit to a Woodfidley that anything was amiss. He huffed and puffed a little—pulling himself together, as Ensie described it, though Maud thought of it as getting up steam—and at last managed to thank Mr. Woodfidley for his congratulations in a pompous little speech which bestowed on the engagement a father's unqualified approval. One could only be thankful, he said, that one's daughter had betrothed herself to so excellent a man as Donald Crouch—a good Christian, a zealous priest, a young man whom it was a privilege to know, and one who would never disgrace her.

All this was directed against Mr. Woodfidley and his daughter Annabel; Annabel had married ambitiously but was now back on her parents' hands and her ex-husband was believed to be leading a criminous life on the Riviera. It was Mr. Woodfidley's turn to be silent; but before he could move away out stepped Ensie, taking the bull by the horns, as she expressed it, and somehow making it clear to her Papa that she had over-heard his praise of her beloved Don.

"Of course he couldn't go back on what he'd said," she told Maud. "He had to go on pretending that he knew all about it and to go on being nice about it. And I asked Mr. Woodfidley to come to tea, and he came, and I slipped away and rang up Don, and he came too, as quickly as he could, and Father had to be awfully nice to him because Mr. Woodfidley was still there. Afterwards, of course, Don had a long talk with Father, explaining why we hadn't told him at first."

"How did he explain it?" Maud asked.

"Well, I wasn't there. But I think he said he was so afraid Father wouldn't approve and he had wanted to win his friend-ship first—and so on." Ensie became purposefully vague, slur-ring over the details of a scene in which Don had come near to having the worst of it. "Father wasn't so nice as he had been, just at first, but as Don says it must have been a shock for him, but anyway he couldn't turn him out after being so nice to him in front of Mr. Woodfidley, and Don was very patient and for-bearing and he explained that we knew how dreadfully Father would miss me but we weren't going to be married for ages. And that sort of thing."

"And are you officially engaged, now?"

"Yes, sort of. Don says we won't put a notice in the papers yet because Father is still sulking. Well, Don doesn't call it sulk-ing, but I do. Don doesn't have to live with Father," she added thoughtfully.

"Poor Ensie. But it was lucky your Papa met Mr. Woodfidley and had to pretend he knew all about it, because now he can't go round telling people that he didn't. He'll have to get used to being congratulated, and he won't be able to say that you've de-ceived him."

Ensie looked quite shocked and began to explain that Don would never, never deceive anyone, but Maud cut her short.

"It's all right, I think Don's wonderful. Do you realise that he has healed the breach between your Papa and Mr. Woodfidley, just as he said he would? Only not in the way he'd planned to. But it was because of him—because you were engaged to him—

that Mr. Woodfidley spoke to your Papa and talked about burying the hatchet. And now he's committed to burying it, just as your Papa is committed to knowing all about your engagement."

Don really was wonderful, Maud repeated, telling Cousin Alice what Ensie had told her that afternoon. Or if he wasn't wonderful he was lucky, and in either case he would surely end up as a bishop, respected by all. Cousin Alice did not seem as thrilled by the story as Maud had expected, but she said rather sententiously that it was pleasant to know there was one feud the less in Glaine combe.

"It wasn't exactly a feud," Maud argued. "Just a violent exhibition of temper."

"That's how they begin."

"Yes, I suppose so. . . . Do you think Charles and old M. will ever make it up?"

"Is that the next task on your list? I don't want to interfere, Maud, but you'll be starting another quarrel if you're not careful. In fact, I think you have."

When people said they didn't want to interfere they always did, and Cousin Alice was no exception to the rule. She faced Maud across the kitchen table, when the cups for the bedtime hot drink and the go-to-bed biscuits had just been set out, and emphasized her remarks by slowly waving the tin of Herb-Soma she held in her hand.

"I think it's because of Charles that Con wants to get rid of you," she said. "It's not like her, you know . . . but people do horrid things when they've persuaded themselves that the end justified the means."

"Wants to get rid of me!"

"On the other hand, it may be because of me. It's probably that too. And that's my fault, because I have given in to her for years and she felt quite secure till you came, and naturally she thinks now—Oh well, it's obvious, isn't it? But I think it really began when you started going out with Charles. And I do feel—"

"But what's obvious? *What*, began?"

Cousin Alice gave the Herb-Soma tin an impatient shake.

"My dear Maud, don't pretend you don't know what I'm talking about. Can't you *see* that she's trying to drive you out? Haven't you noticed how things break and fall over when you go near them? Hasn't it ever occurred to you that Con has planned it all? Pre-arranged accidents, stage-managed calamities, organised discomfort . . . so childish, really, but I suppose she thinks it will get you down. Or get me down."

"Golly!" said Maud. "How—how monstrous of her."

But the iniquity of Con's behaviour did not seem so apparent to Alice, who added tolerantly that Con would never do anything really hurtful or frightening.

"And in a way, Maud, it's your own fault. If you'd only listened to me, about not getting involved with Charles—"

"But what's that got to do with Miss Conway? You said it was because of old M."

"Well, yes, I did. And so it was, as you could see for yourself. But it had to do with Con as well."

An extraordinary idea struck Maud, which yet seemed so obvious that she wondered why she hadn't thought of it before.

"She's his ex-wife," she exclaimed, and was almost disappointed when Alice said briskly:

"Of course she isn't. Don't be so silly."

"Well then—"

"It was her sister," Alice said. "Her half-sister, really—but Con was very fond of her and of course she blames Charles . . . though between you and me Claire was very stupid to marry him. Oh dear, I promised not to speak about it. I promised Con that if she would be absolutely silent I would be too. It was the only way I could bind her to silence."

"But why did you want to?"

Cousin Alice said sadly, "Slanders cost money. When Con starts talking about Charles her tongue runs away with her. And once before, about something quite different, she got sued for slander . . . oh, long ago, before we came here, but of course I was frightened she might be again, when Charles came back to Glaine and she threatened to tell everyone how badly he'd treated her sister. So I made her promise not to talk about it at all."

"I see."

"But didn't Charles tell you?"

"No," said Maud, thinking of the depths of lurid wickedness Charles's silence had seemed to conceal.

"No, I suppose not . . . he doesn't come out of it very well," said Alice, reducing the lurid depths to shallow, muddy ponds.

"I do think *you* might have told me," Maud protested.

"But you see, dear, Claire is dead."

Cousin Alice seemed to think this explained everything.

"She died quite soon after they parted," she went on. "In an aeroplane crash in Italy. So naturally Con feels very strongly about it and the danger of slander is greater than ever. I'm sorry. I suppose it would have been better to tell you—but I'd promised. It was a pact between us—not to mention it. And now I have."

Maud thought about her own promise to old M. How difficult vows of silence were, what troubles they could make for one!

"But it hasn't made any difference, has it?" Cousin Alice asked anxiously.

It was true that it hadn't made any difference in the end, Maud thought, but it had at the beginning. She had seen Charles as a hero, and the mystery surrounding his past, the suggestion of some dreadful scandal that could not be spoken of, had undoubtedly coloured her picture of him and helped to sustain it. Without his attributes of mystery and wickedness Charles wouldn't have seemed so romantic; his obsession with his boyhood and his limited Feniston outlook would have been evident right from the start. It was mostly her own fault, of course, for leaping to conclusions, but it was partly the fault of Alice and Con, for leading her astray.

Still, she had to admit that she had seen Charles in broad daylight, as it were, long before the veil of mystery was dispersed by Cousin Alice. She had seen him, she had listened to him, she had retraced her steps and discarded her illusions. . . .

"No," she said honestly. "No, it hasn't made any difference, really."

CHAPTER TWENTY TWO

"It's Lucas who's coming," old M. said. "So we shan't need the ghost's room after all. He can sleep in the little dressing room next door to his father."

Maud felt thankful that the ghost's room would not be needed, not because of possible reprisals by the ghost, but because the floor was quite rotten in one corner where the rain had leaked in. She wrote "Bed in dressing room" on her list, and reminded her employer that the farm bailiff was still being difficult about providing more milk over Easter. Old M. said he would have it out with him today. Feller was just being awkward, he added, because he resented losing the two men; but after all, who paid them? And anyway, it was only for a week.

Maud did not know much about farming but she suspected that the absence of two of his farm labourers, even for a week, might well make the bailiff feel resentful. Still, it had been a good idea. She looked out of the window and thought that the two men had really done marvels in tidying up the garden; but she wondered why one of them was now busily watering the empty borders, while the other brought him supplies of water, in leaking cans, from the tap under the terrace wall. March had been a dry month, but surely it wasn't usual to water gardens in April? Especially when there was nothing growing in the newly weeded beds.

"I told them to do that," old M. said, standing beside her. "Get the ground soft, I said. Then we'll shift some of those daffodils that are just coming out in the shrubbery. Make the place look gay."

"There won't be time."

"Oh yes, there will. Good thing we got the new pump in. Couldn't have done all that watering with the old one."

The new electric pump had been installed two days earlier and already old M. thought of it as his own idea. It pumped twice as fast as the old one and there was always plenty of water; the well had never been known to dry up even in a dry summer, He was pleased as a child, and he had bathed morning and evening to test the pump's automatic behaviour; no need to watch the dingle-dangle now, because the pump would switch itself on when the tank got low. Maud guessed that he had ordered the watering simply to give the pump some more work. She hoped he would not be very cross when the bill for electricity came in.

The gardeners went on watering; Hat was commanded to wash the windows, and then the car; Mrs. Hat and Who's-it, stimulated by the excitement, drew buckets of water and washed everything they could think of—the stone floors in the back premises, the chequered marble floor in the hall, the drawingroom chair covers, the chintz curtains in the bedrooms, all their clothes, and themselves. The pump pumped incessantly, and Maud feared that all this washing would distract the staff from more essential tasks. But everything was ready in time, as far as it could be. There were still many things lacking for the proper entertainment of a house party, but she had done what was possible and they would just have to manage. After all, she thought, they were Fenistons (even the wife of Little James was a distant Feniston cousin), so perhaps they would put up with the inconveniences, for the pleasure of revisiting Glaine.

They were to arrive on Friday afternoon. Little James and his wife were coming with Penelope and Agatha, by car; Noel Humby and his son Lucas were coming by train. Although she was dying to see them Maud thought she would be *de trop* at the actual moment of reunion, but old M. wanted her to stay so that he could talk to her while he waited for them to arrive. So she kept him company, watching at first from the windows of the long gallery, where she had waited with him for Oliver (and how long ago that seemed), and then following him downstairs when he thought they might come by the narrow lane through the woods at the back of the house; a lane which was never used nowadays, but of course they wouldn't know that, and which could not be seen from the gallery windows. It was Penelope and her companions they were waiting for; Noel Humby and Lucas would not arrive till after tea.

Old M. stood in the porch, looking down the drive. The encroaching undergrowth had been cut back and the worst of the ruts had been filled in, the ironwork of the porch had been given a coat of paint and the newly cleaned windows shone in the sunlight. To the approaching guests it wouldn't look too bad, Maud thought, and she glanced with affection at old M., who didn't look too bad either. He was wearing a tidy suit and a gaily embroidered waistcoat which had mysteriously escaped the ravages of the moth, and his new boots. Not the pair that had recently come from the bootmaker's but its immediate predecessors, which had been maturing on the boot-rack in his dressing room for the past two years. Old M. treated his boots like wine and laid them down two or three years before he intended to use them.

"You look most impressive," she told him.

"What's that—hey?"

Pretending not to hear, he nevertheless looked pleased, and unbuttoned his coat so that she could see the full glory of the waistcoat, and told her his Aunt Sybil had embroidered it . . . yes, the one who had left him all her books.

"I was always her favourite," he boasted.

"How nice to be a favourite nephew."

"Very nice," he said, exultingly. His laugh rang out, high and clear and triumphant. A startled blackbird flew out of a rhododendron bush, and steps sounded faintly on the terrace to their left.

"Can't be coming that way," old M. muttered.

He walked out of the porch onto the drive, and at the same instant Charles Feniston turned the corner of the house and came striding towards him.

It was an intrusion so unexpected, so flagrantly against the rules, that Maud could hardly believe her eyes. But as Charles came nearer she saw that he was in a towering rage, past caring about rules, or simply forgetting all about them because his mind was full of something else. He strode up to old M., opened his mouth to speak, and then noticed Maud in the porch and hesitated, perhaps to revise the manner in which he had been about to address his uncle. Her presence, she felt, was an additional grievance to what he already had to bear.

Charles's hesitation gave old M. the chance to speak first, and he did not waste it.

"Go away," he commanded, waving his arms as if to shoo Charles off the premises. "Whatever it is, I haven't time to talk to you now. I'm busy—important business—don't want you here anyway. Not a moment to spare. Go away at once!"

"I'll go when you've turned off that damned pump," Charles said loudly.

Even old M. was temporarily silenced by this odd request. His arms dropped to his sides, he peered at Charles in a baffled way, and it was left to Maud to ask why.

"Why should he? It isn't doing you any harm."

"Oh, isn't it?" Charles retorted. "That pump of yours"—he seemed about to describe it, and then decided not to—"that pump is taking all my water. *My* pump is out of action. My well, up by the bothy, is bone dry. The whole combe will be dry if you don't show a little elementary commonsense. Pump, pump, pump, from morning to night—oh yes, I've heard all about it, I know it's automatic and pumps faster than any pump that ever was"—Maud wondered what grapevine brought Charles such reliable information—"but it won't do it for long, at this rate. *Your* well will be dry too."

With a house party arriving at any moment this was a more alarming prophecy than Charles could guess. Old M. was visibly shaken, and in quite a mild voice he pointed out that the Glaine well had never dried up within living memory.

"It's never before been fitted with a super-efficient, fully automatic pump so that you can pump out the whole of the winter rainfall in four days and turn the lower garden into a giant's mud pie. And slosh gallons of water over the floors. And do more washing than three laundries put together. And wallow in deep baths six times a day. While I am being ruined," Charles added bitterly. "All my seedlings and early lettuces half dead—not a drop of water anywhere—the greenhouse like a bit of the Sahara!"

Maud was fascinated to observe that Charles was now waving his arms about, to indicate the extent of the disaster, and speaking in an abrupt, incoherent, exaggerated manner, just like his uncle. But the imminent ruin of a nephew who was the very reverse of "favourite" left his uncle unmoved.

"Stuff and nonsense!" he said. "And don't come here insulting me. Had enough of that in the past. I told you—"

"Oh, I don't expect you to believe me. Or to care twopence if you did. But don't say I haven't warned you—just carry on with your pumping and you'll soon see I was right—bad luck on old Oliver if the whole thing blows up while he's here!" Charles looked round at the newly painted porch and shining windows, the fresh gravel on the drive and the resplendent waistcoat on old M. "Pity to take so much trouble for Oliver," he said, "and then blow him sky-high before he's had time to appreciate it."

Evidently Charles's grapevine had its limitations, it had told him about the pump but not about the house party. Nevertheless he seemed a little puzzled by the extent of the preparations made for Oliver; he looked again, more searchingly, and stared over Maud's head trying to get a glimpse of the hall. But old M. said "Bah!" very loudly and moved back into the porch, blocking Charles's view.

"Bah! Nonsense! Pump couldn't blow up if it tried. Never heard such rubbish in my life!" He turned to Maud and asked, in the rumble he thought of as a whisper, "Is it working now?"

"I don't know. Shall I go and see?"

Charles said, "Better go and turn it off. Just to give Oliver time to get settled in."

Old M. said, "I shall do exactly as I please. No business of yours anyway. And don't stare like that—nothing wrong with the house—hey?"

Maud said nothing at all, though she felt she ought to. For while Charles continued to bait his uncle by staring into the house, and old M. nervously turned round to find out what he was staring at (cracks that heralded the disintegration of the plumbing?), she could see a large, old-fashioned car coming slowly up the drive, crammed full of Fenistons and their luggage. It crunched gently round the last bend and drew up in the middle of the gravel sweep. The male Feniston—Little James—sitting beside the chauffeur took off his hat and tried to look as if he were bowing. The three female Fenistons in the back raised their gloved hands in gestures of greeting. The chauffeur, entering into the spirit of the thing, blew a single, melodious toot on the bulb horn.

Charles and old M. swung round. The surprise must of course have been much greater for Charles, but even old M. was taken aback by the apparition which had suddenly materialised in the middle of his drive. For an instant Maud watched a tableau: the Fenistons in the car bowing and smiling, the Fenistons by the porch showing blank astonishment, superimposed on ill-temper. Then old M. pulled himself together and became a welcoming host. Ignoring Charles, he walked over to the car and assisted his guests to alight; he shook hands, and even submitted to being kissed—though this seemed to startle him—and listened attentively to three shrill voices telling him how wonderful it was to be back at Glaine.

"Well, I'm damned!" said Charles, coming to life again after an interval during which he seemed to have been turned, like Ensie, to stone. "Penelope, old Agatha, Little James—and that must be his wife. . . . Luggage enough for a month—and he's obviously *expecting* them . . ."

He drew nearer to Maud, who had withdrawn in the porch but could not bear to retreat further. "Of course that accounts for the pump," he said, in a tone of relief. "Why on earth didn't you tell me?"

"He made me promise not to tell anyone."

"But I was worried. I really thought old M. had gone clean round the bend—putting in a new pump, and madly washing and watering everything within reach. Then, when my own well began to dry up, I rather lost my temper. I wouldn't have been so hard on him if you'd only *told* me why he needed the pump."

"I'm sorry, but I couldn't."

"I do think Oliver might have mentioned it. He told me he was coming for Easter, but he never breathed a word of all this."

Before she could stop herself Maud said, "Oliver doesn't know."

"What! Do you mean—"

"I mean it's to be a nice surprise for him."

"Ha!" said Charles, appreciatively.

She had known he would be enthralled. But she had not fore-seen that he would show such obvious delight at the thought of Oliver's discomfiture; a delight which somehow recalled the many anecdotes in which Oliver had been the booby, and the endless talk about his own childhood at Glaine, and Annabel's soulful sympathy for the boy who hadn't grown up.

"I think we'd better go," she said, hoping that if she went Charles would accompany her.

But Charles meant to stay, and the presence of other return-ing exiles made his own position less awkward. Or so he seemed to think, for he stepped forward quite boldly as the party of Fenistons approached the house. It was hardly surprising that the leading member of the party, a large, elderly woman with a purple toque and yellow wash-leather gloves, should at once hail him as Oliver.

The returning exiles, luxuriating in their emotions, had car-ried old M. along with them to stand on the terrace and look down across the lower garden at the famous view of the combe. He was now bringing up the rear, with Little James, and so was spared the annoyance of hearing Charles mistaken for Oliver. Old Agatha—Dear Cousin Agatha, as Charles greeted her—was quickly corrected by her sister Penelope, who pointed out that it could not be Oliver because Marius had just told them that he hadn't yet arrived.

"Stupid of me," said Agatha, not at all abashed. "Of course I see now—you are Charles."

"Dear Charles—how delightful to meet you again," said Pe-nelope.

The wife of Little James, joining them, prepared to echo this sentiment (a weak face, Maud thought, and a born echoer of other people's views), but before she could speak old M. walked past her and addressed Charles in less complimentary terms.

"You still here?" he said.

Unlike Mr. Martin he cared nothing about keeping up ap-pearances. Maud looked round with interest to see what the oth-er Fenistons were making of it, and was surprised to catch glanc-es of relief and tiny triumphant nods being exchanged between

Agatha and Penelope, and Little James and his wife, respectively. They seemed to be saying to one another, "I told you so."

"The pump—" Charles began, as if he hoped to start another argument.

"We'll go indoors," said old M., turning to his guests. "Expect you want tea. Long drive. Come along, all of you. Oh, and this is—"

Maud's presence was by no means unwelcome; she could be introduced, praised and used as a diversion. But old M. was anxious to get the guests indoors, and he glanced uneasily over his shoulder, not at Charles but down the drive. Maud knew that Oliver would be the next arrival and she guessed that old M. was belatedly worrying about how he would react to the nice surprise if he drove up now. Perhaps, too, he felt unhappy about exposing Oliver to the ridicule of his watchful cousin Charles.

The luggage had been unloaded, and Hat, disguised as a staid English manservant, had helped to carry it in. But Agatha evaded old M.'s shepherding hand and walked back to tell the chauffeur the whereabouts of the stable-yard, and Little James strayed off for another nostalgic stare at the famous view, while Charles, seizing his chance, lured Penelope away to look at something on the other side of the drive. (Maud noticed that Penelope went reluctantly, as if she no longer felt it necessary to make a fuss of Charles.) Old M. grew agitated and rushed about, waving his arms and calling to one Feniston after another, offering them tea, rest, a sight of their bedrooms, anything to get them indoors. They were Fenistons, obstinate and perverse, and they refused to be hustled.

"Maud will see to the car," old M. said. "Or Charles." His face brightened; clearly this was a happy inspiration. "Charles, get in the car and show the man where it's to go. In the old coach-house, next door to mine. *You* know."

It was like Danegeld; the bribe of admitted kinship and familiarity was given to get Charles out of the way.

But it came too late. Oliver must have been pleased to find the drive so much improved and cleared of infringing bushes, and he swept round the last bend at a dangerously high speed—dangerous because he could not have foreseen that the gravel sweep would be dotted with people and blocked by another car. He trod hard on the brake and swerved sharply, missing his cousin Agatha on the near side and her car on the off, by inches. He drew up with the bumper a yard away from the wife of Little James and sat silent, presumably speechless, while the squeaks of alarm died away and changed their note and became a shrill feminine chorus of welcome.

"Ah! Oliver at last," said old M., moving forward. But Charles got there first and held the car door open, so that Oliver had to get out. Cousins converged on him from all sides, but something restrained them from shaking hands or attempting to kiss him as they had kissed his father. They stood round him, at a safe distance. Maud wondered if they saw him as a volcano that was about to erupt.

"Speak, Olly, speak," Charles said mockingly. "Do you need to be introduced?"

"Nice surprise for you, Oliver," old M. shouted, across the intervening heads.

To Maud's ears it was a shout for help, an appeal for forgiveness, and a despairing explanation, all in one. And Oliver—the other Oliver, who was neither obtuse nor unkind—heard it too, and responded.

"Of course not," he said to Charles.

"A *very* nice surprise," he said to his father, reminding Maud that neither of them really wanted to revive the family tradition of being at daggers drawn.

"An unexpected pleasure—" he started to say to his first cousins once removed; but the rest of his greeting was drowned by theirs, as they closed in to embrace him. It was manifest to all of them—and that included Charles—that Oliver and his father were on the best of terms and that a surprise planned by old M. for Oliver could not be other than nice.

CHAPTER TWENTY THREE

A RING AT the bell, late at night—or at least near the hour of bedtime—was so unusual that Alice and Con instinctively braced themselves to hear bad news, if only about their neighbours. (Fire, burglars, a ghastly accident.) But Maud, without stopping to think, said, "I expect that's Oliver," and had reached the sitting-room door before she realized that this conjecture was neither plausible nor soothing.

"Oliver! But did you know—"

"Why should he come here, at this time of night!"

"I don't know that it's Oliver, but I think it is," she said firmly. "I expect he just wants to talk. Don't wait up. We shan't be long."

She shut the door on further explanations; the explanation that mattered must be given to Oliver, and it mattered more than anything. It didn't seem to her at all odd that Oliver should turn up "at this time of night," nor did it seem odd to go out and talk to him instead of asking him in, and the fact that it might seem odd to Cousin Alice and Miss Conway entirely escaped her.

But it had not escaped Oliver, whose first words were a prepared speech about a rather urgent message for Maud which his father had asked him to—

". . . Oh, it's you!" he said, peering into the ill-lit hall. "No—there isn't any message—that was just because I thought they'd be sure to open the door. I thought they'd wonder why. . . . But never mind about that now. I had to have a reason for seeing you, because I'm quite in the dark. . . . No, I don't mean that—I mean I've simply *got* to talk to you about it. It's terrible. It's the end. Do you realize—? Oh, Maud, why in heaven's name didn't you warn me, when there was time to stop it!"

The volcano which had lain dormant in the afternoon was making up for it now, and Maud glanced nervously over her shoulder in case the noise of the eruption brought Con and Alice on the scene. "I'll come out, we can't talk here," she said, and Oliver said, "Yes, do. I brought the car, we can sit in it. No—you'll be cold. Get a coat. Will you be cold? It isn't really very cold. I think there's a rug in the car. I do apologise for dragging you out like this. . . . Do get a coat, Maud."

"Do be quiet, or they'll come out to see what's the matter."

The volcano suppressed itself, with difficulty, and Maud snatched up the first coat she could find, which was Alice's, and stepped out of doors. Oliver shut the door behind her with a bang, and drew excruciating squeaks from the garden gate as he dragged it wide open (the inhabitants of Combe Cottage never opened it more than halfway), and slammed the doors of the car, first on Maud's side and then on his own; and while he did these things he continued to walk on tiptoe and to speak in a whisper, so as not to attract the attention of Alice and Con. But at last they were settled in the car and he could speak in a normal voice; normal, at least, for a Feniston faced with a crisis.

"I suppose he swore you to secrecy," he said.

"Oh, Oliver, I'm so dreadfully sorry! It was so stupid of me. I see now that I ought to have told you, promise or no promise. But I *had* promised—"

"Yes, yes, I realized that. All this stuff about a nice surprise! And you couldn't know, of course, what was behind it."

The relief of finding that Oliver had not misjudged her, had not thought she was being insincere or laughing at him, was so great that Maud immediately felt that all their troubles, Oliver's as well as hers, were over.

"Thank goodness!" she exclaimed happily. "I thought you wouldn't understand."

"Understand!" To her horror Oliver gave a loud groan. "It's you who don't understand," he cried. "Not that one expects you to, of course, with your limited knowledge of my father's motives. But I do assure you that there's nothing—absolutely nothing—to thank goodness for. On the contrary, one can only deplore the badness—no, I suppose that's too strong a word. . . . But he's doing it for fun. For fun!"

"Yes," said Maud. "Yes, I felt that, too. But I don't see where the fun comes in."

"And Noel Humby as well!" Oliver said wildly. "He arrived after tea, with a great gangling creature called Lucas—"

"Your second cousin."

"I know, I know. One sometimes wonders—"

"Oliver. Stop saying *one*. And don't groan."

There was a moment's tense silence, and then, to her surprise, Oliver laughed.

"It was unconscious," he protested. He groaned again, experimentally, and Maud groaned in reply, to show him how it had really sounded, and after a short competition in dismal moaning and groaning, she was able to point out that no house party, however ill-chosen, could justify the production of such horrible sounds.

"You don't know anything yet," Oliver said. "But that's my fault, for sitting here groaning instead of telling you. I ought to have told you before—then you'd have seen what he was up to, and it would have made things easier for you. You must have had a frightful time, preparing for all this, and coping with him. . . . Yes, I know you're fond of him, but all the same—"

"All the same—Well, never mind that. Tell me now."

"I don't know how you can put up with him," Oliver said angrily.

He paused, and then mumbled, "Or with me."

Maud felt a strong desire to assure Oliver that she found it quite easy to put up with him, but she did not know how to express herself without saying more than he perhaps bargained for. Uncertain, stupidly tongue-tied, she let the moment go by, and after another pause Oliver remarked, in a detached way, that that was neither here nor there.

"What I came for, was to ask your advice," he went on hurriedly. "I'm quite sure they've all been got here on false pretences—that's where the fun comes in, for *him*—and the question is, ought I to warn them or just sit back and wait for the balloon to go up? Of course, they might not believe me—I don't knows what he wrote to them."

"I don't either. And I don't know what you're talking about. But I felt that, too, that he was planning a rather unkind joke."

"A very unkind joke. They think the house party signifies a change of heart, and that he's going to hand over large lumps of Great-Aunt Sybil's fortune. You know about that? That she left him all her money?"

The youngest of the three little owls, Maud remembered. "Yes, he told me," she said aloud. "He called it a tidy sum."

Oliver laughed. "Aunt Sybil called it her 'little all.' She made her will years and years ago, and left him her little all because he was her godson."

"And her favourite nephew."

"Well, perhaps. And perhaps it *was* a little all, when she made the will. But she lived with her two sisters and they both died before she did, and as they were both childless widows they'd left her their money—and one of them was the widow of an immensely rich man. So it wasn't such a little all, in the end. And my father came in for the lot."

He told her what old M. had come in for, and she gasped. Oliver's despairing rage, while he watched Glaine falling into ruin, was understandable now; and all old M.'s frugal habits, his hatred of signing cheques, his fury when Hat asked for a rise, his obsession about saving stamps that had escaped the postmark, his indifference to charity appeals, blended together to form the single word: miser.

"Oh yes," Oliver said. "It was certainly a tidy sum."

"Still, why should his cousins expect to be given a share?"

"Because Aunt Sybil had second thoughts before she died. She was their aunt too, and she talked about leaving them legacies—she even got as far as writing directives in a little notebook. Mind you, they were working on her all the time. I believe Agatha and Penelope rented a house in Hastings, just to be on the spot, and Noel Humby's wife talked of taking up nursing again so that she could nurse Aunt Sybil. And they all thought, in the end, that she *had* made a new will—there was a shattering rumpus when she died and they found that she hadn't."

If a Feniston could describe it as shattering, she thought, it must have been a rumpus indeed.

Alice had somehow persuaded Con not to sit up, but she could not persuade her not to ask questions at breakfast. Maud's replies made even Alice look sceptical, and Con gave great snorts to show her utter disbelief. That Oliver should turn up late at night and that Maud should sit in the car with him for at least an hour, merely to discuss certain difficulties about the house party, wasn't a tale that would hoodwink a child of ten, Con said afterwards; and it was perfectly clear that Maud was playing a very deep game.

Encouraged by Alice's scepticism at breakfast, Con developed this theme at some length as soon as they were alone. First it was Charles and now it was Oliver, she said; and what they saw in Maud one couldn't guess, but there was no doubt that *she* had realized which side her bread was buttered. Oh yes—a winter away from home had opened her eyes! And what Alice ought to do—for, after all, she really owed it to old M.—was to make some excuse and send Maud back to her people; they were home from Africa now, and Alice could write, to the stepmother and give her a gentle hint. It would be far better for old M. to lose a secretary than to face—well, trouble, later on.

"It wasn't Charles, ever," Alice said. "She only saw him, at first, as a romantic adjunct to Glaine. . . . So you needn't have worried."

"I'm not worrying! I couldn't care less."

"And if it's Oliver, I'm not at all sure about the butter. Or about the deep game. No, I'm *quite* sure about that. It won't necessarily be buttered, and it certainly isn't deep. . . . Isn't it strange, Con, that we should talk about bread and games and children of ten, when we're trying to discuss life? Life in terms of a nursery tea-party. Though of course there ought to be cake, if it's a party. At Wolfering we used to have lovely sponge cakes on our birthdays, covered with pink icing."

"Puppy's very fond of sponge cake," Con retorted, fending off Wolfering.

"Then couldn't you make one for tea on Easter Sunday? It would be something to do with the eggs."

"No, I'm not doing the flowers for Easter," Ensie explained. "I did them at Christmas, you know, and Don thinks it might look a bit like favouritism. And Mrs. Manchett-Jones has offered to provide seventeen arum lilies. *I* call that bribery. I'm sure I don't know where she's got them from. Seventeen is such an odd number."

"No odder than other odd numbers," said Maud.

Ensie did not reply; her attention had been attracted by the ringing of a bicycle bell in the lane behind them, and she exclaimed raptly, "That's Don!" As Maud looked back, Don came pedalling swiftly round the bend, slowed down outside Pixie Cot, and then saw them ahead and sped on to join them. They were rather short of greenery for the church, he explained, and he had offered to pop round to Glaine gardens and see if there was any to be had. Ensie said she too was on her way to the gardens, to buy an early lettuce because their own were not ready. Maud suspected a plot, but said nothing, though she was a little vexed with Ensie for thinking up the need for a lettuce and dragging her along to buy one, when they had previously arranged to walk down to the sea. Ensie and Don did not want her, and she could have gone for a walk by herself; she would have preferred to keep away from Glaine, because she did not want Oliver to think she was hanging about to see the balloon go up.

But it would be unlikely to go up today, and in any case it would go up indoors, probably in the library (old M. had made a point of getting the library cleared and the piles of books stacked at the far end), and Oliver would be too deeply involved in the rumpus to care whether she saw it or not.

Old M., on the other hand, was quite capable of sending for her, so that he should have an audience for his biggest and unkindest joke.

It troubled Maud to think that she had helped, though unwittingly, to make the joke possible. Her letters to Noel Humby and the other cousins had sounded a note of warm human interest which had misled them into thinking that old M. had mellowed, and had thus laid the foundations for the house party; and perhaps it was the renewed contact with his relatives, by correspondence, that had roused old M. from his seclusion and inspired him to take his revenge. That was what Oliver thought he was doing: paying them out for their bitter criticisms in the past, amusing himself by listening to a competition in flattery, and maliciously looking forward to their disappointment when they learned that he did not intend to part with a penny of Aunt Sybil's fortune. Thinking back, remembering old M.'s hints and chuckles, and taking into account his miserly nature, Maud was sure Oliver was right.

Charles could be seen from the lane, but to reach him they had to walk up the back drive and enter the walled garden. Following Ensie and Don along the upper terrace Maud was interested to observe that the soil looked no drier than usual; but Charles, catching her eye, thanked heaven that it had rained during the night. He grudgingly admitted that a few early lettuces had survived the man-made drought, and he led them back towards the long rows of cloches where these lettuces were growing. "I'm quite surprised to find you here, on a Saturday," Ensie said; but Maud was not at all surprised. She had known that Charles would be keeping as near to the house party as he could get.

The real surprise came a moment later. As they walked back, facing the door in the high wall, it was flung open and old M. stepped through. He held it open, and one by one the members of the house party entered the garden: Agatha and Penelope, Little James and his wife, Noel Humby (recognisably a white rabbit) and the great, gangling creature who must be Lucas. Oliver came last, looking careworn. But after sending a thought-wave of sympathy towards Oliver, Maud had to admit that old M. was also looking careworn. And even the guests, streaming along on a flood of reminiscences, had the air of being desperately determined to keep afloat, as if they had lost some of the buoyancy which had been theirs last night.

"Hrrm. Hey—Charles! There you are," old M. stated unnecessarily. Instead of glaring he seemed positively glad to see his nephew, and a few seconds later Maud realized why. "Showing them over the place," old M. continued. "Been everywhere else—naturally want to see this. Happy memories for all of us. Now you take them round."

He stepped aside, bumped into Don, and instantly began to talk to him, leaving his relatives in Charles's hands. After a moment's uncertainty it grew clear to them that Charles was back in favour, and Agatha, speaking for all of them, assured him that they were longing to know all about his market-garden. So enterprising of him to start it—so nice to think that the dear old garden wasn't being wasted. He must show them everything.

"Respite," Oliver whispered, drawing Maud aside. "I didn't expect such luck, though. Do you think we could slip away, while they've got their teeth into Charles? . . . No, I suppose it wouldn't be fair on *him*."

He nodded towards old M., who was still using Don as a conversational sheet-anchor.

"Not fair on your father? But, Oliver, you said last night—"

"I know, I know. But I didn't realize, last night—I didn't realize—" The owl blinked apologetically, and then became indignantly human. "They're too ghastly. Jealous, greedy, sycophantic, discontented! And worst of all, such unbelievable *bores*. Yes, I know he deserves it—but all the same!"

Maud remembered how Oliver had stood by his father on other occasions; how forbearing he had been about the library key, and how quickly he had responded to the shout for help yesterday afternoon. He had inherited the Feniston temper, but it was linked with a kind heart, which shyness—and a Feniston upbringing—had taught him to conceal. He was behaving quite wonderfully, she thought, and then she found herself wishing that he would behave less wonderfully, forget about helping his father, and abandon the house party to its fate.

"Of course you must stay," she said emphatically, thrusting the wish away. Oliver looked distinctly disappointed.

"Not that I can do much, except hang around and help to take the strain," he said. "I suppose that's something. I suppose it's all I'm good for, really—I mean, I can't prevent him doing these things, or rescue the place from ruin, or—Well, I suppose you wouldn't have been able to come, anyway. I'd forgotten about Charles when I suggested it. I mean, about seeing about the new pump."

Maud feared that the strain had already been too much for poor Oliver.

"What new pump?" she cried. Glancing round, she saw the house party returning from its tour of the garden and Don trying to break away from old M., who had one hand on his arm and the other on Ensie's. Feeling that every second counted she turned back to Oliver. "What's the pump got to do with it? Or—or Charles?"

"He said he was taking you out this afternoon, to see about getting a new pump. And about having his well deepened."

"On a Saturday afternoon!"

"But he said—Perhaps I got it wrong. They were all talking. He must have meant some other day."

He looked puzzled but relieved.

"I'm not going out to choose a pump for Charles, *any* day," Maud said urgently.

"Oh. But I thought—Stupid of me," Oliver said, in a voice that sounded far from contrite. "If you're not—" He gazed at her anxiously, and then became aware of his relatives advancing in full cry and of old M., who was much nearer, looking round for fresh cover. "I don't care if he *is* in a jam," he exclaimed. "I don't care if—Come along, Maud!"

"Hey Oliver," called old M., quickening his pace.

"Oh, Maud," cried Ensie, "we've simply got to fly. Don can't wait any longer, so I wonder if you could—"

Maud would have brushed Ensie aside, but it was already too late. Old M. had caught them up, and behind him, hot on his heels, came Charles and the house party in close formation, almost as if they guessed that Oliver was trying to escape. There was still the grotto, the dear little grotto, the relatives chorused, and of course there was the rest of the house, the north wing where they had slept as children, the cellars, the attics. . . .

"Oliver can take you round the north wing before luncheon," old M. declared. (Maud supposed the dear little grotto, of which she had never heard, must be a total loss.) "I shall have to rest for a bit. Gammy knee, you know—doctor's orders. You go ahead with Oliver. I want—I just want a word with Maud."

In a moment Oliver was surrounded; Agatha took his arm and Little James pressed close on his other side. He was borne away; and old M., instead of having a word with Maud, turned eagerly to Charles.

"What d'you think of them?" he asked. "Aged, haven't they? Did you notice how Agatha nods her head all the time? Sort of palsy, I should think."

"A pity Noel Humby doesn't do something about his teeth," said Charles. "And you'd never guess that Little James was so much younger than the others."

"He never had much stamina. Doesn't take after the Fenistons. Remember seeing him in his pram—poor colour and wizened-looking, even in those days. And what about that boy of Noel's—hey?"

"Strong i' the arm and weak i' the head," Charles quoted, and old M. crowed his approval.

It was quite easy, now, for Maud to slip away unnoticed. After several years of being not on speaking terms, Charles and his uncle were delighted that chance had made it possible for them to start talking again without going through a formal reconciliation. For a malicious gossip about the family was what they enjoyed most, and each looked on the other as the perfect listener and confederate.

CHAPTER TWENTY FOUR

"I suppose we'll have to walk," said Miss Conway. Although she generally walked to church she stated it as a grievance. At Christmas Oliver had given them a lift, and surely he could do it this time if his cousins were going in a hired car.

"They're going in their own car," said Maud. "Old M. made me cancel the hired car when he heard they were bringing one."

"Probably Oliver is going with them," Alice said soothingly. "You'd better start in good time, Con, if you're wearing your new shoes."

"They're not as tight as all that. Oliver had four people in his car yesterday afternoon, so I should have thought . . ."

Miss Conway's grumbles continued to ripple across the breakfast table, while Maud thought about Oliver and wondered which of his cousins had been wished on to him for a nice afternoon drive. She had not seen the car herself, because she had dodged the afternoon walk with Alice and Con and Wilbraham and had stayed at home, mending her stockings and writing to her stepmother. She supposed that poor Oliver had been given the four most objectionable guests, to get them out of old M.'s way.

"Beds, Maud," Miss Conway said briskly. "Can't afford to be late with bed-making, you know, when we've got to walk to church."

The beds were made, the washing up done, and Maud stood in the hall waiting for Miss Conway, who had had second thoughts about her new shoes and gone upstairs again to change them for a more comfortable pair. Alice was also in the hall, waiting to lend Con a shilling for the collection; for somehow Con always found herself left on Sunday mornings with nothing but coppers or half-crowns. Both of them heard the squeak of the opening gate, and Maud had an instant's wild hope that it might be Oliver escaping from his church-going relatives; but the patter of knocks on the door, accompanied by a kind of yodelling alarm call, told her that it was not. The voice was female. Alice opened the door, and there on the mat, panting slightly, stood Who's-it.

"Please to come," she said, addressing Maud.

"Why? What's the matter?"

"Is the house on fire?" cried Miss Conway, halfway down the stairs. "Get Puppy at once!"

"Please to come."

"No, Con, it's all right. At least, it's at Glaine. They want Maud."

"But why?"

"Mr. Hat said to tell you," said Who's-it, who always referred to her kinsman in this formal way. "To please to come."

If the summons came from Hat that explained why they had not telephoned; it must be something he did not want to reveal to old M. All sorts of crises concerning food or its preparation suggested themselves to Maud and she deemed it her duty to answer the summons, if only to calm Hat down.

"All right, I'll come," she said. "In a few minutes. Quite soon. I'll follow you. On my bicycle."

She intended to wait until the car had gone by, taking the Fenistons to church.

"On my bicycle," she repeated loudly, copying old M.'s technique, and Who's-it seemed satisfied and turned to go. But she hadn't told them *why*, Alice complained; and Con shouted after her, even more loudly than Maud. What had happened, was the place on fire, and—in a lower tone—couldn't she understand English?

"They wouldn't send for Maud to put out a fire," Alice commented. "It's probably something quite trivial and they just don't want to bother old M. with it. Foreigners often tend to lose their heads."

Who's-it had a freakish ability to overhear and understand what she was not expected to. She stopped at the gate and looked back reproachfully.

"Not to disturb. Not to report wrong things," she said. "The lady. The bathroom. Is wrong things not to be report. So please to come."

She pulled the gate to behind her and disappeared down the lane.

"Whatever did she mean?" Miss Conway demanded.

"I think she meant that they couldn't tell old M. because he'd said he wasn't to be disturbed, or something like that. But I don't know what she meant about the lady and the bathroom."

"Well! I do think—"

"Con, you'll be late if you don't start now. I'm afraid you'll be late anyway."

"No, I shan't," said Con. But after looking at the clock she allowed herself to be persuaded to start at once. Alice gave her the shilling and Maud brushed her down with the clothes-brush that lived in the hall-table drawer. All Con's outer garments were speckled with white hairs, because Puppy was always moulting.

Five minutes after she had gone they saw the Feniston car pass the gate. It was not possible to identify the occupants but the car did not appear to be full to capacity, and Alice hoped there would be room in it for Con—that was, if they were the kind of people who gave lifts. She started to talk about the people who gave lifts and the other kind, but she soon realized that Maud was not listening.

"All right—you'd better go," she said, and she refrained from adding a postscript about Who's-it being an angel in disguise.

Who's-it must have run all the way back, for Maud did not overtake her. She entered Glaine by the side door and after a short search found Hat in the old still-room, where he was rummaging in a tin box. The still-room like many of the other rooms had become a place for storing bargains from auction sales and other discarded objects, and the tin box contained candles, bits of sealing-wax, a packet of black-edged envelopes, and several bunches of keys. "Will not do," said Hat, tossing the first bunch aside. "Wait a minute, Miss—here is better." He examined the second bunch and held it out to her. "Here are door keys, perhaps to work and perhaps not, yes? After I have sent the young girl to fetch you I remember seeing keys, and then I remember where. It may be that they are the keys of Glaine!"

"Maybe. But why do you want a key? What's happened?"

"The lady is locked in the bathroom," Hat said happily. "The younger elder lady, Miss Penelope. She is gone there after breakfast and the lock of the door is—is—"

"—jammed?"

"Perhaps. It works not. And she complains all the time but Mr. Feniston has said we are not to tell him when they complain. He says he has had enough of these complains and he will listen no more. But I cannot find Mr. Oliver, and my wife and the young girl they say to send for fireman with ladder. But I think not, for Mr. Feniston will not wish to pay fireman with ladder and perhaps he shall make *me* pay. So I send for you. So then I remember the box with the keys and I search conscientiously and I find. Here they are, Miss, and you will perhaps set free the lady, yes?"

"Yes," said Maud. "Well, I'll try."

"These other keys are not of doors, I think. I think you should go now because the lady is complaining loudly. I shall come if you are needing me, but now I must make pudding or all will complain and that is more important, no pudding, yes? Certainly Mr. Feniston shall think so."

The lady was complaining, but not loudly; or perhaps the complaints had been loud to start with and were now diminished by hoarseness or fatigue. Nevertheless the faint wails sounded angry rather than frightened, and it was Maud who felt frightened—though only a little—as she struggled to release an angry Miss Feniston from her prison. She called to her to take out the key, and then she fitted the other keys in the lock from her side of the door, a process which was not made easier by Penelope rattling the handle and shaking the door as each key was tried. Keys, locked doors, furious Fenistons: it seemed to Maud that mischances at Glaine tended to repeat themselves, though with the difference, of course, that Penelope was champing to get out and Oliver had been champing to get in.

The sixth key seemed to fit, and half turned the lock. "That's better," said Penelope, rattling the door madly. "Try again. Try harder!" Perhaps the rattling helped to free the jammed mechanism, or perhaps the house had simply tired of playing jokes on the family. The key clicked and turned, the door flew open, and the prisoner walked out.

"It's intolerable!" she cried. "I have been in there for *hours*." She stood in the doorway, glaring. "Since just after breakfast. And no one taking the *least* notice! Who are you?—oh, you're his secretary, well I suppose it's not your business to look after the locks, but someone ought to have done *something*."

"I'm very sorry," Maud said meekly.

"So you should be."

"Was there no one—didn't they hear you calling?"

"Everyone had gone downstairs, to go to church," Penelope said indignantly. (It must have been later than "just after breakfast," Maud reflected.) "I don't go to church myself, I don't approve of it, I belong to the Higher Branch of Enlightenment and have done for twenty years. There was only that half-witted girl and her father and mother. What use, pray, were *they*?"

"Well, they sent for me. I'm afraid it took a little time, because—"

"They should have informed Marius. Why didn't they? I told them to, several times. Over and over again!" she shouted suddenly, making Maud jump.

"Perhaps they didn't understand. They're foreigners. I'm terribly sorry about it."

"Foreigners. It's so typical of Marius. I suppose he gets them cheap. Oh, I cannot bear it!" Penelope exclaimed. "Glaine—Glaine of all places!"

Maud waited to hear more. She waited for an outburst of loving grief over the deterioration of the family home, and she looked at Penelope with a real sympathy. But the outburst was not quite what she had expected.

"The discomfort," Penelope began. "The *hideous* discomfort. No proper staff—and that girl doesn't understand a word you say to her. Holes in the sheets and not enough blankets, and the window won't shut properly and Agatha says there's a mouse in her room, but I think it's a rat. And making us all wash in the bathroom—can you imagine it! Agatha and me, at *our* age, having to queue up in the passage in our dressing gowns! Oh, I don't want luxury, I've done without it all my life and I didn't expect to find it at Glaine. But I *did* expect to find a reasonable degree of comfort. Other people have modernised their houses, why hasn't he? He could well afford—"

She broke off sharply, evidently reluctant to discuss old M.'s financial position. But the taboo against mentioning money did not extend to grievances, and her sufferings lost nothing in the telling. Nor did the suffering of the other guests. Little James and his wife had woken up to find a jackdaw sitting on the end of their bed; it had come down the chimney, bringing with it half a hundredweight of soot. Noel Humby's son had caught his foot in the hole in his bedroom carpet and had fallen heavily, straining his back. Noel Humby himself . . .

Maud listened to the grievances with outward politeness but inwardly her sympathy diminished; for it grew clear that comfort mattered a great deal to Penelope and that her own dignity and importance mattered even more. She was glad when Penelope remembered the necessity for devoting a half-hour of Easter Sunday morning to religion.

For an adherent of the Higher Branch this seemed to mean sitting in an easy chair and letting Enlightenment flow through one's blankly receptive mind, and it could be done in the drawing room if no one else was there. Maud was sent ahead to spy out the land, and when she had reported that the drawing room was empty Penelope graciously dismissed her, hoping they would meet again. Maud rather hoped they would not.

She turned away from the drawing-room door and walked slowly across the hall. Most of the cobwebs had gone, the brasses and the oak staircase shone with polishing, the black and white marble floor was revealed in all its beauty; whatever the shortcomings of the bedrooms, Glaine was still a house of charm and character. It was a house in which people could be very happy, she thought, and she grew quite angry with the Feniston cousins who grumbled about discomfort instead of rejoicing at being back. But Galloping Grandfather, striking two o'clock, reminded her that it must be well after twelve and that the church-goers would soon be returning. She walked towards the baize-covered door that led to the back premises, and as she approached it was pushed open from the other side and Oliver came cautiously forward.

Maud did not think it funny that she and Oliver should greet each other in hushed voices; her interview with Penelope had shown her why Oliver wanted to avoid his cousins. "What are you doing here?" he asked. "Why weren't you at church?" And Maud whispered back, "Did you come out early? Where are the others?" But whispering was a strain, with so much to say, and Oliver beckoned her through the door to the safe solitude of the passage, where he explained that that fool Lucas had had a pain in his back and had insisted on leaving, and that he, Oliver, had been told by Lucas's father to go out with him and see he was all right.

"Pain in his back!" he said contemptuously. "It didn't stop him walking home. We got here ten minutes ago, and now he's gone upstairs to lie down. And I dodged through the baize door because I thought I heard Penelope nattering to someone and heading this way."

"She was nattering to me. And now she's in the drawing room getting enlightened."

"There's a fearful orgy of enlightenment coming to them," Oliver said. "Unless he just goes sick, to keep out of their way, and sends them home. He's grumbled so much about his gammy knee that I almost believe in it myself. Come into the estate room, Maud. Then I can talk to you."

"You're talking to me now."

"About my relatives—and what a bore you must think me. I've talked about nothing else, ever since I arrived. To you, I mean. And I'd meant to—I'd been looking forward to—That's why I minded it so much when I got here and saw them all. I realized that having them here would spoil everything. They're not like ordinary relatives, one can't get away from them and one lives in continual apprehension." He stopped short, and then said humbly, "I mean, I do."

"What?"

"I do. Not *one*."

"Oh—please go on being *one*, if it relieves your feelings. I don't mind it at all."

"But you did," he reminded her. "And I realize now, listening to Noel Humby, how pompous and affected it can sound. One feels this, one feels that. One hopes the funny smell in one's bedroom is not due to bad drains. Damned cheek!" Oliver added indignantly, in his own person. "It's a perfectly good bedroom-nothing wrong with it at all."

"Oh—Oliver!"

"But really, Maud, they're insupportable. The way they sneer at everything, slyly and pretending not to—except when their comfort-loving natures get the better of them. When I think of all you've done, how you've slaved to get things straight! I don't know which lot is worst, Penelope and Agatha, or Noel and his son, or Little James and that dreadful simpering wife. I had to take them for a drive yesterday and she sat beside me. You'll hardly believe me when I tell you—"

He stopped again, and then to Maud's distress he gave a deep sigh—hardly distinguishable, in fact, from a groan.

"What is it?" she cried anxiously, and Oliver replied:

"Them. I'm talking about them again. Giving you a surfeit of Fenistons. I'm just as bad as Charles."

"Oh no, you're not. You don't use them to glorify yourself."

"Thank you," said Oliver.

He would have said more, but further down the passage a door opened and Who's-it could be heard conversing in her native tongue and rattling plates with carefree abandon, while nearer at hand, though muffled by green baize, an outburst of talk showed that the house party had returned. Reminded anew of passing time Maud said she really must be going, but Oliver said poignantly that this was probably his last chance of talking to her without the house party interrupting, and led the way through a dark little cross-passage that connected the kitchen wing with the other side of the house.

"They won't come in here," he said. "The chairs are too hard for them."

He opened the door of the estate room.

"What is it?" said old M. "Didn't I tell you not to—Oh, it's you, Maud. Come in, glad to see you, wasn't speaking to you of course. Oliver ask you to lunch? Come *in*, Oliver—don't stand there with the door open!"

Oliver put some of his exasperation into shutting the door. "I thought you were in the library," he said.

"Don't bang it like that. You'll bring the place down round our ears."

"I shouldn't be surprised."

"Hey?"

"I'm afraid I can't stay to lunch," Maud said hurriedly. "Cousin Alice—Miss Conway—It's awfully kind of you, but I must get back."

The intervention worked; Oliver and old M. stopped their bickering and spoke with one accord, though each voice interrupted the other. Of course she must stay—meant to have asked her earlier—quite easy to telephone to Combe Cottage—Oliver would do it now.

CHAPTER TWENTY FIVE

TO THE FENISTON GUESTS food was important. They relished it, they treated it seriously, and none of them could deny that Hat was an excellent cook. The luncheon he produced was eaten with reverent appreciation and there was hardly any bickering; the conversation was mostly about food, and they exchanged long, prosy anecdotes about meals they had eaten in the past and vied with one another in deploring the synthetic foods of today. Maud thought it a dull luncheon party, but peaceful, and although she had to sit between Noel Humby and Little James she had quite a good view of Oliver across the table and could compare him, to his great advantage, with his left-hand neighbour Lucas. She did not find the anecdotes about meals interesting, but there was no doubt that Hat's cooking was a nice change from Miss Conway's, and the mood it induced, of well-fed benignity, lulled her into thinking that the house party would settle down to a traditional Sunday afternoon of dozing over books and magazines when it retired to the library.

If she had not thought this she would not have gone to the library. But she had quite forgotten her foreboding that the balloon would go up there and her other foreboding about being called in to act as audience; and as they walked down the passage to the fatal threshold she was only worrying about whether there would be enough comfortable chairs for the dozers and nappers. But old M. had seen to that; a sofa and three additional easy chairs had been imported and set out, with the resident ones, in a semicircle round the fire. The fire was burning well, and the piles of books looming in the library's recesses were impressive at a distance, suggesting scholarship rather than auction-room frenzy. The guests expressed their admiration, tempered by minor criticisms which old M. seemed not to hear. (Rather a draughty room . . . it always had been, but there used to be screens . . . a pity about all those ill-matched bookcases down the middle. . . .) They settled into their places, the three ladies sharing the big sofa. Maud looked across the circle at Oliver; and for the first time it occurred to her that she had made a terrible mistake. For Oliver, frowning and blinking and making furtive discouraging gestures, appeared to be strongly disapproving of her presence.

He didn't want her there; he thought she ought to have withdrawn; it was clumsy and tactless of her to have intruded into a family gathering, even though the family was by no means a united one; he was trying to warn her (and no doubt he meant it kindly) before the rest of them made it painfully obvious that she was in the way; he wished her to go now, as quickly as possible; he didn't want her there. These thoughts whirled through her head like a revolving wheel, which always slowed down at the same point. He didn't want her there.

She stood up, and was keenly conscious of Oliver's look of relief. It was ill-mannered to slip away without saying good-bye or thank you, but she hesitated to interrupt them; a silent, speedy retreat seemed best in the circumstances. She was halfway to the door when old M. looked up and called her.

"Hey—Maud! Can you find that book—the one I showed you the other day? Meant to leave it out but I forgot to tell you. The book about old families that said how the Humbys diddled the College of Heralds over their coat of arms. Should be somewhere over there."

He gestured towards the deep bays at the further end of the room.

"Maud can find anything," he said proudly. "She never fails me."

Amid murmurs of congratulation Maud walked the length of the room, not daring to catch Oliver's eye. She sidled round the great piles of books on the floor and entered the first of the three bays, which was where the book should be if old M. had not taken it out and popped it back somewhere else. Hidden from the family, surrounded by ramparts of books, in her dark little sanctuary which smelt of dust and mildewed leather bindings, she wrestled with perplexity and humiliation. Oliver could not have meant it; he had meant it. He had wanted to talk to her; but he had thought it presumptuous of her to tag herself on to the family. She had woefully misunderstood him. He was a Feniston after all.

"I was there for *hours*," Penelope declared.

She had said it before, but only to Agatha, there had not been time before luncheon to tell the others of her imprisonment in the bathroom, which was quite an adventure in its way and could be made to sound more dramatic than the Little Jameses' adventure with the jackdaw. They had merely woken up to find it there; but Penelope had screamed and rattled the door, had argued with stupid foreigners, tried to send messages to Marius, been freed at long last by that girl's bright idea of trying other keys; and if one of them hadn't fitted she might have been there *now*.

"Stuff and nonsense!" old M. said. "The key sticks a bit—that's all."

"The lock was completely *jammed*. And if you knew about it, Marius, you ought to have had it seen to. A faulty bathroom lock is really the last *straw*."

It was, indeed. Old M. grunted as he slowly got out of his chair, but only Oliver perceived that the balloon was about to go up; and he had been waiting for it to go up ever since they entered the library.

"You've all done nothing but grumble since the day you arrived," old M. stated. "Never heard so much moping and grizzling in m' life. If it isn't this, it's that. Oh yes, I know you've tried to keep it to yourselves, but I've heard it all the same. Heard it going on in corners."

Perfectly true, Oliver reflected. The comfort-loving Fenistons had found it impossible to conceal their distaste for their present surroundings, even though they had every reason for keeping on good terms with their host. Self-control was not their strong point; and, of course, Glaine must have been a frightful shock for them. But they were in for a worse one.

"I'm getting an old man," his father continued. "Wanted to see you all again before I die." (A noticeable wave of interest, disguised as sympathy, ran through the listeners.) "Thought perhaps I'd made a mistake—done the wrong thing. Very difficult position. Hrrm! I used to think about Aunt Sybil—wonder if she was right. . . ."

He looked down, wonderingly, at the hearth rug, and then looked up very swiftly at the tense faces of his relatives.

"I see that she was," he said simply.

"Was what? What do you mean?" the relatives cried in chorus.

"Right to leave the money to me. She knew what would happen if she left it to you. You'd have spent it all—frittered it away on central heating and private bathrooms and new carpets and God knows what! Sheer extravagance—wicked waste of good money—nothing but spend, spend, spend!"

He was still talking, but so was everyone else; the library was filled with wails and protests, arguments and exclamations. In the midst of the uproar old M. suddenly noticed that he was being deserted by the person who should have supported him.

"Oliver—where are you going? Come here!"

"Book," said Oliver. Or perhaps he didn't; with the shouting-match going on all round one couldn't be sure. He circled the family party—all on their feet now and buzzing about like hornets—and stalked off towards the end of the room. A professor, old M. reflected, and a very clever feller; one couldn't blame him for not being good at everything, not good at joining in and standing by. It showed what a clever feller he was, if he could read a book in the middle of all this hullaballoo.

"Maud," said Oliver, edging his way past the rampart into the dusty retreat.

It was dark in the bay as well as dusty, and Maud was standing with her back to him, searching along the crowded shelves for the book old M. had sent her to find.

"I don't think it's here," she said.

"Do you really imagine he's going to need it now?"

"Imagining isn't what I'm here for, is it? He asked me to find the book and I'm trying to."

"A modern Casabianca."

Maud turned round, uncertain whether she was being addressed by an owl or an angry Feniston.

"What do you mean?" she said.

"He stood on the burning deck, you remember, whence all but he had fled. He wasn't doing a bit of good because the ship was sinking anyway, but he'd been told to stay put. And you've been told to look for a book, but commonsense should tell you— Well, just listen!"

The noise of battle thundered down the length of the room, a roar of angry voices all speaking at once as the rumpus gathered momentum. Phrases and slogans rang out above the general hubbub—"Your moral duty . . . Aunt Sybil's dearest wish . . .

disgraceful behaviour!"—but already the massed attack against the head of the family had been disrupted by wrangles and skirmishes among the attackers. Old grievances were being recalled, old feuds revived. It was a family row on the biggest scale, and everyone was well supplied with ammunition.

"Don't pretend to be deaf," Oliver said. "It's appallingly obvious that no one is going to settle down with a nice book after this."

"I couldn't help it! How could I refuse when your father told me to get it? I tried to slip away. I did try."

"Oh, I'm not saying you could have gone then. But for heaven's sake stop looking for—"

"But that's what you did say," she cried. "Or what you wanted, anyway. You wanted me to go away."

She stared at Oliver, willing herself to see an exclusive, unreliable Feniston instead of a lovable owl. For she had come to love the owl too much to be able to bear his rejection of her, but if she identified him with his family it might be possible to meet pride with pride and to think of her wretchedness as justifiable resentment.

"Of course I did," said Oliver, obstinately continuing to look like the nicest owl in the world. He added bitterly, "Are you surprised?"

"Oh no," said Maud. "Not really. It's a family party after all, so naturally you didn't want outsiders."

"Outsiders!"

"Well, I am one. I'm not a first cousin, or even a second cousin twice removed. I know you've talked to me about them, but I suppose that's different from having me here while it's going on."

"Quite different," he said.

"I suppose you guessed that they would—that I should be in the way. You knew the balloon was going to go up, and you minded having an outsider here watching it. No . . . I'm not at all surprised."

Oliver said loudly and violently, "I *didn't* mind!"

He moved impetuously forward and collided with a pile of books, which toppled over and made another small rampart between himself and Maud. "An outsider! How could you sup-

pose . . ." he cried across it. "I didn't mind . . . I only minded because I thought it would put you off having anything to do with
us. . . . Marrying into the family, and that sort of thing. . . ."

Maud gazed at her owl in loving astonishment and said,
"How perfectly ridiculous."

Oliver stepped forward again, kicking books aside and tram-
pling them underfoot in a way that would surely have horrified
a real professor. Shaking in sympathy, the other books that
formed the high, outer rampart of the sanctuary suddenly col-
lapsed and came tumbling down behind him. A cloud of dust
arose and hung in the air, and through the gap in the rampart
Maud had a brief glimpse of the Feniston relatives in battle order. If they happened to look round they would be able to see
her and Oliver, dustily embracing.

"An outsider. Darling, if you'd stopped to think," Oliver said.
"No, no, I didn't mean that," he added anxiously. "It was all my
fault. I mean—well, what I really mean is, will you marry me?"

"Yes," said Maud; and once again she did not stop to think,
although—just like Ensie—she had not expected the proposal
and could have described it as a complete surprise. But then no
one would have expected a proposal to be made in such circumstances, with a full-scale family row going on with undiminished
vigour in the same room and both the interested parties bogged
down in books.

"What a fool I am," Oliver said a moment later, suddenly
becoming aware of the room's other occupants, whose presence he had temporarily forgotten. "What a place to choose!
We must escape. How can we escape? Do you think that end
window will open?"

They extricated themselves from the books and crossed the
room stealthily, without attracting attention. But the nearer
windows would not yield to Oliver's tugging, and the fourth—
which, as he reminded Maud, had been opened quite recently—was in full view of the combatants. To leave in an orthodox
manner by the door would have been just as easy but the idea
did not occur to Oliver and Maud, whose present state of mind
was romantic rather than practical.

"Oliver," said old M. "Hey—Oliver!"

Then he noticed Maud. He'd clean forgotten about her and now he wondered where she'd been all this time. For some reason it crossed his mind that she was supposed to be delicate, or had been delicate once, and almost immediately he knew why he'd remembered it; and he hoped she wouldn't heel over before Oliver got the window open.

Fresh air and fainting were linked together in old M.'s mind, the one being a cure for the other, so naturally the sight of Oliver struggling to open the window, and Maud waiting beside him, suggested both a swoon and its remedy.

"Feeling faint?" he called, not without sympathy.

The relatives, hoarse and exhausted, were rather glad of a diversion. There was a general turning of heads towards the window, and even a murmur of commiseration.

"Hey—you feeling faint?" old M. repeated.

"No. Not in the least degree."

"Don't be a fool, Oliver, you know I didn't mean you! Why should *you* feel faint—hey? Get the window open and give her some fresh air."

"Just what I'm trying to do," Oliver replied cheerfully.

"Can't you see it's bolted at the top? Can see that myself from here."

"So it is. It wasn't like that last time I opened it."

"Must be something wrong with your eyes. Hey! what do you mean by last time?"

But the french window flew open, and in an instant Oliver and Maud were out on the terrace; in another instant they had walked away, right out of sight. Old M. had not expected them to do that, he had pictured Maud sitting on a chair by the open window, and he had been about to rebuke Oliver for not getting her a chair before he started fiddling with the catch. Rather to his own surprise he found himself saying something quite different; though Oliver was no longer there to hear it.

"Feller can't help his eyesight, really. Should probably need spectacles myself if I read as much as he does. He's a professor, you know."

"And a most eligible young man, with all Aunt Sybil's money coming to him," Penelope said acidly.

Old M. pretended not to hear. He'd heard enough, the explosive joke was over, he'd bamboozled the lot of them into flocking round him for the pickings and he'd had the fun of watching them when they learned that there weren't going to be any, but now he only wanted to be rid of them; which he soon would be, for they had all vowed they would leave at once. Relatives were necessary, without them he wouldn't be the head of a family, but they were better kept at a distance. And he had spent far too much on entertaining them, and on installing the new pump. Still, the pump had done the trick and forced Charles to make the first move, and that was a good thing because now he would be able to talk to him again.

"Eligible young men often seem to make rash marriages," Agatha remarked, backing Penelope up. "I hope he doesn't disappoint you."

With this parting shot she left the room, following the others to find out if they really did mean to leave that night.

"Marry in haste, repent at leisure," old M. said, thinking of Charles. "That's what I told him—and I was right, too."

Then he saw that Agatha had gone, and realized that she had been talking about Oliver, and his spurt of anger at her presumption was succeeded by the thought—his own idea, of course—that it was quite time Oliver found a wife. Or rather, had one found for him; otherwise he might pick someone wholly unsuitable as Charles had done, and bring his father's grey hairs with sorrow to the grave.

A pity Maud was delicate, because he'd once or twice thought she would make a good wife for Oliver. Nice girl, respectable background, everything in her favour really, except for that regrettable tendency to faint. But it would never do to introduce a delicate strain into a family that prided itself on its physical stamina.

She was only twenty. He wondered if she would grow out of it.

In the north wing, where they had gone to take refuge from the house party, Oliver was telling Maud that he hadn't hoped, hadn't dreamed . . . that, in fact, he had not really intended to propose to her so soon, and Maud was assuring him that the preliminary period of courtship, which he had planned to start this Easter, would have been quite unnecessary—as he could see for himself. Neither of them spoke lucidly, but the explanations and assurances seemed perfectly intelligible; for Oliver and Maud were in the happy state where misunderstandings do not exist. Even the exterior problems seemed to dwindle into insignificance when they discussed them, just as Little James's indignant voice had dwindled into silence when Oliver shut the door of the north wing on the scene in the hall.

They had come in from the garden to find the relatives all gathered in the hall, arguing about the propriety of leaving at once; and the only way to escape had been to treat them like ghosts and walk straight through the group, up the stairs, and into the safety of the north wing. Little James had voiced the general demand that Oliver should *do* something, produce timetables, sandwiches for the journey, apologies for an intolerable affront; but Oliver's calm unconcern with a house party of ghosts had somehow discouraged pursuit.

"Still, I suppose I shall have to do something," Oliver said now. "Oh, not sandwiches, they'll swallow their pride instead and stay at least till tomorrow. What a ghastly evening it will be."

"Then what will you do?"

"Give them some of the money, I suppose. When I come in for it. *If* I come in for it. He may change his mind and leave it all to them. The future," Oliver said happily, "is entirely unpredictable. Do you love me?"

"Yes."

"I can't believe it. You have to go on saying Yes. Enough to live in the Midlands instead of at Glaine?"

"Yes."

"I hope you always speak the truth, darling."

"Yes, yes, yes, yes," said Maud.

"Of course he might agree to turn this wing into a flat for us. Then we could live here in the vacations and come for weekends."

"But would you like that?" she asked doubtfully.

"You mean: would it be nothing but bickering with Father—"

"—and groaning over the cobwebs. Yes, that is what I mean."

"I do not groan. At least, I never shall again. It's all going to be quite, quite different. In this cosy flat, playing with the rocking-horse . . . and with—"

"—our little ones."

"And with our little ones. Giving them rides on the rocking-horse. Aren't we looking rather far ahead? Still, I don't mind that, I only hope the rocking-horse survives for our grandchildren. Well, as I was saying, it's all going to be quite different."

"Yes," she agreed fondly.

"I wonder how long you'll go on saying Yes to all my statements. But seriously, I *shall* be different, now that you've promised to marry me."

"Yes. But not too different, Oliver darling."

"Of course, Father is impossible sometimes," Oliver admitted. He looked at her anxiously. "And of course, I'm impossible too."

"No, no, no, no," she said.

THE END

FURROWED MIDDLEBROW

Made in the USA
Middletown, DE
28 January 2023